Praise for

"This nov
tory in sp
1950's. Hi
~~ D.S. H

"The Recto
to take us
salvation f
Richard L.
Millenniun
to Michael'

"It is rare t
happened
and every
the chara
Michael")

"If you lo
mail, you'l
its proport
swilling po
Mary Ma
~~ Rheta
Second Con

More comments can be found on Michael's website at
http://www.michaelthompsonauthor.com
Also by Michael Hicks Thompson
DAVID—The Illustrated Novel, Volume I
DAVID—The Illustrated Novel, Volume II
The Parchman Preacher (being replaced by *The Rector*)
Dinner With David ben Jesse (*Dinner With Destiny*, anthology
from Amazing Phrase Publishing)
The Actress, sequel to *The Rector*, due for release in 2016
Clouds Above, due for release in 2017

The
RECTOR

 SHEPHERD KING PUBLISHING, LLC

The RECTOR

A Christian Murder Mystery

MICHAEL HICKS THOMPSON

First in *The Solo Ladies Bible Study* series

 SHEPHERD KING PUBLISHING, LLC

⬛ SHEPHERD KING PUBLISHING, LLC

2795 Lombardy Avenue
Memphis, TN 38111
michael@shepking.com

ISBN: 098452827X
ISBN: 9780984528271
eBook ISBN: 978-0-9845282-8-8
Library of Congress Control Number: 2015917162
Printed in the United States of America
Author website: www.michaelthompsonauthor.com
All scripture quotations are taken from the *NIV Spirit of the Reformation
Study Bible*, Copyright © 2003 by Zondervan, Richard L. Pratt, Th.D.,
General Editor.

Dedication

To Michael Jr., Kyser, and Charles,
three great sons who give me joy.

With special thanks to Jerry Gramckow, my publishing editor, who brought vast value, and to Caitlin Alexander, for the same reason. To the beta readers whose feedback provided many suggestions, my heartfelt gratitude goes to Fred Acuff, Rocky Blair, La Una Brubaker, Judge Gerald Chatham, Mary Call Ford, Sandi Hughes, and especially Emily Kay. Emily, I couldn't have righted all the wrongs unless you'd pointed them out. To Disciple Design for a dramatic book cover, and Nick Nixon for the interior images, "Thank you. Well done."

Author's Note:

The main suspects are introduced in the first three chapters. After that bit of backstory, I hope you'll find yourself on the roller-coaster ride of your fiction reading life.

Also, I have a confession. I wrote a novella, titled The Parchman Preacher, *in 2014 ... it was a mistake. I should have been more patient and written the whole story; and I should have made more changes to that little book.*

Now I have. I hope you enjoy
The Rector.

Still, there are more important books to read than
The Rector.
Twelve are listed at the end of this book.

Characters in order of appearance:

Judd Insner *–Part-time coroner & meat market owner*
Martha McRae *–Boarding house & newspaper owner*
Charlie Parker *–Charlie's Place, barbeque restaurant*
Oneeda Mae Harpole *–Martha's friend*
Betty Crain *–Bible study leader*
Mary Grater *–Married to Capp Grater*
Capp Grater *–Lumber business; richest man in Solo*
John "JJ" Johnson *–Owner, JJ's Honey*
Andrew Dawkins *–Local farmer*
Freddie Carpenter *–Postmaster*
Sheriff Butch Turnbull *–Bethel County Sheriff*
Thomas Cain *–The second rector*
Adam Davidson *–The third rector*
Annie Insner *–Judd's wife*
Emily Norton *–Calvary secretary*
Sonny Sartain *–Parchman prison inmate*
Frank Acuff *–Prosecutor*
Arthur Bernstein *–Defense attorney*

Part I

Late 1954

*For out of the heart come evil thoughts,
murder, adultery, sexual immorality,
theft, false testimony, slander.*

1

The First Rector

"IT'S TRUE, MARTHA. He died of a massive heart attack," the coroner told me. "My assistant was here during the autopsy. The little twit must've run out and told everybody in town."

Word spreads fast in Solo, Mississippi.

Our rector, Pastor David Baddour, was found slumped over his plate at Charlie's Place in Greenlee, thirty miles north.

Mighty young to die of heart failure, I thought.

———

"Yeah, he'd been in here before," Charlie Parker told the police. "Always sat right there at the counter. The man loved my barbeque ribs. Didn't know he was some sort of priest, though. Never wore one of those white collars ... you know?"

None of the locals knew him, or had any idea what he was doing in Greenlee.

I had an idea why he was in Greenlee, and I knew him well.

Goodness, the man was only thirty-two, healthy as a mule—one reason why his death didn't sit right with me. I had my own reasons to believe he was murdered. And my suspicions of who did it—just not how it was done.

⸻

I was in my newspaper office the next morning, ready to write Pastor Baddour's obituary when Oneeda Mae Harpole strolled in. She was my friend and Solo's busiest gossip.

She plopped down in my creaky guest chair and proceeded to stare at me—her usual way of letting me know she wanted to talk. I paused to learn what gossip or opinion she'd brought.

She leaned so close I could smell her Juicy Fruit gum. "Martha, I hope you're not writing some puff-pastry story about the preacher. You should tell the truth. Father Baddour was seeing a married woman."

"What? We don't have any facts, Oneeda. Only rumors."

"Remember? Betty told us in Bible study. She saw him go into that Alamo Motel with some woman," Oneeda reminded me.

"And you trust everything Betty says? People see what they want to see. Besides, this isn't some feature story about Father Baddour's death. It's his obituary."

Oneeda brushed make-believe lint from her skirt and stood to leave. "Well, *I* believe he was seeing some woman."

I watched Oneeda walk out, knowing she was right. Betty Crain had told me privately, after one of our Bible studies, she happened to be in Greenlee one Saturday and saw Pastor Baddour drive into the Greenlee Alamo Motel with a woman—a woman who looked like Mary Grater, one of our Bible study regulars married to the wealthy Capp Grater.

"It was Mary, I'm telling you, Martha, it was *her*," Betty had told me.

Me? I prayed it wasn't Mary. And I couldn't tell Oneeda any of this. The phone line would be jammed for days.

———

Returning to his obituary, I hit a snag. *What title should I give the man? Preacher, pastor, rector, priest, father?*

As old-school Southern Episcopalians, we called him "Father" in conversation with him. But when talking about him we used "pastor," or "preacher."

I decided to go with "Rector David Baddour." *More appropriate for an obituary*, I thought.

———

Close to ten o'clock, not yet finished, I locked the *Gazette*'s doors and walked home to change into something black for the funeral.

I was on the roadside when a car sped past, leaving a cloud of dust and cotton lint hanging thick in my face, smelling like harvest season. It made me think of life in Solo. What a for-gotten little place—center of the Delta, nothing but flat land for miles and miles in every direction. Our views were of corn and cotton fields and roads that hadn't been repaired in years.

Only 310 souls called Solo home. We were a speck of a town—too small for any stop signs, much less a stoplight.

We did have one claim to fame. Solo was the closest town to notorious Parchman Farm Penitentiary, ten miles south. For our entire lives Parchman remained a mystery. We'd all heard unsettling stories about the hardened criminals there. And their publicized escapes.

Growing up in Solo, I remember the older boys taunting, "Those bad men are gonna break out and come straight for you, Martha!"

Believe me, a young girl can have nightmares from such teasing.

The diocesan bishop usually officiated a rector's funeral, ac-companied by a cadre of priests in tow to pay their respects. But I didn't see any flowing vestments at Pastor Baddour's funeral.

Finding Oneeda, I asked her about it.

"They're all in Hawaii for the national convention," she said. *I knew she would know.*

Still, plenty of people attended the graveside service. We had all circled around the casket for the final rites when Capp Grater, our church warden, stepped through the crowd, placed a hand on the wooden casket and announced, "We gather to-day to put to rest Father David Baddour, a man who loved this congregation so much he wanted to be buried here, in Solo, next to his beloved Calvary Episcopal Church. Father Baddour came from the world of big city life, yet he visited our sick, our hurting, and yes … our lonely."

Capp Grater paused, looked to the sky as if speaking with God Himself, then turned a noticeable scowl toward his wife, Mary.

I peeked. Mary's gaze never left the orange and yellow fall leaves beneath her feet.

Poor Mary, I thought.

Me? I'd rather die a widow than be married to Capp, wealthy or not. 'Course he was never interested in me any-way. Mary was a looker. She had a figure. I had hips for the two of us. Put on some lipstick and makeup and she looked like a million bucks while I couldn't care less about cosmetics.

My gift was writing. I studied English at Ole Miss for two years, but dropped out to marry Shorty McRae, my high school sweetheart. That's when I began writing stories—so-cial goings-on, obituaries, weddings, those sorts of stories—while Shorty sold ads and handled the printing for our *Bethel County Gazette* weekly newspaper.

Neither of us knew he was born with a heart defect. Shorty passed four years ago. We had a good twenty-one years to-gether (never could have babies), then he was gone. I was a devastated thirty-eight year old widow.

My Bible study friends pulled me out of a long, two-year self-pity party. Life goes on.

Thank goodness Shorty left me with some insurance money. And there was the *Gazette* newspaper and our two-story brick home, which I turned into a boarding house for extra income. Most of my renters were come-and-go Mississippi officials visiting Parchman for one reason or another.

Having Pastor Baddour as a full-time boarder was a Godsend. Not one for chitchatting, it was still nice to have a man around the house. Then he was gone, too.

I couldn't listen to Capp Grater groan on about Pastor Baddour without wondering if Capp had something to do with the preacher's death. That's what made me think about Mary—how she'd met Capp up north in Phillipsburg on one of his lumber mill business trips. When they married none of us in Solo were invited, even though we'd been dear friends of his first wife, June. She died of cancer several years back. Their two daughters lived out west with families of their own.

While Mary Magden Grater wasn't a true Southerner, she learned to conquer cornbread as well as any skillet cooker in Bethel County. Except that's not what bowled us over about her. It was her church attendance. If Calvary's doors were open Mary was there; and Capp, too, if he wasn't hunting some mammal or fowl in season.

Looking up as Capp concluded Pastor Baddour's homily I said a silent prayer for Mary, praying Betty was wrong about seeing our Bible study friend and our preacher walk into that motel room together. And I prayed for Pastor Baddour's

family—whomever, and wherever they were. He'd never mentioned any kin.

When the service concluded, Capp announced we were all
invited out to his house for the "after" lunch.

Most folks believed the best home cooking could be had
after the body and the bereavements had been put to rest.

2

After the Funeral

THE GRATER HOME could accommodate most of Solo if needed, and that day it did. The men filled their plates with fried chicken, greens, potato salad, Mary's cornbread and headed for the screened porch. We ladies waited our turn for the finger food, congealed fruit Jell-O and deviled eggs.

Deviled eggs. It was a bad omen I couldn't have imagined at the time.

While the other women gathered in the garden room, I stood near the porch door and picked at my food, eavesdropping on the men. I wasn't able to make out everything they said but it surprised me to learn they weren't talking about the sudden death of our young rector. Instead, they were discussing our church delegate's visit to the diocesan headquarters in Salem. They thought our delegate was supposed to meet with the bishop and formally request a new rector.

(Thinking back on it, we were all naive when it came to the process for obtaining a new rector.)

I overheard one man say, "Johnson's not polished enough to deal with such educated clergymen."

"I agree. We shouldn't send him," another said.

"Johnson never got past the eighth grade. The bishop will think we're a bunch of hicks."

"But, fellows, we did elect him as our representative three months ago." That voice I recognized: Andrew Dawkins, vestry member and local cotton farmer. A good man.

"Electing John was a mistake," Capp Grater said. "None of us had any idea Father Baddour would pass so sudden. I think we should elect a new delegate."

"Johnson looks like a grizzly in overalls. And smells like one." I recognized that voice, too—Judd Insner, our part-time coroner and local butcher—the one who'd told me Pastor Baddour died of heart failure.

Another man said, "I don't want nobody in overalls representin' our church in Salem."

This is pitiful, I thought. I'm not sure who's worse, men or women, when it comes to judging others by their appearance.

They were talking about Johnny Johnson. Most of us called him JJ because that was the name of his bottled product—JJ's Honey, sold and consumed all over the Mississippi Delta.

Only Capp Grater referred to him as John, not JJ, not even Johnny. I had long believed Capp thought the use of nicknames was an admission of friendship. And for JJ, friends were in short supply, but I felt fortunate to be one of them.

Enough of their trash talk. I stepped out onto the porch and faced them.

"You men … you're pathetic. You elected JJ. Don't you dare take this away from him."

"Martha, this is none of your business," Capp said, staring me down.

"Of course it is, Capp. I'm a member of Calvary, just like you."

"You're not on the vestry, and this is a vestry issue."

"Nonsense. The vestry should consider what the church members want. It's called democracy."

I'd never gone toe-to-toe like that with Capp. I was happy to see JJ come through the porch door and stand beside me; but he was focused on the men, not me. And he did smell like honey. Sweet honey and sweat. His reddish beard sparkled with tiny droplets of golden nectar. His tall, lanky frame reminded me of a red-bearded Abe Lincoln.

When one of the men said, "Johnson, I hate to say it, but you're just not our man to meet with the bishop," JJ's eyelids narrowed into thin slits.

But he didn't flinch. Neither did he torch them with angry words. He simply said, "Gentlemen, I 'pologize for my tard-e-ness. A coyote got into some o' my bee boxes and I had to shoot him before he did any more damage. I'm sorry I missed the good preacher's funeral. That's all I got to say."

The men stared at JJ for five seconds, an awkward eternity to my mind. I suppose their tongues were too thick with guilt to utter a word.

Capp broke the silence. "John, do you own a suit?"

JJ had always attended church in black trousers, a tattered tan coat with elbow patches hung over a plaid shirt. That day he was wearing work clothes. Overalls.

"I do," he said. "I shoulda worn it today. I was too—"

"—No-no, it's all right," Capp interrupted. "I just wanted to know if you own one, if you have one."

Judd Insner piped up again. "JJ, I know it takes a lot to manage a bee and hog operation. I can't imagine you taking a few days off."

"If you're askin' me if I can go to Salem and talk with the bishop about a preacher replacement the answer is 'yes.' Besides, as the church's delegate, it's my job. You elected me. My sons can take care of the bees and hogs."

Andrew Dawkins said, "JJ, I'll be glad to come over and pitch in at your place while you're gone."

"Me, too," I said.

JJ thanked us and turned back to the men. "Besides, gentlemen, I ain't had my vestry training yet and I'd like to do that while I'm there."

Every man's face was a blank stare. I loved it. By their silence they were agreeing to send JJ Johnson to the diocese as our church representative.

I left the conversation when the men began giving JJ ideas for the sort of priest they wanted. I wanted to check on Mary. She was in the kitchen preparing more food trays.

"What can I do to help?" I asked.

"I'm fine. I just need to make sure those men out there are satisfied," she said, placing more fried chicken on a silver platter.

Something about the way she said "make sure those men out there are satisfied" stuck with me.

—∞—

Later, driving home, I couldn't get her "satisfied men" remark off my mind. I remembered Mary's life story like it was yesterday.

It was a Thursday, three years ago in Bible study, when she poured her heart out. We were studying the book of Hosea. I suppose the story of Gomer set her off, because she broke down in tears and told us incredible tales of her former life as a prostitute in Phillipsburg.

She ran away from home at fifteen, became homeless, hooked up with a pimp, and sold her body, two, three times a day. She told us stories I was not prepared to hear, would never forget, and certainly wouldn't repeat.

We were speechless.

But not for long.

Truth is, we itched to know more.

"Thank heavens I never had babies," she said. "I couldn't let a child grow up in that environment." She lowered her head, reluctant to say more. Candor was a quality I always admired about Mary.

And it was easy to see how her innocent bedroom eyes, plump lips, and pleasing demeanor could lure the lust out of any man's heart, though she did look older than her twenty-seven years. But even at that young age tiny crow's feet crept from the corners of her dark eyes. And no wonder—she'd lived a life most women don't live in a lifetime.

"So when did Capp become a customer?" Oneeda asked, unable to think before she spoke.

Mary's eyes pleaded with us. "No, it's not what you think. He was in Phillipsburg for a lumber convention. I was a model, working the trade show. Well, truthfully, my plan was to meet some new customers and make a little extra money. Anyway, we bumped into each other at the food court during lunch, both of us looking for a place to sit. So we sat together and ate. He was very polite. Never asked me out or anything like that."

I wondered if this was the same Capp Grater we all knew. To us, Capp appeared to be the most attractive and virile womanizer in Bethel County. He reminded us of a tall, handsome movie star. We just never could agree on which one.

Oneeda wanted to get back to the "extra money" talk: "Then how did you and Capp get together? You know ... to do it."

Every face zeroed in on Oneeda's.

She held her palms up and her eyes wide open. "How else am I supposed to ask the sex question?"

"Sex" was one of those unspoken words. But our piety was more show than righteousness, because we managed to smile at Oneeda as if to say "forget it," and turned back to Mary, eager for her to tell it all.

"There was no sex," Mary said softly. "Never has been."

Never? Now we were salivating.

We didn't need to say a word. Mary had seen our surprise. "Not once," she said, avoiding eye contact. "He can't … a hunting accident."

"I remember hearing about that a few months after June died," said Betty Crain, our Bible study leader and host. Betty was the most religious one in our group.

Mary continued, "He told me it happened crossing a fence. His shotgun went off and, well, the blast hit him … in his privates," she whispered in a weakened voice.

"How awful," Nora Beasley blurted. Nora was in charge of our church bookstore, and very librarian-like.

"His gun collection, they're his babies," Mary said, glancing at each of us.

Before I could ask about the firearm collection, Betty jumped in: "Go back to the lumber convention, Mary. What happened?"

"Well, we had lunch three more times," she said. "On the last day he told me about the accident. He said he was seeing a doctor in Phillipsburg to fix things. You know, back to normal. Then he asked me to dinner. We talked all night. That's when I told him about my job, my profession, *every*thing. I just knew he would run away as fast as he could. But it didn't bother him. I think he actually felt sorry for me."

She wiped away a tear.

"I didn't see him again until he called three months after the convention," she said. "He wanted to come back and see me. He said he was fixed. You know, his manhood and all. But he wasn't …" she trailed off, reaching for more coffee.

"And that was *it*?" Oneeda asked in shock.

"Oh, no," Mary said, straightening up. "We sat in bed and talked. That's when he proposed. He said he'd take me out of that life and make me the happiest person in the world if I'd leave Phillipsburg and come live with him in Solo." Her eyes widened while she stretched out her arms and said, "He never told me this house was so big, though."

We looked around and nodded in agreement.

"And then you married. In Phillipsburg," I said, smiling for her.

Mary nodded and blushed like a new bride. "Yes, we married a few weeks later—just us and a witness."

"Then what happened?" Betty asked.

Mary reached for a biscuit, turned it between her fingers. "Well, there's not much else to tell. When Capp brought me here, I stayed in bed for weeks. To get clean, you know. I thought I would die from the DTs. And Capp kept going back to Phillipsburg for more operations. We had hoped he could be fixed. It never worked out, though."

"So you were an addict, too?" Nora asked, surprised pity in her eyes.

"I'm a recovering alcoholic."

"That's terrible. I'm so sorry," Oneeda offered.

"The devil's elixir," Mary said, her mouth clenched.

Then her lips spread into a heart-warming smile. "There was this one Sunday, when I attended Calvary. I'll never forget it. I felt so uncomfortable, walking into such a holy place. But you ladies ..." she set down her biscuit and reached to clasp my hand, "you were so nice to me. And I surely needed the company of other women. I want to thank each of you for being my friend. More than you'll ever know." She shed another tear.

Us? We were so wrapped up in the illicitness of her story we couldn't shed anything, especially our curiosity.

When she asked if we would promise to keep it all a secret, I knew her story had come to an end.

We agreed, of course, to tell no one.

I began to wonder if Mary, after three years of Bible study, had cherished our companionship more than the lessons. And none of us had ever asked her the most important question of all, so I did.

"Mary, are you certain of your salvation?"

"I think so," she said, her eyebrows squeezed together in uncertainty.

I was about to pursue her lack of conviction when Betty Crain glanced at her watch and announced, "Ladies, I don't want to be late for my beauty parlor appointment in Greenlee. Next time, maybe we could meet at your house, Mary. Would Capp mind?"

"I'm not sure," Mary said, her face clouding. "I mean no disrespect, but Capp … he's like two kinds of chocolate—milk and dark. He can change from one to the other with no warning. I could never be comfortable if you ladies were there. I'm sorry."

We never did meet at Mary's house for Bible study. And only much later did I come to know the state of her soul.

Those memories of Mary's past faded when I turned off Highway 333 and entered Solo. But I did wonder how little it might take to bring out *dark-chocolate* Capp. If he was dark enough to commit the most heinous crime of all—taking a priest's life. Then I remembered what Judd Insner told me. "He died of a heart attack." *What could I do about that?*

Early the next morning I headed to the *Gazette* to finish Pastor Baddour's obituary.

"Heart failure." That's what I printed in the *Bethel County Gazette*, along with a few other facts I could recall about the preacher, which were less than adequate given he had lived under my roof for three years. He was such a quiet man.

That same week, a church meeting was held to give all Calvary members an opportunity to tell JJ what sort of preacher we wanted, so he could convey our requests to the bishop in Salem. There was no shortage of suggestions.

"Look at these hymnals," Oneeda said, standing, waving one in her hand for everybody to see. "They're worn out. Pages are missing. We need a preacher who can get us new hymnals."

"We need a rector who'll get involved with our children," one father said. "Our teenagers are gittin' into liquor."

"Precisely," Betty Crain said. "If this new rector could get us a ball field with night lights it'd keep our kids occupied and off the highway between here and Green-lee."

Several more church members told JJ what sort of rector we needed while he sat and listened carefully to everybody's suggestion.

Then Capp stood. "That's all well and good. However, what we really need is somebody who'll have a family, build a home and settle down. No offense, Martha, but it's not right for our preacher to be living at your place."

I kept my mouth shut. But never was I going to turn down a renter because he was single and needed a place to sleep and eat.

Young Freddie Carpenter, our postmaster, spoke his mind. "To me, where the preacher lives is not as important as getting this roof fixed. Every time it rains I leave the post office, come over here and put down buckets. This is God's house, and I think it's an embarrassment to God."

Betty didn't bother to stand when she thundered: "Well, Freddie, you certainly know about embarrassing God. We all know about your drinking problem."

There was silence. She turned to look at everyone. "Well, it's true," she said.

True or not, it was an awful thing to say. Her pious attitude had always been a mystery to me. I thought it was a cover for some insecurity.

I checked on Freddie's reaction. His cheeks were bright red, his eyes glazed over.

Betty had indeed said what few men would ever say to another man. Men are reluctant to interfere with another man's means of escape, no matter what path the destruction may be taking them down. And Freddie was on that path. It was no secret our postmaster swigged homemade liquor all day from little bottles he kept hidden in the back room.

The poor boy lost his parents in an automobile accident when he was in junior high—the worst tragedy Solo had known. Freddie moved in with his grandparents, three doors down from Shorty and me. He spent many an afternoon in my kitchen, eating cheese straws and rambling on about his future prospects in life.

Freddie finished high school (not a common achievement), got his degree from Delta State, and took a U.S. Postal Service training course. Capp Grater pulled a few strings to help him land the job of Solo postmaster.

It was time for somebody to divert the attention from Freddie, so I stood and addressed the congregation. "This is not complicated. A married man with a family might accomplish what all of us want. And I don't care if he rents from me or not—or if he holds a fundraiser for a ball field, and another fundraiser to fix the roof. I'll be first in line to contribute. So I agree we should ask the bishop for a married man."

Betty Crain stood again. "Martha, given our past experience with an unmarried rector, that is exactly how we should phrase our request to the bishop. It would accomplish what we need—a preacher with a wife ... and children, if possible."

"I agree," Capp said, then turned to JJ. "John, will you see to it the bishop knows of our desire to have a married man?"

JJ stood to answer. "Well, sir, I was thinkin' more about a Bible man who could teach us about Jesus," he said. "I s'pose he could be a family man, too. I'll do my best."

Two weeks later, JJ left his family, bees, and hogs for a trip to Salem's Cathedral.

On his visit he learned about the inner workings of the Episcopal Church and vestry duties. However, his time with the bishop proved to be a more memorable experience. As JJ recounted later, Bishop Plunk told him that forty-four percent of Episcopal churches are without a rector ... or have one only part-time.

The bishop said he'd notify JJ when a rector became available. Then JJ gave me the grave news: "We'll have to use our vestry members for Sunday sermons until we can find a replacement."

We had no recourse other than to wait. For the next few months, various members of our vestry delivered the sermons.

Solo's part-time coroner-butcher, Judd Insner, was the first. His sermon from Nehemiah involved rebuilding the wall of Jerusalem. It was an appropriate message for what we in Solo were about to encounter. Betty Crain spoke from the book of

Ruth. Andrew Dawkins delivered more than one heartfelt sermon. As did Capp.

After each service, we'd all address the vestry speaker and say what a fine sermon they'd given. It was the polite thing to do. Still, we left empty. We all wanted an ordained preacher.

Near the end of our four months of vestry preaching Capp delivered another sermon. It was from Exodus, on the seventh of the Ten Commandments. Adultery.

The next day, Mary called me in a panic. She wanted to talk. "At your house, Martha, not mine," she said, her voice trembling.

We sat in the parlor. She wasn't able to make eye contact or speak. Her bedroom eyes turned to mist. Then the dam broke. I moved beside her on the sofa, hoping to console her.

"I'm here, Mary. Tell me. What is it?"

She could barely get the words out: "Martha, I—I had an affair. With Father Baddour. I'm going straight to hell, I just know it." She took a tissue from her purse and bawled.

So it was you in Greenlee, I thought.

Mary dropped her chin and whimpered, "I guess we were both lonely, I don't know. Such a good man. Now he's gone. I feel so ashamed, so guilty."

I wasn't about to judge her or tell her how wrong she'd been. She knew.

Finally, she stood and we hugged.

I took her arms and held her so we could be face to face when I asked, "Does Capp know?"

She pushed me away and crumpled back in the chair. "I'm not sure," she said, shaking her head. "Except his sermon yesterday … on adultery."

"I remember it."

"Why would he choose that topic, Martha? On the way home after church he asked me about it."

Mary closed her eyes and took a deep breath. "Capp said the whole town seemed to miss Father Baddour. Martha, he asked if *I* missed him."

"What did you say?" I asked, hoping with all my heart she'd answered "No".

She stared out the window. "Nothing," she said. "I didn't say anything. I guess that's why he gave me the silent treatment all afternoon and last night."

I put a hand on her shoulder. "Everything will be all right. Give it time and he'll realize how much you love him."

After she left, I watched her walk to the street. I'd never seen her so slumped over. I was worried for her.

After making fresh coffee, I retreated to my special spot—the kitchen table—and pondered. *Surely Capp must have known about the affair. But did he have anything to do with Father Baddour's death? How difficult would it be to have his body exhumed and re-autopsied,* I wondered. *Another autopsy would put this whole notion to rest—prove for certain whether it was a heart attack or something more horrid.* But I was concerned it would turn into some trial and drag Mary's past through the mud of public ridicule.

Yet, I ached to know the truth. *What harm could it cause to merely ask about an exhumation?*

The next day I hustled over to Judd Insner's butcher shop to ask the question.

Judd was in the back, standing beside his chopping block. A deer carcass was sprawled across the table.

"Exhume the body?" he bellowed. "Whatever in the world for?"

He drove his meat cleaver into the wooden block with a sharp *thunk*, wiped both hands on an already crimson-stained apron, then turned to face me.

I flinched, and searched for the most sincere voice I could find.

"Judd, I think there's a strong chance there may have been foul play."

"Don't be ridiculous, Martha. I did the autopsy myself. Remember?"

He turned away, grabbed the cleaver and raised it above his head. With a loud *thwack* he cut off a hind leg, signifying to my mind there was no more to discuss.

His back was to me when he spoke in a blasé tone, "Besides, you'd need consent from the deceased's family and a court order from the district judge."

I don't think Judd liked people questioning his work. And by the looks of things, he was in no mood to help.

Since I didn't have time to pursue this suspicion on my own, I put Pastor Baddour's cause of death on the back burner … until I could come up with a new plan.

3

The Second Rector

ONEEDA WAS VISITING. We had finished supper and were clearing the kitchen when a knock sounded at the door.

Drying my hands on a dishtowel, I thought, *Unusual for anyone to drop by after dark.* I stepped into the hallway. Oneeda was peering through the curtains at a man wearing a clerical collar. Even odder was a man of the cloth coming by so late.

With no hesitation Oneeda opened the door, delighted, and said, "You must be the new rector. We've been praying for a new rector. I'll bet you're here to rent a room. Come in, come in."

Finally, a new preacher, I thought with satisfaction, watching him step across my threshold.

"Ma'am, I can't tell you how glad I am to hear you've been praying for a new rector," he said to Oneeda. "And, yes, I *am* looking for a room to rent. I saw your ROOM FOR RENT sign outside."

"Oh, I'm not the owner," she said, giggling. "My name is Oneeda Mae Harpole."

As I walked closer, Oneeda introduced me. "This is Martha McRae. She's the owner."

Whether they stay months or one night, I want to know everything possible about the people sleeping under my roof.

His clerical collar made a positive first impression. He introduced himself as Father Thomas Cain. He seemed intelligent, in his lower thirties, with eyelashes as long as my late Golden Retriever's. Maybe his eyelashes stood out so much because he was bald. Shorty was slick on top, too. But unlike Shorty, Pastor Cain stood six feet tall. I thought I could see straight through his crystal blue eyes. At the same time, I imagined he could see through mine, all the way to my soul. I flipped my hair back, thinking it might look better behind my shoulder—an instinct ingrained from my high school courtship days.

The three of us sat in the parlor.

"Tell me about yourself, Father Cain. Where you from?"

Thomas Cain told me all about growing up in St. Louis, his mother and father, their factory jobs, his brothers and sisters, seminary training ... pretty much the same type of information Pastor Baddour had given me when he needed to rent a room three and a half years before.

I poured a glass of sherry for Oneeda and me and offered him one.

"Oh, no thank you. I don't drink," he said.

"I'll bet you have a family coming to join you later, don't you?" I asked, eager to celebrate.

"Ma'am, God has given me a family wherever he sends me. My flock."

Rats, not a family man. I knew the church would be disappointed. But I liked his "flock" answer.

"Do you snore?" I asked. (Always one of my first questions.)

"Ma'am, I'm not sure. I sleep alone, so I truly don't know."

"Well, nose tape can help. I have some in the medicine cabinet."

"Sorry, did you say nose tape?" he asked, touching his nose.

"Yes, I've discovered that stiff, electrical tape stretched across the bridge of your nose can help with snoring."

"That's good to know. Thank you," he said.

"What about flatulence?" Oneeda asked without hesitation, smacking on her gum.

"About *what*?" he asked, shaking his head.

Mortified, I kicked Oneeda's foot. "Father Cain, Oneeda is asking if you have stomach issues," I added.

He chuckled. "Ma'am, do you have something for that?"

Goodness gracious, did the good Lord ever give you a pair of beautiful eyes, fella. His crystal blue gaze made it impossible not to grin.

"I do, in fact. I have a home remedy in the cabinet, in your room."

Rushing to change the subject from gastric issues, I added, "I hope you're not a sleepwalker. Had one of those once. Scared the daylights out of me. He was some bigwig out of

Salem. Always stayed with me when he visited Parchman. You do know Parchman is only a few miles down the road?"

"Yes, I've heard about it."

"Anyway, this sleepwalker, he always wound up in the kitchen with the fridge open, staring inside."

"No, I'm certainly no sleepwalker. I can guarantee that one."

"Oh, and you should know, we have a party line here in Solo. Will you need to make calls at night, or receive any?"

He cocked an eyebrow. "A party line?"

I chuckled. "A party line is where folks in the same area share a telephone line. They can hear your conversations, and you can hear theirs."

"I don't expect to receive any calls, no ma'am—or make any, especially since you've told me we're all one big party here." His broad smile was contagious.

We all laughed.

Oneeda couldn't contain herself any longer. "Are you a celibate priest?"

"No, ma'am, I'm an Episcopal priest."

Surely he knows what celibacy means. He must be pulling our leg.

Oneeda blurted, "Well, I knew one Episcopal priest who wasn't celibate."

"Oneeda, let's not talk about that right now," I said.

I turned back to Pastor Cain. "Tell me about your prayer life."

"Sorry. My prayer life?"

"How often do you pray?"

"Oh, all the time."

"Do you pray out loud?"

"I'll keep it quiet," he said, amused.

"Father Cain, you can see that most of my questions have to do with any potential annoyance my house guests might cause the other boarders and me. I'm not concerned about how late you stay up to read the Bible, or meditate, or anything like that. I just don't much care for noisy renters. I require peace and quiet."

He met my gaze. "Ma'am, I assure you I won't cause you any problems with noise. I believe peace comes from above."

I was pleased, and offered him the extended-stay plan. Seven dollars and fifty cents a night. He was grateful for the discount and accepted.

"Oh, by the way, which way is the church?"

Oneeda was quick to say, "It's three blocks to the right, on the next corner. I'll take you there." She was itching to be the first to show him our beautiful church.

"Oh, no thank you. I can manage," he said with a bright smile toward Oneeda.

He was sincere, charming, and exhibited all the traits of the perfect rector. Finally, we had our new preacher. And I'm sure he had no clue how lucky he was, living in tranquil Solo as rector of the oldest existing church in Bethel County.

Calvary Episcopal Church was built in 1856. Soon to celebrate her 100th anniversary, she remained on the original site—center of town, opposite the vacant train depot.

Generations of Bethel County's worshipers held fond memories of her white clapboard exterior and four wooden arches spanning the width of the nave. The deerskin wall sconces spread their golden hue upward into the rafters and mingled with the multi-colored light from the stained-glass windows, imported from Pennsylvania. Visitors to Calvary always said our church gave them an old-world feeling, adding reverence to their worship.

Our new rector spent three days holed up in his Calvary office. The Saturday night before his first sermon, he paced the floor above me.

When the congregation filtered into Calvary's nave at ten o'clock the next morning, we noticed a disturbing change. The crucifix on the sanctuary wall behind the altar was covered in a dark red cloth.

Whispers and murmurs rang through the nave until the procession began and we stood to sing. I figured Pastor Cain would soon explain the meaning of the draped cross.

He stood to read from the Book of Common Prayer, recited the Collect for Purity, followed by the Collect of the Day prayer. His voice was gravelly, but he was powerful in expression. He spoke with conviction, careful to pronounce every word.

Lay reader Andrew Dawkins read the First Lesson, we sang a hymn, and Betty Crain read from the New Testament.

Another hymn and Pastor Cain stepped into the pulpit. Head down, he opened his Bible and said, "The reading today is from First Timothy, chapter five, verses twenty-four and twenty-five: 'The sins of some people are conspicuous, going before them to judgment, but the sins of others appear later. So also good works are conspicuous, and even those that are not, cannot remain hidden.'"

Lifting a hand to address us, he announced, "Brothers and sisters—"

Brothers and sisters? Now that's a Baptist thing, I thought. But I didn't have time to dwell on it.

"—my name is Father Thomas Cain. I am pleased to be with you today. As your new rector I intend to teach you something about the cross behind me, the cross you can't see. And one day, when I believe this entire congregation has come to recognize the fruits of this world, I will remove the cloth and you can look upon it again, knowing that the man who was up there is coming back to do battle. And we must be ready."

His sermon was on the fruits of labor and the rewards we would receive if we could bring societal change into a "Godless culture." He reminded us: "Good works cannot remain hidden," and he added Scripture about rewards for our good works, like health and happiness.

Pastor Cain was forceful, raw, and convincing. I could've heard a pin drop.

But he did miss a few beats in the Order of Service. I thought he might be ill. He looked pale.

As I walked outside behind Capp and Mary, Capp told Father Cain it was the best sermon he'd ever heard. "What a joy to hear about God's rewards for those who believe," Capp remarked.

On the church steps Capp stopped to invite our new rector out to his place for lunch.

"I'll need directions, and please, I hope it's a light lunch. I haven't been feeling so well this morning." He placed a hand over his stomach.

He looks ill. I should remind him about the medicine cabinet.

4

Infatuation

OVER THE NEXT few months, Preacher Cain settled into his role, faithfully visiting the sick, talking to the school boys at chapel devotions, dropping in to visit the other widows of Solo. He even raised a few thousand dollars to build a new gymnasium and ball field. And his Sunday morning Order of Service became like clockwork, never missing a beat.

He captivated the whole town. Myself included. And for good reason. Folks from around Bethel County heard of his sermons and came to sit at his feet. As we grew, there was a pride at Calvary—something we had missed for a long time. I listened carefully to his sermons. Most were what I called "bless*ed* promise" preaching. He said we'd all be blessed with whatever we wanted if we prayed hard enough and gave generously to God's church. So we prayed and gave.

During the week, I would leave breakfast for him each morning, and he'd return after dark. Most nights he told me he had already eaten supper. *If he wants to talk, he'll say so*, I thought. He was a lot like Pastor Baddour—no small talk, studious, always reading something in his room.

One morning, I was dusting and found three expensive suits in his closet, all bearing a Nelson's store label. *Surely he doesn't earn enough money to pay for these*, I thought. *Maybe he's rich.*

I was inspecting one of the suits when the door opened. He startled me.

"A gift from Capp," he said. "He thought I should have some decent suits. He's a mighty fine fellow, you know." Those crystal blue eyes bore into mine. "I get the feeling you don't care much for him, though," he said.

"Who, Capp? No, no, he's fine," I said, replacing the suit in his closet. "He saved Mary from—" I stopped, realizing Mary's past was none of his business.

The rector's brows rose. "What about Mary?" he asked.

"It's nothing. Mary was just a little lost, and Capp gave her a new life, that's all."

Pastor Cain smiled. "If you don't want to tell me about Mary that's fine. What can you tell me about Oneeda?"

"Oneeda is a good friend," I said, surprised he had asked about her. "She's a little flighty, but a good soul. Why do you ask?"

"Oh, it's nothing. Just curious, that's all," he said, and left to prepare his sermon.

—◆◆◆—

Oneeda and I sat together most Sundays. It wasn't long before she began staying behind, talking with the rector. Walking home, I would turn around to see them laughing, touching each other's arms to make a point. My suspicions of a possible infatuation were growing by the week.

One Sunday lunch, when Preacher Cain was out at Capp's, I asked Oneeda about it. That conversation turned out to be stickier than the Delta humidity.

"Martha, I'm the happiest I've been since Bobby Joe left me," Oneeda said.

"That's why I'm worried. You seem to be smitten with our new preacher, and maybe encouraging him a little too mu—"

She cut me off and huffed, "—Look, I may be spending time with him, but it doesn't mean I'm taken with him. Every church needs an encourager and I merely encourage him to keep being a good preacher."

It wasn't the kind of encouragement I had in mind.

"Oneeda, remember when he first arrived?"

"Of course."

"You asked him if he was a celibate priest."

"I did not."

"You did, Oneeda. And I'm guessing you were wondering right then and there if he might replace Bobby Joe."

"Don't be ridiculous," she said, flushing.

Oneeda wasn't a beautiful woman. Neither was she unattractive. I'd always figured God gave her an around-the-clock metabolism. She could eat like a horse without gaining an inch in her hindquarter. I could see how Pastor Cain might be attracted by her physical features, even at five years his senior.

"You mentioned you've spent time with him. May I ask if you're seeing him on the side so to speak?"

Oneeda threw her napkin on the table, pushed her chair back with force and stood. "I will not sit here and be judged by you. You, of all people."

"Of all people? What's that supposed to mean?" I asked.

Oneeda stormed out the front door. She did have one parting remark: "You just want him for yourself. That's what I mean. Stay the hell out of my business."

Well, that settles it, I thought. Oneeda was obviously madder than a wet hen and protecting her interests in this man. Then, too, I had to ask myself … *Was I interested in him? Was she right to think so?*

I wasn't sure. But I did recognize a certain tingling when near him.

A week later, I carried my supplies upstairs for dusting and cleaning. Opening the door to Pastor Cain's room, I almost stepped on an envelope. Even before picking it up, I detected the strong scent of Oneeda's favorite perfume, Tabu. The envelope was drenched in it. It was addressed to *Thomas*.

I stared at it, wondering what to do. Leave it on the floor? It wasn't mine. *But Oneeda … she's getting in over her head*, I thought.

I decided to leave it. To forget about it. *She's a grown woman. I'm poking my nose where it doesn't belong.* I placed it back on the floor and began dusting the room. Every so often I'd glance back at the envelope. The smell of Tabu followed me everywhere. I looked at my watch. *Five o'clock. Thomas won't be home for another hour.* I packed the cleaning supplies and grabbed the envelope.

Five minutes later I was at the post office.

"Miss Martha, it's good to see you," Freddie said. "What can the U.S. Postal Service do for you today?" Freddie was a young, moonshine-swilling man in his mid-twenties who wore glasses as thick as his curly black hair.

"Freddie, I need to know—" The words wouldn't come. I swallowed. "I need to know if you can open this. But only if it can be resealed."

Freddie pushed his glasses up the bridge of his nose and reached for the envelope. "Well, it doesn't have a stamp on it, so there's no law against opening it."

"Can you reseal it?"

"Yes'um, of course," he said.

Taking the envelope, he stepped behind the partition. I started to walk around, but he stopped me. "Best if you don't come back here. Federal regulations and all ... you understand."

"How long will it take, Freddie? I need to get back home."

"Just take a minute, Miss Martha," he said from behind the wall.

I counted the minutes on my watch, and soon heard a whistling sound from the back.

That's a teakettle, I thought. Another minute passed. He reappeared at the counter.

"Here you go," he said, handing me the open envelope.

I turned my back to him and pulled the letter out. There was no question it was Oneeda's handwriting. When I saw what she'd written, I felt queasy.

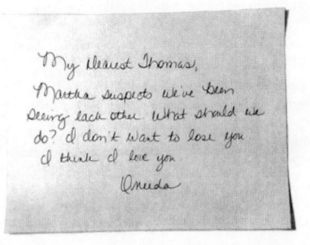

My dearest Thomas,
Martha suspects we've been seeing each other. What should we do? I don't want to lose you. I think I love you.
Oneeda

I inserted the letter back in the envelope and handed it to Freddie. "Thank you. Can you reseal it now?"

A few seconds later Freddie returned and said, "Here you go, Miss Martha."

At home, I slid the letter under Pastor Cain's door. I began to walk down the stairs when his door opened. My grip was on the handrail as I turned to see him holding the envelope to his nose.

"Why, Martha, this smells so good. Thank you."

I willed my heart to stop racing. "Oh, it's not from me. It's—Oneeda's. It's from Oneeda."

"Ah," he said, a frown on his face. "I thought it might be from you. We should have a chat sometime, you and I. You know, we've never sat down and talked much, have we?"

"I'd like that," I said, looking down at the floor. I raised and said, "Tell you what. I'll cook you a big breakfast tomorrow and we can sit and talk. How's that?"

"I look forward to it," he said.

I sensed his eyes following me down the stairs.

———

Sometime in the middle of the night I woke from a nightmare: *Pastor Baddour was stretched out on Judd Insner's chopping block. The preacher's chest was open. Judd was holding a beating heart in his hands.*

———

Three eggs over medium, bacon, grits, and biscuits with JJ's Honey waited for Pastor Cain on the dining room table.

"Ah, the sweet smell of bacon in the morning," he said, striding into the kitchen. "Best alarm clock a man could have."

I was surprised to see him in my kitchen. "Oh, good morning," I said. "Breakfast is on the table. I'll bring coffee in a minute."

"I'm very sorry, I didn't mean to intrude on your kitchen," he said in a polite voice.

"No bother. Just have a seat in the dining room."

I kept reminding myself this morning's talk was to be about Oneeda. I brought coffee out and returned to clean the kitchen. A few minutes later, Pastor Cain shouted through the swinging door, "Martha, these eggs and bacon are fit for a king."

"Thank you," I said, walking back into the dining room. I removed my apron and sat opposite him. He smiled. I smiled back. He was digging into his breakfast, but I didn't think he'd mind talking while he ate.

"Father Cain, you mentioned yesterday you wanted to talk."

"I did indeed," he said, swallowing a forkful of eggs. "Please, call me Thomas."

"Thank you, I will. In fact, I have something on my mind, too," I said.

"Oh? Well, good. See, that's a start," he said. "Ever since I arrived, I've had the feeling you were avoiding me. Please forgive me for being so straightforward, but if you don't mind, I have a serious question to ask first."

With a sip of coffee, I peered at him over the cup's rim. "Please do."

"Good. You see, Martha, when I opened that letter—the one from Oneeda—I felt strangely curious about something."

Coffee sloshed out of the cup as I set it down. *Surely he couldn't tell if the letter had been opened. Could he?*

"Oh, and what was that?" I asked, wiping the table.

"Well, I need your advice. It seems Oneeda may be … oh, how would you say it … obsessed with me. Is that the right word?"

"That's it exactly," I said, excited he had brought it up first.

"Then you know what I'm talking about. I believe Oneeda thinks I may have some sort of romantic feelings for her."

Exhaling a sigh of relief, I said, "I think you're right. She hasn't been herself lately."

"Oh? How so?" he asked.

"She's a sweet person, with a heart of gold. And easily taken advantage of, I'm afraid. I'm concerned about—"

"Are you afraid I'm taking advantage of her?" he interrupted, asking with raised eyebrows.

"I don't know. Are you?"

He put the fork down and wiped his mouth. "Martha, I have no … what is the word I'm looking for?"

I waited.

"Carnal," he blurted. "I have no carnal interest whatsoever in Oneeda. She's sweet, and good company. She makes me laugh."

I smiled and said, "Me, too."

5

JJ's Honey

O NE SATURDAY AFTERNOON in August I drove out to JJ's to pick up a new batch of honey for Pastor Cain. All my renters loved JJ's Honey.

JJ was shooing off his hounds as I drove up the dusty driveway. He was pleased to see me. "Martha, don't let these mutts jump on ya. They'll get that purdy dress dirty. Come on inside. I have plenty more new batches this time."

He led me to a building behind his house, the same place I always came when I needed honey. I could smell the sweetness long before we entered his jam-packed storage room. There were shelves and shelves of honey jars, each shelf and each bottle labeled by date and grade. Some were raw, the combs still inside. And there were a variety of amber colors, without a speck of comb.

"My favorite is the thick honey, this one with the comb inside," he said, pride in his voice.

"I've never tried that one," I said. "Tell you what, give me one of those, and two of the pale ambers on the end."

"Good choice," he said.

JJ wrapped and packaged the jars in a box while I inspected the honey-collecting equipment, as I'd done many times before.

"Martha, since you're here, there's something I want to say, if you have a minute," JJ said over his shoulder, sounding proper.

"Of course. What's on your mind?"

"I'm sure you know, we don't come to hear him preach anymore. I still go to the congra—congra—"

He couldn't get it out. "Congregational?" I asked, trying to help.

"Yes. The meetings. You were there, last week. Most folks seem to like this preacher. And you know he and Capp are attached like two peas in a pod. You remember how that meeting was all about raising more money for a ball field and gym. And I agree. It's a good idea. We need to give these young ones somethin' to do at night." The way he furrowed his eyebrows showed he was concerned—most likely for his own two teenagers, Jake and Jimmy.

"I know, and Father Cain is all for it," I said.

"Oh, he's all for it, for sure. And he does a lot of good for Solo. But Martha, there's somethin' about this preacher ... I can't put my finger on it."

I leaned back against a work counter. "Hmm. But I guess it's hard to argue with the projects he's undertaking."

"Yeah, you're right. But more important, we need a preacher who'll teach us the Bible. All he wants to talk about is money. And you remember one of the first things he did when he took over Calvary … he turned our church library into a money-making trinket shop."

JJ folded the flaps of the box and reached for a roll of tape. "And have you noticed he ain't bald by nature?" JJ said, shaking his head. "He shaves his head. He could have a full head of hair if he wanted. Seems mighty strange to me."

"I've noticed that, too … Look, JJ, I understand how you feel. I'm not sure about him either, probably for different reasons, though," I said, thinking of Oneeda's infatuation. "But JJ, the diocese in Salem says he checks out. You said so yourself … You know, it might help if you came back and talked to him about what's bothering you. He'd listen to a man like you."

JJ scratched his head and sighed. "I ain't about to ask him why he shaves his head."

"No, I mean talk with him about his preaching. Whatever's on your mind."

"All I got from those sermons was dead orth-e-doxy. And a bunch of hullabaloo—all his talk about riches if we'd just walk the straight and narrow. And give more money to Calvary. I don't think he'd listen to me. I'm not educated like him. Don't matter anyway. We have church services here at home now."

I remembered Pastor Cain's sermon on Sunday. He had indeed preached again that if we prayed long and hard enough, God would bless us with whatever we needed—"Money for a mortgage, pray for it. A new gym for our kids, pray for it. New streets, pray for it. Need a new car? Pray for it." Whatever we prayed for, if we were sincere enough and gave to the church, we would receive it. Never before had I seen Calvary's congregation happier, and billfolds lighter.

"I agree with you, JJ. But look, we need all the good men we can get in Calvary on Sundays."

He turned away for more tape. I sensed he didn't want to continue with my pleading.

To change the subject, I said, "That reminds me. Did you ever ask if the bishop confirmed Father Cain's appointment to Calvary?"

JJ put the box down and turned to me. "Forgot to tell you. I did. The bishop told me the Episcopal Church does have a priest by the name of Thomas Cain. Fact is, he said there are two Thomas Cains in the Episcopal Church. Said one of them was being relocated. He couldn't remember if it was for Calvary or somewhere else. Said he'd get back to me. Never did, though, so I figured Father Cain was the new rector. Stands to reason."

"Should you follow up with him, just to make sure?"

"Been meaning to. Just keep forgit'n." He handed me the box and said, "Well, I guess we got you all fixed up. You let me know what you think about the honey, okay?"

"Thanks, I will. JJ, there's something else you might ask the bishop. I need someone in Salem to tell us the name and whereabouts of Father Baddour's next of kin. Will you ask him about it?"

"I will. I certainly will," he said.

"Good. Now, how much do I owe you? And don't tell me it's free."

"Martha, how many times I gotta tell you? My honey is your honey. Now go on, git outta here, 'fore it gets dark." He laughed. "I know you ain't one for drivin' at night."

Placing the jars of honey in my pantry, I thought about Pastor Baddour's death again. I had hoped my suspicions would go away. But they didn't. It still added up to foul play, with Capp in the middle.

I shouldn't let go of it. But how can I get at the truth without dragging Mary's past into it?

To know for sure, his body would have to be exhumed and autopsied again. There was one problem. It'd be impossible without the permission of a next of kin. If JJ couldn't get that answer from the bishop ... well, I didn't know what I'd do. *He's bound to have family somewhere. Where can I look on my own?*

I remember thinking, *There's one source I can use. My newspaper. I can write about the speculation of a Baddour relative.* News of an exhumation—especially of a priest—would reach the Associated Press. If they ran a national story, thousands would read it. Hundreds of thousands. There must be a relative who'll make the connection and come forward.

But then a judge will need to sign off on it. I'd have to reveal Pastor Baddour's affair with Mary. Otherwise, what reason would the judge have to unearth him? At some point, all fingers would point to Mary—my friend—the former prostitute who had an affair with a priest. The public knowledge would devastate her.

My mind was spinning. I needed a plan. But first, I needed some sherry.

6

The Postmaster

WHILE I FOCUSED on the exhumation, something nefarious was brewing elsewhere.

Greyhound delivered Solo's mail every morning around ten o'clock, five days a week. Freddie would take the mail inside and dump it on his sorting table. Most of the mail was placed into the recipient's keyed lockbox in the lobby each morning.

In the afternoons, Freddie delivered the remainder to the rural roadside mailboxes. He always stashed a few jars of moonshine underneath the front seat for his ride through the county.

But Freddie's alcoholism wasn't his only addiction. He had an uncontrollable urge to know things before other people did. If a piece of in-coming mail looked interesting he'd heat up his teakettle on a small electric hot plate and use the steam to loosen an envelope's glue enough to pull the letter out, read it, reinsert it, and seal it with new glue.

He never did anything with the information, though, because as he told me later, "None of it was very interesting. Except for the letter I steamed open for you."

"Oh, I didn't realize you'd read it," I said.

Freddie didn't say a word. His cheeks turned pink, signaling he regretted having confessed to reading it.

I decided to ignore his transgression. "Freddie, you haven't been to see me in quite a while."

"Miss Martha, I've been meaning to. Guess I've been too busy."

I smelled the scent of moonshine on him. I hated that odor. Any whiskey, consumed over time eventually seeps through the skin, leaving that man or woman smelling twice as bad as the alcohol that went in. Moonshine is the worst.

One morning in September a letter from the bishop addressed to Mr. John Johnson fell from the mailbag onto Freddie's sorting table. After steaming it open, he realized he had hit the jackpot of useful and interesting mail.

Freddie did something he'd never done before. He redirected the letter to Capp Grater. He knew mail tampering was a federal offense. Much worse was delivering it to someone other than the intended recipient.

If Freddie hadn't been so enamored with Pastor Cain, circumstances might have taken a different course. He'd heard Capp and Cain were best friends. Freddie figured

Capp Grater would know what to do with the letter. After all, it was Capp who got Freddie the postmaster job in the first place.

Freddie hung his TEMPORARILY CLOSED sign on the door, and drove out to Capp's house to deliver it.

Standing on the threshold of his front door, Capp read the letter. The gist of it assured John Johnson that the diocese was doing its best to find a replacement rector.

> Mr. Johnson ... demand is greater than the supply ... we still have faith a part-time priest can be found ... Please tell your congregation to remain patient, and trust in the Lord.

"Don't say a word about this to anybody. Understand, Freddie? This must be a mistake. I'll take care of it when I get back from Phillipsburg." Capp's husky voice meant serious business to Freddie.

(So Freddie kept it a secret. Until one day when he was in hot water and told me about it.)

―――

I was down with a stomach bug one Sunday and couldn't make it to church. Mary stopped by that night to bring chicken soup and check on me. I asked her to pull a chair beside my bed and tell me some news. Reluctant to sit or talk, she kept shifting from one foot to the other, fidgeting.

"Oh, Martha," she finally blurted, "I've been trying so hard to be good, to forget about Father Baddour, to commit myself to Capp. But the way he looks at me sometimes, the suspicion in his eyes ... like this morning, after Father Cain's sermon on adultery."

"He preached on adultery?" I asked, a little surprised.

"Yes. And afterwards Capp invited him out to our house for lunch," Mary said. "Capp seemed to relish asking him about the sermon. And those eyes of Pastor Cain ... he kept looking at me, like he knew something. Then Capp suggested I give them some privacy. They shut themselves in the library. Martha, I eavesdropped on them. I could hear everything they said."

"What did you learn?"

Mary told me she was afraid that Capp was going to talk about divorcing her. She was relieved to hear that they talked about something else—the letter Freddie had brought to Capp.

She said Capp confronted Father Cain. "As warden of Calvary, I'm obligated to show you this letter, Thomas, and ask if you really are a priest in the Episcopal church."

Mary heard the unfurling of paper. There was silence for a few seconds.

"Capp, this is some sort of mistake. Yes, of course I'm a priest. Why else would I be here in Solo? Look, this is obviously an administrative oversight. I'll call Bishop Plunk and get this straightened out. In fact, I'll have him send you a letter confirming my appointment."

Capp seemed pleased with the rector's response. "Thomas, I was hoping you'd say that. I was going to contact the bishop myself, but you've suggested it. I'm glad you did."

"Well, good. Now … where's that bourbon you have hidden somewhere? I could use a shot," Cain said, snickering. (I remembered my interview with Cain. He had said he didn't drink alcohol.)

Mary said she heard footsteps, and the clinking of glass. Cain said, "Capp, we make a good team. Don't go and mess it up with some wild suspicions. You had me worried for a minute there. By the way, how'd you get this letter?"

"Freddie, the postmaster, brought it to me," Capp said.

When Capp started talking about his gun collection, Mary rushed away from the door. She figured they'd go there for an hour while Capp proudly explained the history behind each gun, as he had done once with her the day she arrived in Solo as Capp's new bride.

<hr />

I wasn't there to witness what happened the next day but Freddie remembered every detail.

Pastor Cain parked his red Buick in front of the post office. Freddie, with a clear line of sight to the car, grabbed a bottle of mouthwash and rinsed. He made sure the little moonshine bottles were tucked away. He had already finished two bottles and felt ready to tackle the day.

Freddie stood behind the counter as the preacher strode in.

"Father Cain. It's good to see you."

"You, too, Freddie."

"You haven't set up a postal box since you've been in Solo. I'll bet that's why you're here."

"No, Freddie, it's not. May we sit in your office?"

"I guess so. The feds don't allow civilians in the back. But I suppose they'd make an exception for you, being a priest and all."

"I'm sure they would."

Pastor Cain walked around the partition. Freddie took a seat. Cain didn't. Cain towered over him.

"Freddie, I'm going to ask you a question."

Looking up through his thick glasses at Cain, Freddie said, "Of course, sir, anything."

"Good. Good. Now Freddie, you see all the mail that comes into Solo. So I have a very important question to ask. By any chance have you come across any letters from the bishop in Salem? Any at all, even if they weren't addressed to me."

The fuzz on Freddie's forearms sprung straight up. He so wanted to reach for one of the little bottles under the counter. He couldn't help himself. He glanced at them.

"Freddie, Freddie," Cain *tsk-tsk*ed. "You wouldn't happen to have some of that homemade shine here, would you? Even a priest could use a taste of libation from time to time."

Freddie couldn't help himself. He peered at the bottles. But he was too nervous to move. Cain bent down and took one from the shelf. He unscrewed the cap and swigged. Freddie's head jerked back, surprised that a priest would swig moonshine like that.

"Ohh, that's fine stuff," Cain said, handing the bottle to Freddie. "Whew! Here, go ahead, you next. We won't tell anybody what we've been doing, will we?"

With shaky hands, Freddie reached for the bottle.

"No'sir," he said, downing the last of it.

"Ohh, man," Freddie said, exhaling and shaking his head from the brain burn.

"Now Freddie, back to my question about any letters from the diocese."

Freddie said he didn't wait for Cain to repeat the question. "Yessir. A letter came in a few days ago. I took it to Mr. Grater. I'm sorry. I didn't know what else to do."

"That's okay. You've told the truth, and that's what counts." (Of course, Cain already knew Freddie had delivered the letter to Capp. Evidently, he was testing Freddie.) "Tell me, was it addressed to John Johnson?"

"Yessir, it was."

"What was Capp's reaction to the letter?"

"He told me not to say a word to anybody. Said it was all a big mistake, a misunderstanding in Salem and he would take care of it."

"Good, good. I knew I could count on Capp."

"You and Capp, y'all are good friends, aren't you?" Freddie asked.

"Yes, we are. Now Freddie, this is important information we've been sharing, and I thank you for telling the truth. But if you see any more letters from the bishop, I want you to bring them to me, not Capp, or anybody else. Will you give me your word on that?"

"You have my word, Father. And, please, forgive me for reading it."

"I forgive you, son." As Cain turned to leave, he pat-ted Freddie on the shoulder. "You did good, Freddie. You did good."

Freddie had no idea Capp and Cain had already talked about the letter.

Several weeks later another letter addressed to Mr. John Johnson crossed Freddie's sorting table. He put out the TEMPORARILY CLOSED sign and started to leave for Calvary, but hesitated. Holding the letter in his hand, staring at it, he couldn't help himself. He had to open it.

Before steaming the envelope he needed to calm his nerves with some steam of his own. While the teakettle was heating he gulped two of the small moonshine bottles. The whistling kettle signified it was time to loosen the glue and open the flap. He pulled the letter out and read enough to realize it should be rushed to Pastor Cain.

Cain was in his office when Freddie appeared at Emily's desk. Emily Norton had been Calvary's secretary for twelve years. Cain waived Freddie in and shut the door behind them. Emily moved closer and listened to everything through the drafty door.

"Freddie, you look like you've seen a ghost," Emily heard Cain say.

"You instructed me to bring you any letters from the bishop. Here," Freddie said.

Cain must've gleaned the gist of the letter in a matter of seconds. (While Emily didn't see the letter, we later learned its implications.)

... happy to report that your new priest will arrive in Solo in early October ... Rector Adam Davidson answered Calvary's calling ... comes highly recommended. —Bishop Theo Plunk

Emily remained at the door, peeking through the crack. After folding the letter and placing it back in the envelope, Cain turned and walked to the chair behind his desk. He sat, twirled around, and stared out the window.

Freddie asked, "Are we going to have two priests at Calvary now?"

Cain ignored his question. "Freddie, did you read this letter?" he asked.

"Yessir, I did. I—I know I shouldn't have."

Continuing to stare out the window, Cain said, "Freddie, you've committed a federal offense. Mail tampering. That's how the federal government will see it."

Freddie said, "I—I don't—"

Cain spun his chair around. Emily jerked back, startled, when Cain raised his voice and said, "Do you realize you could go to Parchman for this? You don't want to go there, do you, Freddie?"

"But you asked me to bring you any letters from the bishop. Why are you talking about prison? What are you saying, Father?"

"I'm saying you can't say a word about this to anyone. Do you understand?"

"No, of course not. I mean yes, I can't say a word to anybody," Freddie said.

"Now, I want you to go back to the post office and do ... do whatever it is you do."

"Father Cain, help me. I don't understand any of this. Why are you saying these things? Will you help me?"

Through the crack, Emily saw Cain smile and say, "Yes, I will help you, Freddie. But from now on you must do everything I tell you to do."

"I will. I promise."

After Emily told me about Cain and Freddie's meeting, I asked her: "What did Freddie mean about "two priests at Calvary?'"

Not able to see the letter, she had no clue what it meant.

7

JJ's News

JJ CALLED THE NEXT Monday.

"Martha, we need to talk, but not on a party line. It's important."

"Okay, where?"

"Not your house, and not the church," he said.

"Your place?" I asked.

"I'll be here," he said, and hung up.

We sat on a bench outside his factory. He didn't say a word. Not right away.

"Tell me, JJ. What is it?"

He rested his back against the wall, crossed his arms, and stared at the horizon. "I called the bishop this morning to follow up on the Cain situation, but he was in some sorta meetin'. So I spoke with one of the assistants. Remember when I told you there were two rectors named Thomas Cain?"

"I do."

"The bishop had told me one of 'em was being transferred. I thought it was here in Solo."

"I remember," I said, eager to hear more.

JJ dropped his arms and turned to face me. "Martha, you ain't gonna believe this, but that assistant told me Thomas Cain took a church in Indiana. Not Mississippi."

An awful dread ran through me.

JJ shook his head. "I don't believe our Father Cain is the real Father Cain. And that ain't all. I learned that the bishop mailed a letter *weeks* ago. Martha, I never received any letter."

"JJ, Emily told me about a letter Freddie delivered to Cain the other day. It may have been the bishop's letter meant for you. And knowing Freddie, he probably read it first. He could be in trouble, JJ."

"We need to stop Cain," JJ said, his brow wrinkled in concern.

I placed a hand on JJ's shoulder. "We should be careful with him. The bishop's letter is the proof we need. Something's not right. We need that letter."

"I'll ask the bishop to send another one. He won't be pleased though," JJ said, shaking his head.

"We can't wait any longer. We need to get the letter now. Somehow. But look, ask him anyway, just in case. And ask him again about Baddour's family, would you?"

Pastor Cain wasn't the only priest on my mind. Things hadn't been right in Solo for some time. And it began before Cain's arrival.

"I will, Martha, I will," JJ said. "I never asked why you need to find his family."

"I need his next of kin to get a new autopsy."

"You're gonna dig him up?" asked a surprised JJ.

"I'm gonna try."

Unfortunately, JJ didn't wait for a confirming letter from the bishop. He arrived at Calvary the next Sunday for one sole purpose. After the service ended, JJ stood to face the congregation and shouted, "Friends and fellow believers, please allow me to speak about somethin' so important it can't wait 'til our next church meetin'."

I alone suspected where he was headed. I was proud of him. Part of me wished he had waited until he had the letter. But Holy Spirit had something else in mind.

"I've spoken with the diocese in Salem," JJ told the congregation. "They don't know of any Thomas Cain being appointed to our church. Fact is, they said Father Thomas Cain took a church in Indiana, not here," he shouted, turning around so everyone could hear him.

The congregation was too stunned to utter a word; until Capp Grater stood and pointed his finger at JJ.

"What are you saying, John?" Capp demanded.

"I'm saying that man ... that man there, is not Father Thomas Cain. He ain't who he says he is."

Several members came unglued—shouting at JJ. I looked to catch Pastor Cain's reaction. He remained stoic, staring at the floor with closed eyes. *Is he praying?* I wondered.

More stood and shouted. I couldn't hear everything being said, but there were plenty of angry faces and loud talk. My heart sank. *JJ is going to lose this battle*, I thought.

Cain took the water pitcher off the lectern and rapped the thick bottom with a fountain pen.

"Listen to me, people. Listen to me. Brother Johnson is right. I *am* a deceiver."

He stepped down from the raised dais, on a level with us. Everyone hushed.

He studied our faces, and announced, "In fact, we are *all* deceivers! Are we not? Every one of us. Nobody is perfect. So I applaud my brother ... Brother Johnson." He turned his attention to JJ, yet spoke to the crowd. "But what John here failed to tell you is that there are *two* Thomas Cains ordained in the Episcopal Church. Don't you suppose the other Thomas Cain might be in Indiana right now?"

Cain moved toward JJ, extending his right hand in friendship. "All you have to do, Brother Johnson, is ask the bishop," he said in a pacifying tone.

But JJ stopped him from coming closer. "The diocese didn't say nothin' 'bout the other Thomas Cain taking a church," he said to Cain.

JJ's voice became like that of a prophet. He turned to the congregation and shouted, "Behold, I am telling you, friends, our true rector has not yet come. This man is an impostor. Beware. You've been warned."

Me? I thought he'd been overcome by Holy Spirit. He'd never sounded so forceful.

But the congregation ignored his prophetic warning. They loved Pastor Cain and had grown offended by JJ's accusation.

Normal, post-World War II working Americans, overcome by rage, rushed JJ, took hold of him, and ushered him outside. It was an ugly scene to witness in God's church. Some of us watched, stunned, frightened by what was happening to our one hundred years of peaceful worship.

Because of our spat, Oneeda and I hadn't sat together for weeks. But as they took JJ out the front door, I looked to find her. We met in the aisle. I thought she might faint.

"What happened?" she asked, fanning herself with a church bulletin.

"JJ's different, Oneeda. He's not like any of us." It was all I could think to say.

We walked outside in a daze and watched as JJ's family put him into their truck and drove away.

After the commotion, Oneeda turned to me. "Thank goodness they didn't lynch him."

I was about to tell Oneeda that I would be going out to JJ's house to be with the Johnsons at such an awful time.

"Martha, can we go to lunch? Just the two of us?" she pleaded.

I could tell there was something weighing on her. "Of course. Where should we go? Greenlee? You wanna go to Greenlee?"

"Sure," she said.

She didn't care where we ate. She just needed to talk.

The congregation remained outside, milling around, discussing the event, as Oneeda and I slid into her car.

On the ride to Greenlee I talked about JJ and his bravery for confronting Cain.

After a couple of minutes, she said, "I don't want to talk about JJ. I want to talk about that snake," dabbing away tears with a tissue.

"Snake?" I asked, surprised by her sudden mood swing.

"You were right, Martha. Father Cain is a two-timing lizard."

"What happened?"

"I dropped by his office the other day. Emily wasn't at her desk, so I thought I'd go in to see him. The door was cracked open. I saw him with Betty. I saw them kissing, Martha. I saw him kissing Betty. Ohh, what a fool I've been."

"Oneeda, you're fortunate. You found out now, rather than later. I tried to tell you. Something's not right about the man. He's been bringing expensive clothes and other stuff home. Claims they were a gift from Capp, but I doubt it."

Oneeda sniffled. "He was wearing a new blue sweater when I saw him with Betty."

"Are you sure it was Betty?"

"Positive," Oneeda said with certainty.

Betty Crain. I remembered her piousness when she'd told me the story of seeing Mary with Pastor Baddour in Greenlee. A wicked thought crossed my mind. *Betty deserves what she'll get if Cain turns out to be the bad apple I suspect he is.*

In Greenlee, I pulled up to Charlie Parker's Place, the lone restaurant on the outskirts of town. We'd eaten there several times over the years.

"Why are we going here? This is where Father Bad-dour died," Oneeda said.

"I know. I wanted to come here."

It was as though my subconscious was reminding me there remained a missing piece of the puzzle, the one that would make sense of his death.

"Do you mind?" I asked.

"I guess not."

After we'd relaxed in a booth, I pointed to the counter stools. "Oneeda, he was right there, slumped over his plate."

Oneeda leaned in and asked, "You don't suppose that woman was with him, do you?"

"I doubt it. She would have been questioned," I said, thinking it was a good thing Oneeda didn't realize Mary had been to Greenlee with the rector or the whole town would know.

Fortunately, our food arrived, and there's nothing to compare with barbeque pork ribs and potato salad to lighten a wounded spirit. Oneeda's mood improved and we began to laugh about how man-gullible all of us can be as we get a bit older.

A man wearing a white apron approached us. "You ladies sound like you're enjoying the food. I'm Charlie Parker, the owner. How are the ribs?"

"They're delicious," I said, while Oneeda continued to chew and nod her agreement.

"Thank you," he said. "It's all about the quality of meat. I get mine from a butcher down in Solo. He delivers every Saturday, trimmed and all." He wiped his hands on his apron.

"Really? Oh, my name is Martha McRae, and this is Oneeda Mae Harpole."

"Pleased to meet you. I've seen you ladies in here before. You from Greenlee?"

"Actually, no. Mr. Parker ... would you mind showing me your kitchen?"

"Don't tell me you're a meat inspector," he said, a twinge of anger in his tone.

"No, no, I'm not," I said, smiling.

I whispered, "But I *am* writing a cookbook (not all together a falsehood; I *had* considered it) and would like to learn your secret."

His huge round face lit up, "Well, in that case I'd be proud to show you. Come with me."

Oneeda looked at me like I'd lost my mind.

"I'll explain later," I whispered in her ear, and followed Mr. Parker into the kitchen.

"First, I like to rinse the meat and parboil it for ten minutes," he said. "Then we work my special dry rub into the meat. After that—"

I was too anxious to wait for the lesson. "—Pardon me for interrupting, but tell me about the butcher from Solo. Does he ever come back here in the kitchen?"

"Oh, yes, ma'am. He smokes the ribs himself. He'll stay here all day Saturdays and help. It's one reason I keep buying from him."

"Oh, really?"

"Yep, Judd Insner. Good man," Parker said.

"I figured it was him. Thank you, Mr. Parker. I think it's time Oneeda and I got back home."

His forehead wrinkled, and he placed a hand on the meat, "But don't you want to hear how we *cook* it?"

"Oh, I think I know. You cook it over apple wood at 250 degrees for five hours."

I left Charlie Parker standing there, as immobile as his slab of ribs.

I'd found another piece of my Pastor Baddour puzzle. But I wouldn't be mentioning any of this to Oneeda. Rumors have a way of spoiling a good plan—a plan I didn't have at the moment.

8

The Gazette Story

WHEN WE RETURNED from Greenlee I dropped Oneeda off at her house and headed straight for the *Gazette*. I couldn't remember what day of the week Pastor Baddour died. *Was it on a Saturday?*

I searched for obits from November, 1954, and found it. He'd died on Saturday. November 20. I needed to find out what Judd had done to the meat, and *why*.

Leaning back in my chair, I pondered. Which comes first? Chasing Father Baddour's murderer, or dealing with a possible imposter priest. Two dilemmas. I decided the priest situation was more urgent. To think that our priest could be a fraud was a scary thought. Judd and the meat poisoning could wait. *I need to get that Bishop letter and force Cain into the open.*

But how? I dwelled on this for an hour.

Finally, an idea came.

I inserted a blank sheet in my typewriter and began writing a story the likes of which I'd never written, much less published. I wrote and revised until midnight. My working headline? *"Solo's Mysterious Rector."* The next day I picked it up again and agonized over every word—not knowing if I had enough facts, or even enough speculation to bring such a public accusation against our rector. In my gut—as a reporter—this felt wrong. In my heart, it felt right.

Late that afternoon I settled on a new headline: "Saint Or Deceiver?" To be fair, I included Pastor Cain's good works—his pastoring to widows, the sick, and all he'd done to help Solo. There were plenty of good works to write about. I gave him his due. But I also wrote how the diocese had never confirmed any Thomas Cain as our rector. I praised JJ for warning us in church and I defended his actions. I thought it best to use that angle rather than a direct character assassination. I didn't write about his expensive suits or womanizing ways. The story closed with these words: ... *assuming his real name is Thomas Cain.*

I knew a story like this would be awfully sour news at diocese headquarters—only a little prick is required to burst a rotten tomato. It would certainly force Cain's hand.

Still, I was conflicted. If JJ's and my speculations didn't hold up for whatever reason—if we'd both made a big mistake—a libel lawsuit could lead to the next death being mourned in Solo. My *Gazette.*

I needed another opinion. I picked up the phone and called Oneeda. "How soon can you get here?" As flighty as she was,

Oneeda could sometimes think out of the box and conjure up unique solutions. I needed her.

Ten minutes later, Oneeda stood beside my desk, reading the article. Finished, she dropped it on my typewriter.

"Martha, if you print this, you'll be ruined. For heaven's sake, I'm worried you'll disappear."

"Disappear?" I asked, half amused.

"Think about it, Martha. You could be taken and buried out in the cotton fields somewhere."

"Whoever in the world by?" I asked.

"Thomas Cain," she said. "There's something wrong with the man."

"Oneeda, this whole thing is, and always has been, in God's hands." Looking out the window, I silently added, *Dear Lord, I hope JJ was right about his conversation with the bishop.*

Sleep never came that night. *Maybe Oneeda's right. Maybe he is dangerous. Gotta be dangerous if he's an imposter. Then again, what if I'll be destroying an innocent man's reputation? What if one of the Rector Cains is in Indiana and the other one here, in Solo?* While my speculations were strong, my convictions were weak. I needed more guidance.

Taking refuge in my newspaper office the next night, I sat and prayed for it. Three hours later, about midnight, strong convictions took hold.

I prepared the printing plates and filled the press wells with black ink.

Early in the morning, I called Oneeda. "Can you come over again? I need to show you something."

I'd done it. I'd printed it. *The Bethel County Gazette, October 25, 1955.* Front-page headline: "Priest? Or Deceiver?" At the last minute I'd changed "Saint" to "Priest." *He's no saint.* Of that I was certain.

When Oneeda arrived I escorted her to the kitchen and showed her the article.

"Martha, I sure hope you know what you're doing," she said.

"Me too."

By the time Preacher Cain came down for breakfast, the freshly printed *Gazette* was on the table waiting for him, alongside his eggs, bacon, and toast. Oneeda and I came out of the kitchen. I sat down opposite Cain with a Bible on my right, Oneeda on my left—both for protection. I could see Oneeda's eyes shooting daggers nonstop at Cain. He hadn't touched his food. He was too busy reading the article about himself to even acknowledge our presence. I opened my Bible to Second John and read aloud, "'For many deceivers have gone out into the world, those who do not confess the coming of Jesus Christ in the flesh. Such a one is the deceiver and the antichrist.'"

I asked him point-blank, "Are you the deceiver?"

"What do you think?" he snapped. "Now that you've written this garbage in your little rag, everybody will believe it's true. It's in print, for God's sake. The bishop will read it. You call me 'The Deceiver.' You've probably destroyed my reputation."

"Did you not say, six weeks ago in church, that you're a deceiver?" I asked.

"You fool woman. I said we are *all* deceivers, none of us is perfect."

He pushed his chair back with force, and I could feel Oneeda next to me, fidgeting. Cain turned and bounded upstairs. Oneeda and I could hear him opening drawers, packing his belongings.

"Is he crying?" Oneeda whispered.

"Oh, my goodness. Sure sounds like it."

Coming back down, Cain's eyes were indeed misty as he announced he was moving into Capp Grater's guesthouse. For a split second I wondered if he actually might be a priest. Maybe JJ was wrong. Maybe we had misinterpreted our feelings. *Could he really be a priest?*

Something told me to stick with my intuition. A new boldness came over me.

"Wait a minute, Father Cain. I believe you owe me for this month's rent." I was in a daze, a dream-like state, wondering how I had the presence to speak those words to a man of the cloth.

We stared at each other—an eye for an eye—and I willed myself to stay calm. His stare turned into an oily smile—a smile I'd never seen before.

"Don't worry, I'll be back to see you one day, he said." Then walked out.

Humph, that sure sounded like a threat. I knew then—for certain—I'd been right about him.

Oneeda was jumping up and down with victory. "Martha, Solo is going to be famous."

"What?" I scoffed. "Why?"

"Because the *Gazette* will be picked up by the Salem papers, then it'll go out on the wire and go national."

"Oneeda, this is the only issue I printed."

Her forehead was a wrinkle of confusion. "You printed only this one issue? I don't understand."

"Yep. And there it is, right where he left it."

"What's the point then?" she asked.

"Well, for one, I didn't destroy his reputation without proof, did I? Nobody else will see this story."

Oneeda needed a second to process this … then said, "You flushed the dirt-bag out."

"At least now I know he's not a priest. A real priest wouldn't threaten me like that. And certainly wouldn't call me a fool. Not if he knew the Bible."

"What are you going to do?"

"Oneeda, I need your help. There's a letter I need to get my hands on."

"A letter?"

"I'll explain later. If you'll help."

"Of course I'll help. I haven't been this excited in years."

⎯⎯⎯⎯✖⎯⎯⎯⎯

Freddie loved his job even more than he loved moonshine, and if anyone discovered he'd redirected the letter, he'd lose his job.

So Freddie wanted the letter back.

He arrived at Calvary about ten. Emily picked up the phone, rang the preacher, and announced, "Freddie Carpenter is here to see you."

After Freddie walked in, Cain shut the door behind them.

Once again, it was easy for Emily to eavesdrop on the conversation. She even took notes. In shorthand.

"Father Cain, I'm sorry to bother you, but I—I really need the letter back."

"You need the letter back? You - need - the - letter - back? Is that what you said?"

"Yessir."

"And why would I give it to you? What in god's name would you do with it? Take it to Johnny Johnson?"

"Yessir. Those are my intentions."

"Freddie, you've been drinking, haven't you?"

"Yessir."

"I thought so. Let me explain how it's going to end for you, Freddie."

"End?"

"Yes, Freddie, 'End.' You see, the felony we talked about—mail tampering—it's going to end with you in prison. In Parchman. I've told you about Parchman, but I haven't told you what those queers do to pretty boys like you."

"Queers?"

"That's right. You're what they call 'fresh meat.' They will rape you every single day. Do you understand? Can you get a mental picture of that in your brain?"

"You're not going to give the letter back to me, are you?"

"No, I'm not," Cain told him. "Now look at me. Look at me, Freddie! Do you own a gun?"

"Of course. Everybody owns a gun. Why—why would you ask?"

"Do you want to be with those men in Parchman? Do you want to be their little pet? They'll take turns licking and raping you every day for five years."

"No. No. God, please no."

"This may be hard for you to understand, Freddie, but here's what you're going to do. You're going back to the post office … you're going to take that gun … you're going to stick the barrel in your mouth … and you're going to pull the trigger and end your life. Trust me, Freddie, it's better than going to that hellhole of a prison. Do you understand me?"

"But … I'll go to eternal hell if I do that. Father Baddour said suicide is a mortal sin."

"Not if I absolve you and give you permission."

"You can't do that. Can you?"

"Of course I can, Freddie. But you must not write a note of any kind. God doesn't want his name brought into this. Just say a prayer and do it quickly, Freddie."

"I don't understand. I'm so confused. Will you help me?"

"I *am* helping you."

"But if you turn me in for mail tampering … only you know about it," Freddie said. Why would you turn me in?"

Emily said Cain's voice became soothing, "Let's go to the post office together, Freddie. Just you and me. I'll explain it there. We can drink some of your shine and talk about it."

"No," Freddie shouted. Then he turned and ran. As he bolted by Emily and out of the church, she had no idea he was headed to my place.

Emily told me she scooted away from the door and sat behind her desk. When Cain stepped out of his office, she sensed he could smell her fear. "Emily, you're not a person to listen in on a private conversation, are you?"

"No'sir."

"Good. You may leave early today. I'll lock up."

<hr />

Oneeda and I were chopping vegetables for supper. We had known Freddie since he was a young boy. He knew us and trusted us. Thank the Lord he came to us.

But he was a basket case by the time he came through the back door, and stumbled into my kitchen. We helped him into a chair. Eyes swollen red from crying, he dropped his face into his hands, trembling.

"Freddie, what is it? What happened?" Oneeda asked, panic-stricken.

He couldn't talk. We offered him coffee. He guzzled it. After a minute, he stuttered out the story of meeting with Cain and what Cain had told him to do. Oneeda and I looked at each other, our jaws slack, lost for words.

As Freddie gathered himself, he confessed it all—the letters from the bishop to JJ he diverted to Capp, then the second letter to Cain. He told us of the drinking he and Cain had done. After that, he put his elbows on the table and his face in his hands.

"Freddie, listen to me," I said. "You must go back to the post office. You get that gun and you go throw it in the river."

He raised his head to look at me.

"Do you understand?" I asked.

"Yes," he whispered.

"Do it now, Freddie. Go throw it in the river. Then you'll have to keep your distance from Thomas Cain. I believe he's posing as a priest, and I intend to find out why."

"Me, too," Oneeda said, casting a sympathetic smile as she patted Freddie's shoulder.

"Promise me you'll do it," I said, begging.

He dropped his chin to his chest and muttered, "I promise."

After Freddie left, I plopped down in the closest chair I could find, worn out from absorbing this new information.

"Oneeda, what sort of man would say those things?"

"Certainly not a priest," she said.

"The time has come. I need to get that letter."

"But how?" she asked.

"I have a plan. You said you'd help."

"Of course I'll help. Whadda you need me to do?"

I explained the plan to her. When Oneeda left, she was already rehearsing her part.

I needed one more actor for my scheme to work. I went to the back bungalow and sat with Mary. I explained the plan but was concerned about her ability to pull off the "leading lady" role?

"Martha, you don't spend eleven years as a prostitute without learning how to act," she said with confident eyes and a voice to match.

The plan was set for the next afternoon.

Mary met Cain in his office. She talked about the new gymnasium, and how Capp wanted to give more money to the project. Cain was pleased to hear it.

Mary then changed the subject. She told him Capp had been drinking too much.

"You two are good friends," she said. "Can you help Capp? He won't listen to me."

"Of course I will, Mary. You and I both know what alcohol can do to a man," Cain said.

A screeching sound came from the church's side yard, outside Cain's window.

"Is that Oneeda?" Mary asked, feigning shock at the sight of Oneeda standing in the yard yelling her lungs out: "You're nothing but a two-timing lizard, Thomas Cain. You're a womanizing skunk, Thomas Cain. I saw you making out with Betty Crain in your office," Oneeda screamed.

"My god," Cain said, bolting out of his chair, peering out the window. "Is that Oneeda? Somebody get her away from here."

Cain rushed outside.

That's when Mary stayed behind and searched every drawer, every file, every shelf in his office, trying to find the letter. Emily helped.

Cain ran toward Oneeda, shouting, "Oneeda, what are you doing?"

Taking her by the arm he said, "Stop this right now. Everybody can hear you." He scoured the area to see who was close by.

I was hiding behind a hedge, waiting my turn. I came out playing the role of "sympathetic witness"—designed to keep Cain outside as long as possible so Mary and Emily could finish their search.

I said, "Oneeda, tell us what's wrong. Are you hurting?"

She moaned, "Yes, yes," and fell into my arms, sobbing like a two-year-old. Oneeda seemed to relish her moment in the spotlight.

Cain put an arm around her. "Everything's going to be okay, Oneeda. Take a deep breath. I'll give you a ride into Greenlee. You need to see a doctor."

Cain's taking Oneeda to see a doctor wasn't part of the plan.

"No, no, not you," I said. "I'll take her. You just need to help get her to my car."

We walked her three blocks. She cried the whole way, pushing Cain's arm away. She called him a "skunk of a man" at least five times. Oneeda had played the hysterically scorned woman to a tee.

Mary phoned me that evening and described every place she and Emily had searched in Cain's office.

No letter was found.

Much later, though, we learned Cain had been in his office on the party line listening to Mary's description of every nook and cranny she'd searched in his office.

Part II

Son of David

Deliver me from those who work evil, and save me from bloodthirsty men.

PSALMS 59:3

9

The Third Rector

A FADED RED PAINTING of Solo's *Delta Devils* mascot—horns, pitchfork and all—leered from the side of Capp's barn. I often had occasion to reflect on that. Perhaps all of us in Solo had grown too immune to recognize the evil among us. That's why our third rector's arrival in November was unlike anything we'd expected.

His first stop was Calvary Episcopal Church. I know because Nora Beasley stormed into my house that morning, chomping at the bit to tell me what happened.

Nora ran the trinket shop (formerly the book store) in the church narthex and was a faithful attendee of our Bible study group. She wasn't prone to excitement; but that morning was different.

"Martha, Martha," she screamed, bursting through the front door. I ran to the hallway to see what the hollering was about. "Martha, Father Cain just struck a man. It was awful."

"What man?"

"Adamson … Davidson, something like that. I can't remember," she said.

"Nora, here, sit. Catch your breath and tell me what happened. Start from the beginning."

She plopped down, her arms flailing. I'd never seen her so animated.

"I was in the shop when a man walked up and told me to shut it down," she said.

I dropped to the sofa next to her. "Who told you to shut it down?"

"Wait, I'm trying to remember his name … Davidson, that's it. Adam Davidson. He just walked up like he had the authority to do it. He said I should find another place to sell our merchandise."

Nora loosened the scarf around her neck. "Then he wanted directions to the rector's office. Emily wasn't there, so I showed him." Nora took a deep breath. "I don't think this man Davidson was expecting Father Cain to be there, because he seemed surprised."

"Who was surprised?" I asked.

"Davidson," she said. Nora's eyes widened further as she continued. "Anyway, Father Cain comes out to greet Davison right in front of me. Father Cain said something like, 'I've been wondering when you'd get here.'"

"Martha, this man told Father Cain that he was the new rector. Adam Davidson is a priest, Martha."

Now it's becoming clear, I thought.

"It makes perfect sense, Nora. This man Davidson is the true rector. Cain is a fraud."

"Then Father Cain said the craziest thing. He said he could make Davidson rich."

"Rich?"

"Money, Martha. But Davidson … he just kept looking at him, waiting for an explanation. Father Cain invited him into his office and closed the door. Martha, you've seen that door."

"I know. It's as drafty as a loose woman's skirt," I said.

"I could see them talking," Nora said softly. "Father Cain said he had come into some money and wanted Davidson to have it. But Davidson refused. So Father Cain asked Davidson to leave and find another church. He told him Solo already had a priest. He said, 'If you leave now, no one will even know you were here. And no one will be hurt.'

"Davidson said he'd been sent by the diocese. That's when Father Cain hit Davidson and knocked him to the floor."

"Oh my goodness."

"Is Oneeda here? She should hear this," Nora said, scanning the house.

"She's not here, but she'll know soon enough," I said. "Back up. You said Father Cain struck this man? Where? His body? His head? Where?"

"His jaw."

Nora balled a fist, mimicked the striking action, and continued. "Davidson got to his feet and said something about striking his other cheek. Father Cain called the man a fool and knocked him down again. I had to do something, Martha. I thought he might keep hitting him. So I knocked hard on the door and walked in."

Nora was fidgeting. "Martha, remember years ago when Shorty and Bill brought that wild boar home they'd caught in the woods? Father Cain looked like that boar … mad, wild eyes."

She gripped my arm. "I swear I've never seen a man so angry. Father Cain just stormed out, and this Davidson man got up and introduced himself. He said the Salem diocese sent him here to be our rector. Then he asked what Father Cain was doing at Calvary. I just stood there, like a statue. I didn't know what to say, Martha."

"It all makes sense," I said, staring out the window.

But why is Cain in Solo? I wondered.

Nora tapped my arm to regain my attention.

"He said the bishop had given him your name as a place he could stay. He asked for directions. He must be on his way here right now."

"Wait. Who's coming?" I asked, alarmed.

"The new rector, Adam Davidson," she said, in a tone that implied I hadn't been paying attention.

"Goodness gracious," I said, and hurried to the kitchen to make coffee.

I was in a daze when Nora called out from the parlor, "He's here. He's in the driveway."

Nora and I huddled at the front window as Davidson closed his car door.

"Is that him?" I asked.

"That's him. He looks awful," she said. "His jaw is all swollen."

"Look, you go to the kitchen. Let me handle this," I said, moving to one side of the window.

I waited for him to knock.

"Good morning," I said, opening the door.

"Good morning. You must be Mrs. McRae?"

The man before me was not someone you'd pick out of a crowd. Average height, five-foot-ten, brown hair. In his mid-thirties, I guessed.

"Yes, and you are?"

"Adam Davidson. I'm Calvary's new rector. I was told you might have a room for rent."

"I might. Come in and we'll talk."

After he stepped through the door I got a closer look at his face. His jaw was red; there was a cut above his cheekbone. Looked to me like he'd already wiped the blood away.

I took a deep breath. "I've already heard what happened at the church. I think you could use some medical attention."

He winced and raised a red bandana to pat the cut under his eye. "Small-town news does travel fast," he said.

That's when I got a good look at his eyes—brown, deep-set. They would go from smile to concern to sorrow with each shift in the conversation. No way to explain it other than to say that when you meet a genuine person, you can sense it. It's in their eyes. *I will not be putting this man through my usual inquiry,* I thought.

"The closest doctors are in Bethaven or Greenlee," I said. "You want me to get their addresses?"

Trying to smile, he said, "Well, not just yet. Let me see how I feel tomorrow. But I am interested in renting a room."

Too curious to wait any longer, Nora slipped out from the kitchen.

"I should introduce you to my friend, Nora Beasley," I said.

As she approached, he said: "Ah, the lady from church. I want to thank you for helping me."

"Are you okay? Shouldn't you see a doctor?" Nora asked, her puppy-dog eyes staring at his jaw.

"Oh, I think I'll be fine. Mrs. McRae has the name of a doctor in case I need one. But thank you."

He brought his bags in from the car and settled into his room. Nora gave me a significant look before she left; the news of this morning's events wouldn't take long to spread. Pastor Davidson spent the afternoon in his room and came down at four o'clock, asking if I had any coffee. I made a pot, and when he hesitated to sit at the dining room table, I said, "Father Davidson, you are welcome anywhere in my home. Please, sit. Call me Martha."

He asked about rental arrangements. I explained them. He said they seemed fair. Then he asked about Cain. "How did he become Calvary's rector?"

I told him all I knew. It took fifteen minutes.

He listened, absorbing everything, then asked, "So there's been no official confirmation from the diocese—either of this Thomas Cain, or me?"

"Correct. I believe Cain still has the letter confirming your appointment."

I explained my charade in trying to retrieve the letter.

Concern wrinkled his brow. "Mrs. McRae, I must say, that was dangerous. Look, this is an unusual situation, to say the least. He's obviously not a priest. Couldn't you be in danger from this man?"

"I'm not sure," I said, then showed him the *Gazette* issue. "Just yesterday morning, Cain, or whatever his name is, read this and stormed out. He took his belongings, said he was going to stay at Capp Grater's house. He had the audacity to threaten me."

"Then you do need to be careful." He cleared his throat. "I guess the missing letter explains how he knew I was coming. And you say he read this article yesterday and believes his reputation has been destroyed?"

"Right. But nobody, other than Cain and a friend of mine, has seen the article. I printed this one copy to see how he would react."

Pastor Davidson laughed, a twinkle of amazement in his eyes. "Now that sounds interesting. Tell me again why you printed only one copy?"

"To flush him out, of course," I said.

"Mrs. McRae, I applaud your courage. Where did you say this Cain fellow is now?"

"Capp Grater's house. He's our senior warden. He lives outside of town."

"Well, given what Cain is capable of, I'd say we should warn Mr. Grater."

I felt my forehead tighten thinking about Capp. "It won't do any good. Capp has defended him before. He'll just side with Father Cain—or whatever his name is."

Pastor Davidson rubbed his jaw again and gazed out the window, processing this information. He turned back to me.

"Mrs. McRae, tomorrow I want you to tell me all about Solo and our church, if you don't mind." The sparkle in his eyes, and his earlier actions at the church, gave me hope this new rector might bring some *good* to Solo, for a change.

"I would love to, as long as you'll call me Martha, not Mrs. McRae."

"Agreed."

"Good. We can do it over breakfast ... Oh, one more thing," I added, "what title do you prefer?"

"Title?"

"You know—father, priest, rector, preacher? Maybe pastor?"

"Oh, I guess 'preacher,'" he said. "My father was a Methodist preacher. But it doesn't matter much. Just don't call me Puffy." He smiled, rubbing his jaw.

We both laughed. Nora said, "I'll get an ice pack. You could use it."

"Thank you. Then I should to go back to the church. I need to see what sort of library we have."

"Oh, and you're going to find something unusual in the sanctuary," I warned. "Thomas Cain covered the cross with a cloth when he first arrived and hasn't taken it down since."

"With a cloth?" He frowned. "Why?"

"I believe he couldn't stand the thought of Jesus looking over his shoulder," I said, smiling.

"I'll remove it tonight. And, Martha, thank you for telling me all this. Looks like I have a lot of work to do in Solo." His smile was comforting.

Welcome to Solo, Preacher Davidson.

10

The Sheriff

On November 11, the day after Preacher Davidson's arrival, JJ called. His two teenage boys, Jake and Jimmy, had discovered a smoldering car in a roadside ditch between his place and Capp's. The entire car had burned—windows, seats, dashboard, everything—leaving a charred body on the seat springs, slumped over a melted steering wheel. The boys said it reeked of alcohol. They thought a moonshiner was using this back road to avoid the law.

When JJ and I arrived at the scene, Solo's constable, Jerry Webb, was already there. The car was still smoking.

Webb covered his nose and mouth with a bandana and used a crowbar to yank the driver's side door off. Finding a sturdy tree limb in the ditch, he used it to poke at the dead man's chest, moving him off the wheel and backward onto the exposed metal seat springs.

When he pointed to the scorched clerical collar around the corpse's neck, that's when I knew this was no moonshiner. And likely no accident.

Within thirty minutes, both ends of the scene were blocked off with eight police cars from Greenlee and Bethaven.

Bethel County's Sheriff Turnbull, a hefty, no-nonsense man known for busting up moonshine stills, arrived and spent several minutes studying the scene.

"Webb, better go into Solo and get your coroner out here," he said. "We're gonna need him. Tell 'em to bring his camera and a body bag. I'll get hold of my arson specialist. This sho looks like a homicide."

The sheriff turned to address the officers on the scene. "Fellas, we got ourselves a possible homicide," he announced. "And a priest at that. Constable Webb here thinks our victim may be Father Thomas Cain from Solo. What's the name of that church, Webb?"

"Calvary. Calvary Episcopal Church."

I remained quiet. *Let the sheriff do his job. He'll find out about me soon enough.*

"Right. Calvary. Okay, men, let's work it backwards. Start with this crime scene. Creel and Cox, you two go over it with a fine-tooth comb. Martin and Stubblefield, y'all find out where he lives and start interviewing neighbors. Everybody else follow me."

The sheriff led six men to the rear of his truck. "You men split up; half of you take one end of Solo, the rest of you take the other side. Talk to people. Find out what you can. I'll set up a temporary command post in the old train depot. Meet back at five today. Let's git it done, men."

⸺

By late afternoon, everybody was back at the vacant train depot to give their reports. The sheriff had set up tables, typewriters, portable blackboards, and brought in phone lines. I snuck in the back.

"Okay, men, let's go 'round the table," the sheriff said. "Tell me what you got. Bob, start with you. What caused the fire?"

Bethel County's arson expert was a wiry little man with missing teeth. He said, "Gasoline alone could'na made this much heat. Had to be somethin' else."

"Would pure grain alcohol do it?" one of the men asked. "The Johnson boys told me they thought it was a shine-runner."

"It's possible. That stuff ain't as volatile as gasoline, but once it gets going, it can burn hotter'n gas."

"But what's a priest doing runnin' shine?" the sheriff asked in disbelief. "And I wanna know what started the fire," he demanded.

"Probably a cigarette. We may never know," the arson expert said.

"The car wasn't his," I said. "See? It's a Plymouth." I walked closer and pointed at the hood ornament in the photograph. "Father Cain drives a red Buick. The Plymouth belongs to Capp Grater."

"And you are ... who?" the sheriff asked, grimacing.

"I'm Martha McRae. I own the boarding house where Father Cain was staying. Oh, and I'm a reporter." I stepped back into the shadows, not wanting him to kick me out.

"Good work, lady," he said, then turned his attention to the men. "Where's Cox and Creel? Anybody know?" he asked.

"I think they're headed out to the Grater house," Martin said.

I added: "Cain spent last night at the Grater's."

"Good," the sheriff said, just as Judd Insner walked in late. "Whadd'ya got for us, Mr. Coroner? Sorry, I forgot your name."

"Judd Insner."

"Show us what you got."

Insner laid out several photographs and a yellow legal pad.

"Here's a preliminary," he said, tossing photographs of Cain's charred body on the table. "I found a bullet wound in the victim's throat."

"Say what?" the sheriff asked, his face wrinkled like a bulldog's.

Insner demonstrated. "A bullet entered the back of his mouth, and stopped here, at the back of his skull."

"Holy Moses," one of the deputies said.

"I dug the bullet out. Here," Insner said, tossing it on the table. "Looks like a .22 caliber."

"Well, this puts us in a different frame of mind, don't it, men?" Sheriff Turnbull said. "Somebody didn't have much regard for our priest here."

The sheriff turned to a deputy. "Get on the radio and let Cox and Creel know about the bullet. I don't want them walkin' into some sort 'o surprise when they get there. Martin, you take the bullet to Salem and have it analyzed. And Miz McRae, why don't you head on home. One of our deputies will be by later to ask you a few questions."

Turning back to his men, "I'm gonna pay a visit to the Johnson boys and their daddy. He's the honey man, right, Martin?"

"Yes, sir, JJ's Honey. He was at the crime scene this morning."

"That's him," the sheriff said. "Okay, men, we'll meet here again tomorrow morning at five. We're gonna find out who killed this priest."

As I was leaving, Deputy Martin was on the radio calling Cox about the bullet in Pastor Cain's head. He was warning Cox to be careful with Capp Grater.

—⦿—

Mary later told me about Cox's and Creel's visit.

At the front door, Mary—wearing her robe and nursing two puffy eyes—stood behind Capp as he answered the doorbell.

"Mr. Grater, I'm Deputy Cox and this is Deputy Creel. Mind if we come in and have a word with you and Mrs. Grater?"

"About what?" Capp scowled.

"Sir, we discovered a car in a ditch down the road a'ways. We understand it might belong to you. We just have a few questions."

Capp let them in. They all sat in the living room. Mary witnessed the entire series of events.

"Mr. Grater, let me start by asking if you're missing a car by any chance."

"I don't think so." Capp's eyebrows carved a deep furrow in his forehead. "Mary, be a dear and go out back, would you? See if any cars are missing."

Mary was walking out of the room when she heard Capp ask the deputy, "Is the car damaged?"

"Sure is," Creel said. "Burned to the ground. Along with the body."

Mary stopped to listen.

"Body? Whose body?" Capp demanded.

"No positive ID, but it looks to be your church's priest, Father Cain," Creel said.

"Father Cain's body? I don't believe it," Capp said.

"We understand he was here with you last night. Is that correct?" Cox asked.

Mary returned on the heel of Capp's last comment. "Father Cain?" she asked. "You said there was a body. What's going on?"

"Mary, just go check the cars, okay?" Capp said.

Mary looked out the kitchen window and reported back. "Yes, your Plymouth is gone. But Father Cain's car is here." She couldn't keep the tremble from her voice. "What's going on, Capp?" He didn't have a chance to answer.

"Mr. Grater, you didn't answer my question," Cox interrupted. "Was he here last night?"

"Yes."

"We need to search the premises," Cox said to Creel.

"I'm inclined to make you get a warrant, but I have nothing to hide," Capp said. "So go ahead, search all you want."

They followed the officers through the house. Mary asked again, "Capp, tell me, are they talking about Father Cain's body?"

Capp frowned at her. "I'm not sure. Thomas and I were up late last night. We drank some. I guess he stole my car and left. I think he realized his time was up."

Cox wheeled around and asked, "What do you mean, 'his time was up?'"

"Last night, he came to tell me he was leaving Solo and going out West," Capp answered. "Look, officer, we were good friends, but he didn't tell me a lot. Just that he was taking over another church because we were getting a new rector. I'll get the letter and show you."

In Capp's study, Mary watched the deputy read the letter.

"This letter says the folks in Salem are still looking for a new rector," Cox said. "And there's nothing in here about Cain going to some other church, either."

"Well, maybe he just mentioned it to me," Capp said, shifting in his chair. He crossed his long legs and grabbed hold of his cowboy boot. "There's a new priest, named Davidson. He's already in Solo. He and Cain had a fight yesterday."

"Who told you that?" Cox asked.

"Cain did. Last night."

"Right," Cox said. "So you were the last person to see him alive."

Mary said Capp's muscle jaw tightened.

"Correction, deputy. The last person to see him alive was the man who killed him."

"Who said anything about a killing? How do you know it wasn't an accident?" Cox asked.

That question turned into a staring contest between Capp and Cox.

Looking back at the letter, Cox said, "This letter is addressed to a Mr. John Johnson. How did you come by it?"

"Our postmaster. He brought it to me."

"That's a federal offense, Mr. Grater. Mail tampering."

"You don't understand. The postmaster knew I should know about this."

"Doesn't matter. It's a federal offense. Now, you say he's the postmaster?" Cox asked, writing in a small notepad. "What's his na—"

"—Cox! Git out here," Creel shouted from the garage. Cox hustled towards Creel's voice; Capp and Mary followed.

As they entered the garage, Creel asked, "Mr. Grater, would you mind explaining why you have a barrel of moonshine in your garage?"

"It's not moonshine, deputy; it's barrel-aged bourbon," Capp said.

Creel turned to Cox and whispered, "Highly flammable."

Capp frowned. "Would one of you deputies tell me what you found down the road there?"

"Soon enough, soon enough," Creel said, tying a card onto the barrel, marking it as evidence.

"Do you own a gun, Mr. Grater?" Cox asked.

"Several."

"We need to take a look at those if you don't mind."

"No gun powder yet," Cox said, after an hour of checking Capp's massive gun collection.

Mary was standing in the doorway of the gunroom, filled wall-to-wall with rifles, shotguns, and pistols.

The deputies were lifting guns off the racks, looking down the barrels, sniffing the chambers. "Mr. Grater, look around and tell me if you notice any weapons missing," Creel said.

Capp surveyed the walls, shook his head, and said, "No, nothing's missing."

"Here's a hook with no gun on it. What's that about?" Cox asked, one eyebrow cocked.

Capp shrugged. "I'm a collector. I buy and sell guns all the time, deputy. I can't remember about that one. I must've sold it."

"Well, Mr. Grater, I'm afraid we need to get a team out here, collect these weapons, and get 'em to Greenlee, maybe even to Salem, and have 'em checked out."

"Checked out for what?" Capp demanded.

"Forensics, sir. I'm sure you're aware of the science. Our laboratory will fire each weapon and determine if the markings on the bullet match the one found at the scene. In fact, one of us is going to stand guard in this room until we can get a truck out here. Don't worry, sir, they're all professionals. They won't put a scratch on any of 'em."

"I don't like it. Not one bit," Capp said, his mood melting into *deep dark chocolate*—so mad, Cox was compelled to ask,

"Mr. Grater, is there something you want to tell us?"

"No. It's just that these guns … they're my babies."

"Mr. Grater, did you ever show this room to Father Cain?" Cox asked.

Capp hesitated and shifted from one foot to the other.

"That's what I thought," Cox said. "Creel, we'll need a fingerprint kit out here, too. Looks like our victim has been in this room."

Capp twirled around, nearly knocked Mary down, and stormed out of the room.

"Mr. Grater," Cox shouted, "can you tell us your whereabouts last night?"

Capp shouted, "I was with my wife all night. Ask her. I've had enough of this. Go get a warrant."

Mary figured he was headed to the bar to pour himself a drink.

"Miz Grater, I need to ask you a question," Cox said.

"Of course."

"Were you with your husband all night last night?"

She kept her eyes down. "Officer, I don't believe you can ask me to testify against my husband."

"That's correct, Mrs. Grater. I was just hoping you would help us solve this."

Deputy Creel walked up. "Mrs. Grater, when I was upstairs a few minutes ago, I noticed two large bedrooms and a smaller guest bedroom out back," he said. "All three beds were slept in. Do you and Mr. Grater sleep in separate bedrooms?"

"We do. Yes."

"Then how could you have been with him all night?" Creel asked.

"Neither one of you has an alibi, do you? Umm, what a shame," Cox said, adopting a sad expression.

Mary closed her eyes for two seconds, willing herself to stay upright and not collapse in a heap. There was more she wasn't telling the deputies, and likely never would.

Mary lived by Oneeda's motto: "There are some things you take to the grave. Everything else is open for discussion."

***

I wasn't surprised when deputy Stubblefield knocked on my door.

Oneeda was at my place again. We'd been in the kitchen, baking pies for a church fund-raiser. The three of us sat in the parlor.

"Mrs. McRae, do you know why I'm here?" Stubble-field asked.

"Well, probably, but why don't you tell me." I was also praying Oneeda would develop a quick case of laryngitis. *Don't need her going off in some wild direction.*

"There's been a death. A man was killed early this morning. Tell me about your relationship with Father Cain. I understand he boarded with you for a pretty long time."

"There was no relationship. But, yes, he boarded with me for several months."

"I'm curious, was your arrangement with him a charitable one? Meaning, did you allow him to stay for free?" he asked.

"Heavens, no. This and the *Gazette* is how I make a living."

Oneeda had been squirming in her chair. Suddenly, she blurted, "That scoundrel left yesterday owing Martha three hundred dollars."

"Is that true, Mrs. McRae?" Stubblefield's gaze promised he'd spot any evasion.

"Not exactly. It was two hundred and twenty-five dollars, not three hundred. And deputy, I was at the scene shortly after it happened. I already know he died in a car explosion. And I'm gonna tell you right now, I never could come to trusting terms with that man. And some-thing else: he's no priest."

"That so?" he said. He leaned his head to one side. "Yet, you did have a motive for killing him."

"There's no motive. And I certainly didn't kill him," I shot back.

Oneeda grew tall in her chair and smoothed her skirt. "I promise you, Martha didn't have anything to do with it. I know for a fact."

What did she just say? I wondered.

"And how do you know, Mrs. Harpole?" Stubblefield asked.

I took in a deep breath.

Oneeda paused, fidgeted a bit, then exclaimed, "Because I was here all night with her."

I almost choked. *Oh, Oneeda, why did you say that?*

The deputy didn't blink. "Okay, ladies, that's all for now. Oh, wait. I do have one more question. Was the other priest, Adam Davidson, here last night?"

"Yes, upstairs preparing a sermon," I said.

"Okay, thank you, ladies. I assume you're not going anywhere soon, right?"

"No'sir," we said in unison.

After he left, I promptly turned to Oneeda. "Why in the world would you tell him you were here last night? What were you thinking?"

"Martha, I was giving you an alibi," she said, pleading with me."

"Why would I need an alibi? I didn't have anything to do with it."

"I don't know why I said it. It—it just came out."

Peg, JJ's wife, told me all about the sheriff's visit.

After Turnbull pulled up to their house, JJ invited him inside.

The sheriff asked, "Your two boys found the priest, didn't they?"

"Sure did. And I was there when you arrived."

"Yeah, I remember you. But you ain't heard what the coroner found, have you?"

"What's that?"

"Well, the good father had been shot in the back of his mouth. It coulda been suicide, but we don't think so. People who shoot themselves don't bother lighting their car on fire. Mr. Johnson, where were you last night?"

"Sure didn't know he'd been shot," JJ said.

Peg offered the sheriff a biscuit with an extra-thick smear of honey. He gulped it down and said, "Mmmm, this sure is good. So where were you last night Mr. Johnson?"

"In Salem, selling some hogs at the auction barn."

"What time did you get home?"

"'Bout midnight." JJ turned to Peg. "Midnight … right, Hun?"

"Sure was. I was awake," Peg told the sheriff.

The sheriff asked to see the sales receipts.

Peg fetched them.

The sheriff studied them for minute. "Mr. Johnson, says here your last sale was at eight-fifteen. How come it took you four hours to get back to Solo?"

"I stopped to eat. Some small town."

"Would that place have a name?"

"Can't recall off hand. But I can sure go back and git it for you?"

"That won't be necessary," Turnbull said. "Maybe later."

Peg served the sheriff another biscuit with honey.

JJ told him about his trip to Salem and how the bishop had promised to send a letter—a letter he had never received.

"That so? Where's the letter now?"

"I'm believin' Father Cain has it. Or, had it, if it didn't burn up in the car."

JJ then told the history of his relationship with Cain and how the church had forced him out.

"So, they tossed you out of the church?" the sheriff asked, half amused.

Peg said JJ didn't flinch, or even reply.

"I take it you and Father Cain didn't see eye to eye on some things?" Turnbull said.

"Nope. Sure didn't."

The sheriff noticed JJ's .22 rifle above the mantel and asked if he could inspect the weapon. JJ didn't object. Turnbull opened the breech and sniffed. He asked JJ why it'd been fired recently.

"Varmints. I need it for the coyotes. They been tearin' up my bee boxes."

The sheriff explained that he'd have to take the rifle in for tests. "To see if the bullet we found matches this weapon," he said.

JJ didn't argue with him.

Early the next morning, Cox came into Solo in search of Pastor Davidson. Not finding him at the church office, he came to my place. The preacher had just finished one of my big breakfasts, and was about to leave when Cox knocked on the door. They sat in the dining room while I eavesdropped from the kitchen.

After Pastor Davidson explained his swollen jaw, Cox said, "So, Father, I still can't understand why you let the man knock you down twice. You get up and—how did you say it—you turned your face and invited him to knock you down again?"

Pastor Davidson simply smiled.

"Where were you two nights ago?" Cox asked.

"Upstairs, working on my sermon."

"Anybody see you there?"

"Only God," the preacher said.

"I see. Do you know where he might be, so I can question *him*?" Cox asked sarcastically. "He may be a material witness in this murder." Cox chuckled at his own cleverness.

"Officer Cox, if you would indeed like to see God, may I suggest you cover your face first."

"What's that supposed to mean?" Cox asked.

"It means neither you nor I could stand in the sight of His presence."

I couldn't believe it … a bright sunshine ray streamed from the window and spread across the room.

"Okay, whatever," Cox said, shading his eyes from the sunbeam. "I'll be talking with the postmaster later. Maybe I can get something useful from him."

<hr />

That afternoon, Deputy Stubblefield interviewed Judd Insner at his store. His wife, Annie, was behind the counter. She confirmed they'd been together the night of Cain's death.

It seemed as though several Solo residents had motive and means for murdering Pastor Cain. And so far, only Judd Insner had a decent alibi.

~∞~

Then it was Freddie's turn.

Freddie remembered his encounter with the six-foot-three tall Cox like it was yesterday. He recounted the entire story in my kitchen. I took notes, and with a bit of creative liberty, filled in some nuances.

At ten o'clock that morning a police car pulled up to Solo's post office. Freddie was in the back. As he peeked to watch the deputy step out of his car, Freddie told me he began sweating. He downed another small bottle of shine, and stayed behind the partition to gather his wits.

The bell above the door tinkled. Heavy boots clomped along the concrete floor.

"Miss Martha, I've never been so afraid," Freddie told me, and continued his story.

Freddie said he heard the deputy yell, "Hello. Anybody here?"

Freddie stepped to the counter.

"Just me."

"And you're the postmaster ... Freddie Carpenter, right?"

"Yessir. In the fletch—I mean flesh."

Freddie had been drinking. *I suspected as much.*

The deputy smiled at Freddie and said there were no re-
strictions on a deputy entering the back of a U.S. Post Office,
so he walked around the partition. His hand rested on the butt
of his pistol.

Freddie's legs were too wobbly to stand, so he sat at the
table. Cox stood, towering over him. Freddie told me it reminded him of Cain's visit.

"Freddie, do you have any liquor back here?" Cox asked,
"Cause I can smell it on you. See, I've been trained to break up
moonshine stills those fellas hide in the woods. You have some
here, don't you?"

"Yessir."

"How much?"

Freddie reached for a miniature on the shelf below. "Here
it is."

"There're only a half dozen little bottles here, Freddie. I
want you to take me to the mother lode, to the big stash." He
gripped the butt of his pistol. "Right now."

Freddie didn't hesitate. He jumped up and led Cox through
the door to the loading dock. Freddie pointed to a five-gallon
jug.

Cox whistled. "Well, well, if this ain't a mother lode of
spirits. Largest I've seen in a while. Whew. Let's go back inside." He told Freddie he'd have the liquor picked up later.

Back at the table, Cox sat, facing Freddie. "All post-mas-
ters are required to have a weapon on the premises. Where's
yours?" Cox asked.

Freddie pointed to a filing cabinet.

"What caliber is it?" Cox asked.

"A .22," Freddie said.

Cox barked, "Show it to me."

Freddie stood and walked to the cabinet. Cox followed, his hand never leaving the pistol butt.

"Show me the drawer. I'll retrieve the weapon myself," Cox said.

Pointing, Freddie said, "It used to be in that drawer."

"What do you mean, *used to be*?"

Freddie didn't reply.

Cox pulled the drawer open anyway. "Nothing here except old files."

"I threw it away," Freddie said.

"You - threw - it - away? There's only one reason you would throw the gun away, Freddie. Where'd you ditch it?"

Silence. Freddie didn't know what to tell him.

"Where'd you throw it, Freddie?" Cox yelled.

"In the river. In the Yazoo River."

"Why'd you throw it away, Freddie? Come on, it'll feel good to confess it. Just tell me. I want to hear you say it."

"I was afraid I'd shoot myself," Freddie mumbled.

"Wrong! You threw the evidence away, didn't you, Freddie? You threw away the gun that killed Father Cain."

"No. I threw it in the river because I don't want to go to Parchman."

Freddie told me he put his face into his hands, sobbed, and leaned against Cox's chest. Cox sat him down in a chair, and began handcuffing him.

Freddie said he was confused.

"What are you doing—why are you handcuffing me?"

"Freddie, you are under arrest for the murder of Father Thomas Cain."

"No. I didn't shoot anybody."

Cox put his mouth into Freddie's ear. "How'd you know he was shot? I didn't say anything about a shooting."

"You don't understand. He told me I was going to prison. To Parchman. He told me to commit suicide. That's why I threw the gun away. I didn't want to kill myself."

Cox got in Freddie's face. "Who told you, Freddie? Satan? Did he tell you to kill the priest, is that it? Did the devil speak to you, huh? Is that what happened?"

The mention of Satan's name sent Freddie's mind far, far away. He stared off into the distance, then straightened and clasped his hands together on the table.

Freddie said to Cox, "You know ... come to think of it, it might have been Satan."

11

Media Swarm

O N THE EVE of Freddie's arrest, the sheriff told his team it was the proudest day of his life. He gave a speech praising his department for capturing the killer, Freddie Carpenter. But the crafty Sheriff, up for re-election, waited two days to hold an official press conference, "to give the media time to git here," he announced.

They arrived like scavengers to dead animals on the highway. They came from Louisiana, Alabama, Texas, even Washington, D.C., headquarters of the Episcopal Church. They poured into Solo while the police celebrated.

"Ladies and gentlemen, this has to be a Mississippi record for solving a murder crime. And Deputy Cox, I'm putting you in for a special commendation."

Freddie was pronounced the killer that day by the sheriff and the media's notepads. They got their story and left.

But they would be back.

When Oneeda and I heard about Freddie's arrest, we were flabbergasted. We felt worse when we learned the evidence rested on the fact Freddie had thrown the murder weapon in the river on the same day Cain was shot. We felt responsible—guilty that our advice contributed to a false arrest.

We drove to the depot to straighten the sheriff out.

When we arrived the place was clearing out. Phones, blackboards, typewriters, all of it was being hauled off. The sheriff was sitting in a corner, rocked back in his swivel chair, his feet on the desk, hands cupped behind his head, looking pleased. "What can I do for you ladies?" he asked, stretching out over his desk. He was giddy, beaming from ear to ear.

"Sheriff, you have the wrong person. Freddie Carpenter didn't murder Father Cain," I said.

"Is that so? And how do you know that?" he asked, leaning back in his chair, folding his arms against his chest.

"Because we told him to throw the gun away. Father Cain, or whatever his real name is, wanted Freddie to commit suicide."

"No kidding?" the sheriff said, puzzled wrinkles forming on his forehead. "And why would he do that?"

"Freddie wanted the letter back—the letter he shouldn't have taken to Cain in the first place," I said.

"Ma'am, I hate to disappoint you, but we already have the letter."

"You have the *first* letter. There's a second letter. It explains—"

"—Look, ladies, it doesn't matter. We have the man who did it. Now, if you don't mind, I have a lot of paper work to do." He stood to shake our hands. Oneeda had already turned to leave; I refused to shake.

"Sheriff, do you realize Thomas Cain was an impostor?" I asked. "He wasn't a real priest."

"That so? Now look, you ladies go on home and tend to your own business. I have this under control. And I'm busy, so y'all need to scoot," he said, waving us off. "You ladies go on home."

The sheriff had his man. For him, nothing else mattered.

Freddie was carted off to the Salem jail.

Oneeda and I were sick with grief.

<hr />

I volunteered to take the postal exams and fill in as Solo's temporary postmaster. It wasn't a difficult job. Open at nine, close at four.

In the late afternoons, Oneeda and I would sit in the kitchen and conjure up ways to free Freddie. But we were as useless as a chocolate teakettle, melting into a dark glum. After hours of thinking and drinking sherry, Oneeda would always say, "Think, Martha, think. We've got to help him."

"I'm trying. I'm working on it."

<hr />

Two weeks after Freddie's arrest, Mary Grater called. "Martha, I'm scared," she whispered. "I need to see you."

When she arrived I was at the front door, waiting for her. "Tea, coffee, anything?"

"No. I just need to talk. I'm terrified, Martha," she whimpered, her cheeks streaked with makeup.

"Come, sit. Tell me. What is it, Mary?"

"It's Capp. I think he may have killed Father Cain."

My back stiffened. "Based on what?"

"Father ... Father Cain came to my bedroom that night. Martha, he ... he raped me." She fell into a chair, sobbed and buried her face in her hands.

"Oh, Mary, you poor woman," I said, holding out my arms. "I *knew* he was a snake."

She stood, and we hugged. I wanted her to feel my lack of judgment, my wordless assurance it was not her fault. After a minute, she felt secure enough to step back.

She wiped her face, and when her eyes met mine I could see how haunted she felt. "I feel so ashamed," she said.

"Mary, there is no way on God's green earth you're going to feel ashamed. I won't let that happen. God won't let it happen. Let's go report this to the sheriff. Together."

Her eyes flashed from haunted to terrified. "No," she said, shaking her head. "You can't tell a soul. He's dead. There's nothing anybody can do now."

I sighed, realizing she was right. We settled in the kitchen where I brewed coffee. We sat for some time before she brought up Capp's name.

Wrapping her hands around a mug, she said, "Capp lied to the police about the letter. And when I saw all those guns again, and then heard Cain had been shot before he was set on fire ... think about it, Martha. Freddie wasn't capable of doing all that. Not only that, but Cain was in Capp's Plymouth. How could Freddie have gotten Cain into Capp's car?"

I nodded. "Do you think Capp knows what Cain did to you?"

She turned and looked out the window. "I've thought about it. But I'm not sure. The next morning, after Cain had gone, I was going to tell Capp, but the police showed up. After that, I couldn't bring myself to tell him."

"Last year, when you told me about Pastor Baddour ... have you learned anything new that would make you think Capp knew of the affair?"

"Nothing. Other than his sermon on adultery." Her eyes widened. "You don't think Capp killed Father Baddour, too, do you?"

I sighed. "I'm not sure. Look, I'd feel better if you stayed here. There's an extra room upstairs."

"Thank you. I don't know what to say. I'm just grateful," she said, clasping my hand like she'd done that day in Bible study.

12

Souls With A Body

Preacher Davidson settled into his ministry, while I settled into a routine of shuttling between the post office and my newspaper.

Mary continued to stay with me, *still afraid of dark-chocolate Capp.*

Every night after supper I would take the dishes into the kitchen, wash, dry them, and listen to the preacher and Mary in the dining room. At first, I was resentful, having to clean the kitchen by myself.

I could hear them talking.

Preacher Davidson used Jesus's name more than any man or woman I'd ever heard. "Jesus is the healer, Jesus is our true priest, Jesus is our only Savior, Jesus is alive now, Jesus is fully human and fully God." Mary had a tough time with that one. But the preacher was patient, never giving her too much in one night.

Me? I would rush the cleaning and sit at the kitchen table, listening to them through the swinging door. I don't think they ever caught on to my eavesdropping. And I didn't care if they did. I was learning too much. I came to realize those revelations coming through the door were as valuable as if I were in Mary's own shoes.

One evening, she told Pastor Davidson about that ugly night with Cain. The preacher pastored Mary, teaching her about grace and forgiveness.

One of his talks with Mary inspired a Sunday sermon. What he said to Mary, and again in his sermon, was a life-changing revelation for me.

"We don't have a soul. We *are* a soul. We happen to have a body," he said. That's when I gave credit to Pastor Davidson for changing my entire view of life. *I'm a soul. I happen to have a body.* It was if a light switch had turned on. I began to see myself—and others—as eternal souls instead of makeup, hip size, or reputation.

And my search for the clues to the unsolved murders and our effort to free Freddie became a spiritual passion for me. It was the evil in the world I was chasing. I became more determined than ever to track it down and bring it to its knees. I felt as though God was using me for this sole purpose.

Night after night, week after week, I'd be in the kitchen washing dishes, listening to Pastor Davidson talk with Mary about her salvation.

One night took on a special meaning. I stood still in the kitchen, listening to her repeat the preacher's prayer of confession and acceptance. I came out and we celebrated. The preacher presented her with a Bible. It was beautiful to witness. She had received Christ's invitation.

A week didn't go by before the preacher started in on Mary about another issue. She was three months pregnant. Not wanting to give birth to Thomas Cain's child, she fought the preacher many a night.

"How can I have a child that'll come from something so evil?" she would throw in his face. She often mentioned a doctor in Phillipsburg who performed abortions.

I'll never forget what Preacher Davidson told her one night. "Mary, inside of you is a living, breathing child of God. Life begins at conception. Life begins when God says it begins. If you abort this child, you'll be killing God's child. That's what abortion is. Let the child live. Martha will help you raise him."

I smiled and nodded. I told her I would be there to help.

She turned to the preacher. "You said 'him.' How do you know it's a boy, Father?" she asked.

"It's a boy, Mary," was all he would say.

Mary wept.

After weeks of turmoil and soul searching, she agreed to have the baby.

———∞———

By then, Capp had become aware of her pregnancy. Soon after, an attorney from Phillipsburg served her with divorce papers.

"Martha, I'm fine," she told me one night. "I'm actually relieved. I have no more guilt. What I did with Father Baddour was a sin and God has forgiven me. If Capp can't forgive me, that's his problem. And I can't do anything about what Thomas Cain did. God will be the judge of him."

———∞———

Pastor Davidson had become accepted as Calvary's rector, priest, preacher, pastor, and friend. Everybody admired him. And his preaching had nothing to do with works leading to rewards. "Only by faith can we be saved and live forever." He was digging the dirt out of the evil wake Cain had left in our minds. Pastor Davidson never stopped preaching God's grace and salvation by faith alone.

Then, one day, he made a strange request of our Bible study group. Pastor Davidson asked if we would bake cookies for him. Dozens of cookies. He didn't explain why. We trusted he had a good reason and obliged. Every Saturday, Mary, Oneeda, and I delivered twelve dozen chocolate chip cookies to his office.

After lunch on Sunday afternoons, he would take the packaged cookies to his car and wave goodbye. He wouldn't return until late at night.

It would be months later before we solved the mystery of the cookies' journey.

———❧———

And there was Freddie's trial. We prayed a good attorney would take his case.

But no experienced defense lawyer was interested in defending a "mentally disturbed priest-killer," so Freddie's life rested in the hands of a public defender.

When the trial date was set for January 15, 1956, I made note of it on my kitchen calendar. In December, Oneeda, Mary, and I gave depositions for his defense.

Freddie's public defender fit the stereotype, looking like a fresh-out-of-law-school kid, fumbling and fidgeting with his papers during the trial. His sole argument rested on a plea of insanity, meant to save Freddie from the gas chamber.

Freddie never took the stand in his own defense. It wouldn't have helped. Our hearts broke each morning when he walked into the courtroom, limping and shackled. His eyes were swollen. We thought he'd been beaten.

The prosecuting attorney was ruthless in his attack on Freddie. He called witness after witness, all of them former visitors to the Solo Post Office. They'd all gotten to know Freddie. And they all testified to his sane mental state. The defense attorney's insanity plea was going downhill fast.

While questioning Deputy Cox—the prosecutor's chief witness—he asked, "Deputy, you say the defendant, Freddie

Carpenter, confessed that he threw the pistol in the Yazoo River around the time Father Cain was murdered, is that right?"

"That's correct," Cox said.

"But the weapon was never found?"

"That's correct."

The prosecutor turned to the jury and said, "Ladies and gentlemen, we don't *need* a smoking gun. By throwing the murder weapon in the river he might as well have admitted his guilt."

Filled with spiritual fortitude, I stood and launched an objection. "Your Honor. That's not what happened."

The *BAM!* of the judge's gavel startled me. He followed with a sharp reprimand. "One more outburst, lady, and I'll have you in contempt of court. If the defense calls you to testify you may speak your mind, but not before."

I bored a hole in the feckless defense attorney's back until he had sense enough to make eye contact. We did lock eyes a few times. And when he had a chance to call his witnesses, he called me.

On the stand, I asked the young lawyer if I might tell the story of what happened. He obliged. I told the jury about the impostor Cain and how he tried to manipulate Freddie into committing suicide. And I told them the truth about the gun—how we begged him to throw it away. Glaring into those jurymen and women's eyes with all the earnestness I could muster, I concluded, "*I* was the one who told him to throw it into the river. Me. There were plenty of people in Solo, and heaven only knows where else, who might've wanted to get rid of Thomas Cain. But not Freddie Carpenter. Not him."

After my impassioned plea, I looked at Freddie. He was listless, bent over, drawing on a legal pad. That's when, for the first time, I asked myself if Freddie might actually be guilty.

The next morning, the prosecutor and the defense gave their summations, and the jury met to decide his guilt or innocence.

Then, there was only the waiting.

⁓

Two days later, the jury came back with a verdict of not guilty—"lack of sufficient evidence." There had been no witnesses to a crime.

Hallelujah!

But our celebration was muted; our boy was too psychologically vulnerable to return home. We found a place where he would be safe. The Waterton Mental Hospital.

But Sheriff Turnbull was left with a quandary. If Freddie Carpenter didn't murder Cain, who did?

13

The Exhumation

B Y THE TIME Greyhound pulled out of Solo in the mornings, I was already sorting the mail.

One day, a special letter floated onto the table. It was easy to spot—the envelope with the distinctive Episcopal Church return address. It was addressed to Mr. John Johnson.

There was one piece of news left to receive—the whereabouts of Pastor Baddour's next of kin. I held it up to a light bulb.

Nope, can't see through it. Rats.

I eyed Freddie's old teakettle. It hadn't been used in months. But I couldn't bring myself to steam it open. So I rushed it straight to JJ's.

A cloud of dust must've created quite a twister behind my Ford because the whole Johnson clan was outside by the time I came barreling up the long hill to their farmhouse.

After coming to a stop, JJ leaned down to my window and quipped, "Where's the fire, Martha?"

I hopped out of the car like a teenager, held the letter above my head and shouted, "Right here, JJ. Right here in my hand."

The entire family—JJ and Peg, Jake and Jimmy, and the three Johnson girls—gathered around as I handed the envelope to JJ. He looked at it and said, "You know, Martha, this is the first letter I ever got from those folks in Salem."

"Go ahead, open it," I said.

"Open it, JJ," Peg said.

"Open it, Pops," the children yelled.

JJ opened the side of the envelope, pulled the letter out, read it, and reported back to me. "Martha, it's from the bishop. He says Father Baddour's next of kin has been located. Is this what you've been waiting for?"

I snatched the letter out of his hands. "Yes, JJ. Now we can have a look at Father Baddour's body."

The entire Johnson clan screamed. Some of the girls yelled, "Lord have mercy." But JJ quickly reprimanded them.

"Don't you girls ever take the Lord's name in vain, ever again. You understand?"

The girls lowered their heads. "Okay, Papa."

The Johnsons are like most of us. Deep down, we want something to cheer about, something to revel in. While the Johnson family wasn't sure of the significance of the exhumation, they were excited to see one. So was I.

All I had to do was contact the name of Baddour's cousin mentioned in the letter.

I reached him by phone two days later. The man had never met his second cousin once removed. Maybe that's why he had no problem giving the judge permission to dig him up.

———⁂———

When the judge's order came through, I thought it was time to bring Judd into this. He deserved to know.

We met in the back of his meat market. His muscular, tree trunk arms reminded me he could whack a deer in two with one blow.

"You'll be able to be there, of course, while the county coroner performs the autopsy," I said as soft as possible.

"But, Martha, Martha, why are you doing this? I told you, I did the autopsy myself. Father Baddour died of a heart attack. My assistant was there."

"Judd, I'm sorry. I asked your assistant about it. He told me he didn't actually see the autopsy. He only heard you say it was a heart attack." (While I had never asked his assistant about it, I suspected as much.)

"Martha, I'm telling you there's no reason to do this," Judd said. Red-faced and round-eyed, it didn't take a psychologist to realize he felt like a trapped 'coon.

"Judd, I was in Greenlee a few months ago. I know you supply Mr. Parker with his meat. He told me you often stay and help him cook …" I trailed off, waiting for his reaction to my subtle insinuation.

Judd's massive right arm crept behind his back to the chopping block. I couldn't see the cleaver, but I knew it was there.

"Judd, Annie's in the front ... Annie!" I screamed. "Come here, please. Judd needs you."

Judd dropped the cleaver on the block and brought his arm back. Both hands fell into his apron pockets. His chin dropped to his chest. He said, "Martha, I think it's time you leave now."

I didn't wait for him to repeat it.

The county coroner and his exhumation team arrived the same day Judd Insner committed suicide. Both events occurred about ten o'clock on February 14, 1956. While the team was digging up Pastor Baddour, Annie found her husband hanging next to the animal carcasses in the 38-degree meat locker.

After that, nobody was sure of anything. We shook our heads and wondered why so much had happened to such a small town.

Three days later—when we thought it couldn't get any worse—Baddour's autopsy findings were the talk of Solo. His body contained potassium chloride. He had indeed died of a massive heart attack, but it wasn't a natural one.

From then on, everybody figured Judd Insner had poisoned Father Baddour.

He must've doctored the preacher's food at the restaurant. But how? Why?

A crowd of locals gathered in front of the meat market. Whispers, questions, bafflement filled the scene. But the sheriff had the final word.

"Folks, the man who killed Father Baddour is on a slab right now in that little building over there. So stop dreaming up any more wild stories about what happened here. Now y'all leave and git on home."

Speculation. It's all I had. And now that Judd was dead, Capp would likely never be brought to trial for the murder of Pastor Baddour. Not unless I presented evidence of Capp's motive to the District Attorney. To do that, Mary's affair with the pastor would come front and center. And the rape would be exposed.

I wasn't sure how I could keep all that from public knowledge.

One day Oneeda turned to me and said, "Sometimes it's best to let sleeping dogs lie."

No matter that the saying had been around for centuries, it was the wisest Oneeda utterance I'd ever heard.

And Mary's wishes were clear. Nobody was to know.

Besides, I had two people to take care of—Mary, and the baby she was carrying.

14

Infamous Forever

ONCE AGAIN, REPORTERS descended like hungry scavengers. Judd's suicide and news of the autopsy brought them back.

We didn't have enough rooms, food, or scuttlebutt to fill their appetites. This time, they had been savvy enough to reserve motel rooms in Greenlee, Bethaven, all the way to Salem.

The first story I read from a reporter's typewriter carried this headline: 'Two Priests Murdered in Solo, Mississippi.' The sub-head: 'Coroner Commits Suicide.' How shocking would that appear to the rest of the world? Two priests murdered in little Solo, Mississippi. *Infamous forever.* It was in print. It must be true. They wanted a story, and they got it.

What stayed out of the newspapers was, to my mind, the real story—Mary's past. She was six months along. Only she and I knew the identity of the real father.

Some nights I couldn't sleep for thinking of Capp going scot-free without so much as a trial for Pastor Baddour's murder. Maybe Cain's murder, too. And the evil … I couldn't stop wondering why all this evil had descended upon Solo.

But I always came back to reality by praying for Mary's welfare, for her sake.

And there was the sheriff … he was back to investigating Capp for Cain's murder. We all knew about Capp's guns, along with the missing one.

Mary had heard from one of her trusted yardmen that Capp couldn't come up with a receipt for any gun sale. That's when a serious investigation began to center on him.

To me, Turnbull was a bulldog. He wouldn't hesitate to arrest the President of the United States if he thought he was guilty of something. This was good news. *I'm going to get some needed help.*

But nothing happened. Sheriff Turnbull wouldn't discuss his investigation. I suspected he couldn't get enough evidence to arrest Capp.

15

Sunday Afternoons

WEEKS TURNED INTO months, and I assumed the sheriff's investigation had gone bitter cold.

On a good note, our little church was bursting at the seams. Word of Preacher Davidson's sermons spread throughout Bethel County. Folks from thirty miles came to hear him. "Salvation through faith alone" was his message for weeks, along with how faith comes only from God Himself. "We can't earn salvation. It's a free gift from God," he kept preaching.

We learned that James's writings on faith and works were not a contradiction to Paul's letters. Sunday after Sunday, he preached, "Faith is not *true* faith without works. Works are merely the *evidence* of our faith. Works don't gain us salvation. Faith alone does."

Our nave for 150 souls soon exceeded its capacity. Calvary had already added an additional morning service, so we began seating people on folding chairs along the chair rail.

A vote was raised among the vestry to add a Sunday evening service, but Pastor Davidson declined, pleading a long-standing prior commitment. In spite of his plea, the vestry approved it.

Oneeda dropped by my place. We'd seen the preacher leave Solo every Sunday afternoon and return late at night. We speculated: *Is he seeing someone, maybe a woman friend in Greenlee or Bethaven? What is he doing with those cookies?*

How and where our preacher spent his Sunday afternoons remained a mystery until two months later, when the answer literally dropped into my lap.

While sorting Solo's mail one day, an envelope with an unusual return address fell onto the table. Having never seen an envelope with a Parchman Farm Penitentiary return address, I was intrigued. Its addressee was strange, too.

I was as close as anybody to represent the Town of Solo, so I opened the envelope.

Handwritten and barely legible, it read:

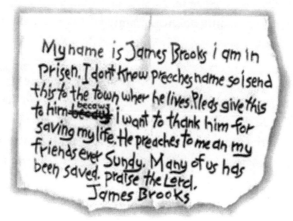

My name is James Brooks i am in Prisen. I dont know preechers name so i send this to the town wher he lives. Pleas give this to him because i want to thank him for saving my life. He preaches to me an my friends ever Sundy. Many of us has been saved. praise the Lord.
James Brooks

I carried the letter home and showed it to Mary. We were stirred by its raw power.

"That's where the preacher goes on Sunday afternoons," Mary blurted, excited to unravel the mystery. "Do you think he has a relative in prison? Maybe a cousin?"

"I hope not. We don't need another Solo media circus," I said.

"But the letter. It belongs to the preacher, doesn't it?"

"Mary, you're right. Let's take it to him," I said, fetching my coat.

We handed Preacher Davidson the letter. He read it, folded it, and put it in his desk drawer. He thanked us and asked if we might keep this to ourselves. We agreed but were still confused.

—◦≋◦—

A few weeks later the largest mailbag I'd ever seen arrived in Solo. Among the Sears catalogs, regular envelopes and post cards, were dozens of letters from Parchman—this time all addressed to: *The Preacher, Solo, Mississippi.* I stacked them, counting as I did. There were twenty-three letters.

Mary had gone to Nelson's in Greenlee to shop for baby clothes. I had to share this with somebody, so I called Oneeda. She came to the post office posthaste. Of course, we didn't open any of them. I put out the TEMPORARILY CLOSED sign, and we took them to Calvary, to Pastor Davidson.

Emily wasn't at her desk, so we walked straight into his office, eager to show him the batch of letters. He was on his knees, praying. We stopped and stood still, not making a noise. I was sure he'd heard our footsteps because he finished praying within seconds of our arrival. As he stood, smiling at us, it was impossible to ignore the worn threads at both knees. I have often wondered why I hadn't noticed it before. The man had spent a lot of time in prayer.

"Well, hello. It's good to see both of you. Come in. Please, have a seat."

We sprinkled the letters onto his desk. After opening a few of them and reading to himself, he smiled.

"Ladies, I've been meaning to talk to the vestry about this. Seems as though my Sunday afternoons have caused quite a stir. It'd be nice if our church members would work with me in this ministry."

He handed us each a letter. We read them. They were similar to the one James Brooks had written, thanking the preacher for saving their souls so they could "live in paradise forever."

After reading more letters I looked at the preacher with a twinge of curiosity. "You said ministry. What ministry is that?"

"The penitentiary. Parchman," he said, smiling.

"Parch-man," I stammered. "What could we do?"

His answer was unexpected. "Bake more cookies and come with me this Sunday afternoon. I'll show you."

"Go to Parchman? Us?" I asked, shocked at the thought. Neither Oneeda nor I had ever set foot there; not once in our entire lives. I'll admit, I was a bit nervous—not for my safety, but for what I might see.

Yet, there was something about Pastor Davidson that inspired trust.

———※———

On Saturday, Oneeda, Mary, and I baked twelve dozen chocolate chip cookies. Mary had no interest in going to

Parchman, and I didn't want her going. Not in her pregnant condition.

It was a short drive. Fifteen minutes. Preacher Davidson did his best to prepare Oneeda and me.

"When we get there, I don't want you to be afraid or surprised by what you see. The prison is heavily guarded. We'll pass through several checkpoints and be searched. Not to worry, there won't be any sort of strip search, I assure you," he said, smiling.

"Praise the Lord," Oneeda said.

My sentiments exactly.

"Your driver's licenses will be checked against your records. Once inside, we will meet with the superintendent. If they aren't under lockdown, we'll be allowed visitation privileges. Usually, I'm able to teach and talk with a number of men in the library," he explained. "Sometimes, I can visit the cell floors."

"But what are the cookies for?" Oneeda asked.

"For the prisoners. Feed them something special and they're more apt to listen. The superintendent will hand them out before we see the men. Today, I'll ask if we might be escorted down one of the cellblocks and talk with some of the inmates. Highly unusual, but he and I have become close friends."

The preacher smiled. "There're a lot of souls to be won in prison, ladies. You'll see."

16

Parchman

IT WAS JUST as the preacher had described. Except for the part about my throbbing heart. He hadn't warned me it would jump into my throat as we left the superintendent's office and stepped through a steel door, where I gazed down two rows of cells stretching a hundred feet on each side. A wooden skylight filled the ceiling between the rows. We were inside Unit 29, a two-story building of wood, grey cinder block, and hopelessness.

The smell of stale sweat and other obscene odors made me want to turn and run.

My next sensation was the silence. An eerie quiet. When the metal doors slammed behind us, I squeezed my eyes shut and felt Oneeda grab my arm. As the reverberation from the door faded, a loud, sinister scream echoed from the far end of the cellblock.

"Who's in my house? Is it the preacher? Is that the preacher man himself?"

I could see the man's face poking through the bars, but too far away to recognize.

Mouthing to us, the preacher said, "Ahh, that's exactly who I want you to meet."

I froze. Oneeda turned to me. "Is that who I think it is?" she whispered. "Is that Freddie?"

I must've looked frightened because the preacher put an arm around me. When Oneeda grabbed the preacher's arm we became a bundle of bodies and nerves.

Pastor Davidson broke it off. "Follow me. Look straight ahead. Don't look at the men. You might see something you wish you hadn't."

We followed him down the long row of cells. As we walked, some of the inmates spoke to him:

"Thank you, sir, for healing me," one man said softly.

"Thank you Father for saving my life," another said, standing in his cell.

"Will you heal me, too?" one man asked.

All of the men were eating cookies. One man tossed a half-eaten cookie on his bunk, jumped off his mattress and grabbed the cell bars, announcing to the entire unit, "Wake up men, the good preacher is in the house. Praise God."

There were cheers, and there were jeers. Some of the prisoners laughed and dog-cussed the preacher with utterances only the devil himself would speak.

We passed a man on his knees, praying. I had to look. Preacher Davidson stopped, too, and said, "This is Arthur. He murdered his wife and children. I'm certain he was possessed by a demon. But God has redeemed him. He's being trans-ferred to Kansas for his execution."

"Is this Death Row?" I whispered to the preacher. He nod-ded. My first thought was, *Why is Freddie on Death Row? Why didn't we know about this?*

Finally, we reached the far end of the walkway. The pris-oner was already standing by his cell bars, one hand noncha-lantly grasping a bar up high, the other hand wrapped around a lower bar, his body leaning sideways, his posture the em-bodiment of arrogance. Scraggly hair covered most of his face. I still couldn't recognize him.

Is this Freddie? I wondered. I glanced at Pastor Davidson. His expression radiated sorrow for the man. I looked at the man behind the bars. His eyes were closed, his mouth con-torted into a menacing grin. When he opened his lazy eyes—those crystal-clear blue eyes that could see through me—I shrieked. Without a blink, his glare slithered over to Oneeda, like an evil snake stalking its prey.

"Martha, Oneeda," Preacher Davidson said, "you re-mem-ber Father Cain. His real name is Sonny Sartain."

With a casual blink, Cain's eyes slid from Oneeda to the preacher, and he spoke. "So, preacher, I'll ask you again, for the umpteenth time. How is Mary? You know I can't wait to get out of here and see her." His voice was hollow, devoid of the slick charm that had brought him admiration in Solo.

"Sonny—" Preacher Davidson started to say, but Sartain interrupted him.

"How - many - times - must - I - tell - you - to - address - me - as - Father - Cain? *Father Cain*," he screamed. "Not Sonny. Not Sonny Sartain. Father Cain. Is that so difficult for you?"

"Sonny," the preacher said, ignoring Sartain's demand, "Mary is in God's arms now. It's where you belong, too."

"Noooo," he said, gripping the bars, "Mary is going to be in my arms. I knew she was crazy for me when Capp told me she was a prostitute."

I didn't say a word. It wasn't the right time to remind him that he'd raped her.

Preacher Davidson turned to us and spoke softly. "I've been by to talk with Sonny several times now. I thought he had been making progress."

Sartain—evidently not wanting to hear any more—spun around in disgust, covered his ears and curled up in a fetal position on the bunk. Preacher Davidson continued, "But I haven't given up hope for his soul."

Oneeda asked the question I wanted to ask: "But Father, when do you know there's no more hope for him?"

"Oneeda, there's always hope," he said.

Sonny Sartain was done talking with us. So we walked away, back to the main door. We stopped when we heard Sartain scream, "When I get out, I'm coming straight for Mary."

Chill bumps ran down my spine. Oneeda grabbed me again and we walked out arm in arm.

Driving back to Solo, Preacher Davidson told us why he had brought us to see Sonny Sartain.

"Martha, I want you to write about the man. Not only so Calvary can learn how easy it is to be taken in by false teachers, but so others might know, too. There's going to come a time when many more are deceived by Satan's demons."

"Why didn't you tell us about him sooner?" I asked.

"Because I wanted you to learn for yourself."

"Who was in the car that burned up?" Oneeda asked.

The preacher told us how Cain had faked his own death the night he left Solo. He stole Capp's car and pistol and drove to Salem, in search of a homeless man. He shot the man in the mouth, and brought the body back to Solo. Pulling off into a deserted cornfield, he dressed the dead man in his own clerical garb. He placed the body behind the wheel and ran the car into a ditch. He dowsed the body and the car with gasoline and turpentine and lit it.

He walked the Delta back roads into Greenlee, tossing Capp's gun and the man's ragged clothes in a creek along the way. He caught the next bus out west to California.

Five months later, Sonny Sartain was captured in Los Angeles and brought back to Parchman to await his multiple murder trial.

In the meantime, Turnbull and his men traced the route Sartain had taken to Greenlee, searching the creeks and found the pistol. His fingerprints were easy to identify—as were the prints in Capp's gunroom.

—⟨≡⟩—

During Sartain's murder trial I learned how he'd escaped from prison, without even the superintendent knowing. And I learned about his reign of murder just before he set foot on my front porch.

"Parchman often sent a busload of inmates to clear roadside trees and bushes," the prosecutor said during Sartain's trial. "On March 10, returning to the prison that night, the bus hit a deer and rolled into a gully. The defendant and one guard, Hershel Stevens, survived the thirty-foot drop, as the bus rolled and crashed in the ravine."

The prosecuting attorney had put together a map showing where it all happened.

The prosecutor explained: "The defendant strangled Stevens at the scene, switched clothes, placed him in the bus, and doused the inside with gasoline from the spare lawnmower cans. Then he set it ablaze. He climbed up the ravine and waited for a suitable victim to replace him at the scene of the accident. The third car that stopped was Sartain's answer—a man about his size, Good Samaritan Bill Waites."

Waites had seen the fire in the sky and drove to the scene to help. Instead, he became the twelfth dead man on the bus. (Waites' disappearance had remained a mystery since the accident.)

The map traced Sartain's route—now driving Waites' truck—from the burning bus to Bethaven, where he spent a night in St. Andrew's Episcopal church.

"The church's rector, Pastor Peterson, was a man of compassion. He had no idea Sonny Sartain was an escaped prisoner, posing as officer Stevens," the prosecutor said. "He let him stay overnight. He later told the police a man named Hershel Stevens had come into his church one night, cold, broken down and crying about losing his wife and family."

What a liar Sartain is, I thought, listening to the prosecutor's account.

"The defendant left St. Andrews early the next morning. With him, he took a clerical collar, a shirt, a pair of trousers, a book—*The Duties of Episcopal Rectors*—and a letter opener. The defendant needed a weapon," he told the jury.

The book. That's how Sartain knew the Order of Service, I thought.

"Pastor Peterson never knew anything was missing. He assumed the letter opener had been lost. From another book in Father Peterson's library, the defendant dis-covered a listing of all the U.S. Episcopal rectors," the prosecutor said. "He found two Thomas Cains, both about the same age as the defendant, Sonny Sartain. He tore the page out of the book so he could memorize Cain's background. He figured it was a good cover—two same last names would confuse anybody searching records for a Thomas Cain."

I figured the prosecutor was explaining everything in explicit detail so the jury would come to realize Sartain's evil mind.

The prosecutor used the map to trace Sartain to Greenlee, where he stopped at the ALL GOOD used car lot. He stabbed the owner, Tyron Good, in the ear with the letter opener, and stuffed Bondo in both ears and his mouth, "so no blood would be found on Tyron Good's floor," the prosecutor said. "Sartain then cemented Tyron Good in the trunk of another car, with lime to cover the odor. He left Herschel Steven's pick-up on the lot and drove off in Tyron Good's red Buick."

Sartain was so clever, he studied Tyron's hand writing and left a note on the door of the sales trailer: *Traded the red Buick today! Gone fishing. Celebrating. TG.*

The prosecutor held the note up for the jury to see.

That little note saved Sartain months of "free" time because law officers spent weeks searching rivers and lakes for Tyron Good's body. Eventually, they assumed he had drowned and disappeared in the river.

"Driving the stolen red Buick across Bethel county," the prosecutor continued, "the defendant stopped to ditch Stevens' clothes in the Yazoo River. The letter opener was in the trousers' pocket. At the river bank he shaved his head and became an impostor priest, clerical garb and all."

The prosecutor even recalled how Sartain had laughed during his interrogation about traveling through the Delta and seeing all the towns' *WELCOME* signs—the *Welcome to Greenlee, Home of the Red Devils* sign; and Bethaven's *Demon Deacons* high school mascot sign. The prosecutor said Sartain had confessed to feeling right at home when he discovered the *Delta Devils* painting on Capp's barn.

In the end, it was the letter opener that got Sartain, the mistake that came back to haunt him.

The trousers had drifted down the river. A boy fishing the riverbank snagged the trousers and took them to his father, who had the good sense to take them and the letter opener to the police in Salem. That little piece of evidence was the beginning of Sartain's undoing.

The inscription on the letter opener—*To our beloved Father Peterson, 1949*—led the Salem detectives to Pastor Peterson in Bethaven.

Pastor Peterson's story resulted in a check of Parchman's records for a possible match to any released prisoners. The detectives spent a half-day showing photographs of former prisoners to Pastor Peterson. They were about to call it a day when the superintendent, "on a whim," showed them photographs of the prisoners who'd died in the bus accident. That's when Pastor Peterson identified Sartain. The photograph was circulated and a nationwide FBI search began.

But they kept it out of the news so Sartain wouldn't get word they were on to him. It took months to capture him and conduct the trial.

⸎

In the third week of August 1956, Sonny Sartain was convicted by a jury and later sentenced to the gas chamber. Executions, however, were always years away, and he would have to wait on death row a long time for his.

I often wondered if it would ever happen. His execution.

The media picked up on Sartain's Solo connection. It made for good copy—an escaped prisoner parading as a priest. And they recycled all the earlier headlines: the unsolved murder of our first priest, a butcher-coroner suicide, and an alcoholic postmaster almost convicted of murder.

But the media hadn't finished with Solo. Not yet.

———

Mary came into the kitchen one morning, sweating, holding her watermelon-size stomach. "I think my water broke," she said, casting a sheepish smile.

I rushed her to the Greenlee hospital, and an hour later she gave birth to a baby boy.

In her hospital bed she pulled the little baby onto her lap, and proudly exclaimed, "Look, Martha, he has ten toes and ten fingers."

"Have you decided on a name?" I asked, while she nursed him.

"I have. His name is Michael," she said, showing me his face for a brief moment.

"That's a fine name. Is it a family name?"

"No," she said, shifting positions with the new baby. "I named him after Father Davidson's brother. He told me he was killed in the war. He told me what it means."

"You mean the name?" I asked, confused.

"Yes, the name. Michael. It means 'Who is like God? No one,'" Mary exclaimed, forming a wide smile.

"No one is like God," I said. "I love it."

She smiled, and let me hold him. He had a full head of black hair, and the most beautiful, crystal blue eyes. I couldn't help but wonder about the genes baby Michael had inherited.

After four days in the hospital, I took Mary and little Michael home to my place.

That week I drove back to Greenlee and purchased a Polaroid camera. I took pictures of Mary and baby Michael. I was starting a photo album for her. I prayed this child would never see, meet, or know his biological father. And I was thankful the media never got wind of the fact Sonny Sartain was the father.

Neither was I finished with Mr. Sartain. I needed answers to a few more questions.

17

Death Row

I HAD AN IDEA Sonny Sartain could shed some light on Capp's involvement in Pastor Baddour's poisoning. *Maybe Capp had actually confessed to him*, I thought.

I believed Sartain might talk to me if he knew I had something he wanted. And I did. I had written to him, asking if I might visit and bring it. Two weeks later, I received word from the superintendent. My visitation was approved.

I traveled alone this time. I was escorted to Unit 29. Walking past the cells without Pastor Davidson by my side, I was petrified, trying to ignore all the nasty comments from the condemned men who had nothing to lose no matter what they did or said—not something I wish to remember.

Reaching Sartain's cell, I pulled the visitor's stool close to the bars. I was determined to not be afraid of him. He was on his bunk reading a magazine. He flipped it around to show me a photograph of a naked woman. I suppose he wanted to shock or embarrass me.

"Do you actually know her, or do you just like looking at the little girl's picture?" I asked.

He threw the magazine on the floor and was in my face before I could move. I refused to let my head jerk backward or show any signs of fear, but seeing half his face poking through the bars, three feet from me, sent such a shock through my nervous system I could feel the hairs on the back of my neck stand on end. But I held steady.

He hissed, "You forced me to leave your place with that piece of garbage story you wrote. I wanted to kill you. And I would have if Davidson hadn't shown up."

Looking him in the eye, I said, "Mr. Sartain—"

"—*Tsk-tsk*, Martha," he interrupted, sneering. "My name is Father Thomas Cain. Remember?"

"What if I refer to you as Thomas?" I continued before he had a chance to respond. "Tell me what you and Capp Grater talked about that last night you were in Solo?"

His eyes narrowed into thin slits. "I might if you give me what you promised to bring."

"I brought it," I said, tapping my purse.

He relaxed and enjoyed telling the story. "That night at Capp's, we got real drunk. I told him I'd overheard Mary telling you about searching my office for that letter. Ha, he didn't even know about any new letter. So I showed it to him. When he realized there was another rector coming to Solo he said there'd be no more money coming from *him*," Sartain snorted.

"You know Mary shouldn't have searched my office like that. And you know about their separate bedrooms, if you get my drift. I was leaving town the next day anyway. So, I paid her a visit. She was a prostitute you know. And you know what else? She appreciated it."

Angry, I slid my stool back. "You're lying. You raped her and you're too ashamed to admit it."

"Martha, do you really think I could feel shame?"

He stepped back and spoke in a soothing, evil tone. "I can't tell you how excited I was to hear about the little boy. What's his name? Is it Thomas, like me?"

I refused to say anything.

"That's my son," he blurted. "I want to see the picture of my son. I know you brought it. Now show it to me."

"You raped her, didn't you?" I wanted him to admit it.

He refused to say anything.

"I brought the picture. But you have to tell the truth. You raped her, didn't you?"

Going back to his bunk, he sat on the edge, lowered his head and rolled his eyes around in circles while rubbing his legs. He began to fidget and rock from side to side. He became like a little boy unwilling to confess his guilt but whose body language was his only way of admitting it. I was looking at a demon-possessed, sorry excuse of a man.

He jumped and squeezed his face through the bars again, his eyes leveled on me. "I've told you *everything*. Now let me see the picture of Mary and my boy. It's the only reason I let you in here." He reached an arm through the bars and held his palm open.

"Hold on. There's one more thing," I said. "Capp Grater confessed to you about poisoning Father Baddour, didn't he?"

Sartain's lips spread into a sinister smile as he pulled his arm back through the bars. "Confessions are a sacred secret between priest and confessor," he said.

"You're not a priest. Besides, that's a Catholic tradition."

Sartain sighed as if he'd grown bored. He gripped the bars with both hands. "No. He didn't confess to killing anybody. Now let me see the picture," he demanded.

"One thing I've learned, Mr. Sartain, is that Satan is not capable of telling the truth. You're lying to me. And I never promised to actually *show* you the picture. I merely stated in my letter I would bring a picture of them. May God have mercy on you." I stood and walked away.

"You stupid hag," he screamed. "Don't you know I'll get you for this? I'm gonna get out of here and come straight for you. Straight for *you*. Then Mary. And the boy. Do you hear me?"

He screamed unspeakable profanities as I walked down the long corridor; but I covered my ears. The men in the cells didn't utter a word. I think they were too afraid of Father Thomas Cain. The last sound I heard was the metal door of Unit 29 slamming behind me.

I left, still not certain Capp had anything to do with Pastor Baddour's murder.

18

Fall, 1958

TWO YEARS PASSED. Finally, there was peace in Solo for the first time in a long time—enough to recover from the drama and have my mind ready for whatever might come next. As long as Sartain was alive, I didn't know what to expect.

I was getting plenty of room rentals, so I borrowed from a Greenlee bank and added a two-room bungalow in the back. It was for Mary and Michael. I never thought it was proper to have a man, priest or not, live down the hall from Mary and Michael. Now little Michael could hop out from his own bedroom and burn off some energy in the backyard, while Mary kept an eye open from the kitchen.

After Emily retired, and moved away, Mary took over as Pastor Davidson's secretary. She would take Michael with her to church. Coloring books and toys kept him busy.

It's true: Intuition is God's gift to women. When the phone rang, I sensed fear on the other end.

"Mrs. McRae, this is Superintendent Harris at Parchman. It's Father Davidson. He's in trouble."

This was not something I wanted to believe.

"You're familiar with the prisoner holding him hostage," Harris continued, his voice shaky. "And I should tell you … Oneeda Harpole is a hostage, too. It's serious. The prisoner is demanding to see Mary Grater and her child. I don't know her, so I'm calling you. It sure would help if you could bring the woman and child here."

Oh, Lord, no, I thought, squeezing the door jam. A dreadful feeling ran through my chest. I remained silent until he finished.

"This man has nothing to lose," he continued. "He's on death row. You have my word; I will not let him harm them," he said, determination in his voice. "I will station her and the child in a secure room with guards, and the prisoner in another room. They'll be able to see each other through a glass window and talk by phone. I swear they'll be safe. Can you bring them to Parchman? The sooner, the better."

"No. I'll never let that beast see her, or Michael. Ever." I replaced the receiver, not even waiting for a response, and stood there, stupefied, trying to gather my wits, my mind lit with adrenaline.

Was I not willing to go because I wanted to protect Mary and little Michael? Or was it something else?

I raced into the powder room and splashed cold water on my face. I had to think.

Looking in the mirror, memories of the cool waters of the Mississippi crossed my mind.

(I was seventeen. On a whim, I bet a friend two dollars I could swim across the Mississippi River. How impulsive I used to be. How confident. I slipped into the river on July fourth, from a sandbar where my graduating class was celebrating Independence Day. Shorty and a friend puttered beside me in a small boat, while the sand dwellers yelled and cheered me on. Halfway across I was exhausted, confused. I wanted to give up, grab the boat rail, have them pull me in. It wasn't the stupid two dollars that kept me going—it was my determination, my commitment to self-respect. By the time I reached the Arkansas side, the current had carried me downstream a mile.)

I dried my face and looked in the mirror again. *What am I doing here at home, holding on to hope that Father Davidson and Oneeda will be okay? I have to do something.* I tore through the phone book searching for Parchman's number and dialed the superintendent.

"Tell Sonny Sartain I'm bringing them." I hung up knowing Sartain needed to believe he was going to see them.

Grabbing my purse, I yelled, "Mary, I have to go. I'll be back later."

The front door was closing behind me as she yelled from the kitchen. "What? … Where?"

I didn't answer.

Going to Parchman without Mary and little Michael would be my middle of the river moment.

My night vision had always been terrible. Speeding toward Parchman, every approaching car appeared as two moonbeams blaring past me at sixty miles an hour. And the Delta highways at night? Like flying on monotonous strips of black ink with no shoulders and witches' ditches on both sides.

Halfway there, a farm tractor with dim headlights pulled in front of me. It was October—cotton-picking season. I yanked the wheel, barely missing the trailer, and dropped into the ditch. At sixty miles an hour mud shot up from both sides, spewing over the car top, covering my windshield as I screamed at the tractor driver. After fishtailing in the ditch, I bounced back onto the road, switched on the windshield wipers and grabbed my heart, pounding so hard I thought it would explode.

After that stopped racing, ten minutes later, I started thinking about Pastor Davidson—how important he'd become to Calvary and Solo. I began to second-guess myself. *Should I have brought Mary and little Michael? Oh, Lord, should I have?*

And Oneeda, my friend. *Why she's at Parchman with the preacher is beyond me.*

Then a more immediate concern struck me—Sonny Sartain. *What will I say when he realizes Mary and Michael aren't with me? Would he do the unthinkable? He must have a weapon to hold them hostage like this.*

There was a darkness over the Delta I'd never sensed before.

I made it to the entrance soon after eight. Parchman was big. Over 2,800 hardened criminals lived in nine different buildings, surrounded by twenty-eight square miles of farmland. It had always been a self-sustaining farming prison, with vegetables, cattle, chickens—everything needed for 3,000 staff and inmates.

The main gate guards were expecting me. They waved me through. I continued a half-mile through the pecan-tree orchard to the last checkpoint before entering hell.

As I opened the car door to greet Superintendent Harris, he barked, "Where's the woman and child?" He didn't bother to ask about my mud-splattered car.

"In my purse," I said.

He looked puzzled. "Let's go," he said through clenched teeth, surely realizing he had to go with what he had—me and a purse.

Three armed guards escorted us down several drab hallways, ending in a twenty-by-twenty-foot, non-descript room with linoleum floors, fluorescent overhead lights, no windows, and one Peavey speaker attached to a cinderblock wall above a grey console desk.

After pointing me to a seat, he said, "Mrs. McRae, I have no idea why I let you in, but you're here now. I'm going to listen in on them in the library. So be quiet. When I feel the time is right—provided there *is* a right time—I'll decide if you should go there with me, in which case let's pray I can explain to this prisoner why the woman and child aren't here. Are we on the same page?"

"Yessir. What's the other option?"

"There *is* no other option," he said, deadpanned and annoyed.

"Okay, but what if there isn't a right time?" I asked. "What happens then?"

"Shut up. We'll cross that bridge when we come to it."

"I sure hope you'll be praying then," I said, mimicking his deadpan—not maliciously, just hoping he would seek a higher power.

He ignored me and flipped a console switch to look at the speaker. At first, we heard nothing.

Then footsteps.

Sonny Sartain's voice crackled through the speakers: "The superintendent's got thirty minutes to git 'em here. Plenty of time, don't you think, preacher? Or maybe you and Oneeda want to meet that Jesus of yours. You see, I got nothin' to lose. I'll be sucking gas down my throat some day anyway. Does any of this make sense to you? Hello … Are you with us here, preach?"

I waited for Pastor Davidson to respond, but he said nothing. I wanted to see inside the room, to check on them. Television was new. Not many homes in Solo had one. *Why didn't the prison have the new device? They could be monitoring every room*, I thought.

Harris must've read my mind. "I'd give anything to see what's going on in there," he mumbled to himself, never removing his gaze from the speaker.

Then Sartain's menacing voice came through again: "You know what, preach, somethin' just occurred to me. While we're waitin' here, why don't you write a letter to the governor? Huh? I want a stay of execution. Yea, a stay of execution. Somebody git me a pen and some paper. The preacher here wants me to stay alive for a while anyway. He's gonna save my soul. Right, preacher?"

Sonny Sartain, when around Solo, could speak eloquently with a modicum of sophistication; but evidently among his "disciples" he chose to mimic their guttural slang.

What a manipulating con man.

I heard shuffling and other indecipherable noises. *Maybe a chair being pushed across the floor?*

Then Sartain's voice again: "Write it down exactly as I say. Dear Governor Coleman … Write it down, preacher," his voice was abrupt and angry. He dictated to Pastor Davidson a letter intended for the governor, explaining why he deserved a stay of execution. I imagined Pastor Davidson at a desk, writing every word from Sartain's dictation.

But where's Oneeda? I wondered.

I whispered to Harris, "Is Oneeda in there?"

"Yes," he said, his neck craned upward, never taking his eyes from the speaker.

"Is the team in place?" he asked one of the men.

"Yessir," a guard replied.

Then the speaker came alive with Sartain's voice, "Now, sign it."

A few seconds passed. Then Sartain spoke—his voice level, even-pitched, like he was reading something: "Even - though - I - walk - through - the - valley - of - the - shadow - of - death - I - will - fear - no - evil ..." His voice trailed off. "What's this? You stupid idiot," he shouted, and cussed like a foul-mouthed sailor. "You're in *my* house. Not yours. You wanna' see death valley so bad let's do it right now."

Superintendent Harris shoved his chair away from the console, his eyes boring a hole in one of the guards, "Get the team to the door. We're going in. Now!"

"No, wait," I said. "Let me go. I have something that might work."

"*You* have something that might work?" he said, sarcasm punctuating his disbelief.

"Yes, I think so." I pulled the photograph of Mary and Michael from my purse and showed it to him.

"What? This is the woman and boy? You think a photograph will satisfy this maniac?"

I was so nervous and shaking, it was difficult to get the words out. "Yes, I do."

"*Baam!*" We heard the sound of something crashing to the floor. We both locked eyes on the speaker.

"Let's go. *Now*," Harris shouted to the guards.

Superintendent Harris, four armed guards, and I sprinted down the corridor, through a door to the outside. High-tower perimeter lights lit the ground as I huffed and puffed to another building. One guard remained stationed at each door, holding it open for us to rush through. Down a short corridor, then a long one. We stopped in front of four more guards, all holding sawed-off shotguns, all standing stiff with their backs pressed against the corridor wall, no one facing the door; two on one side of the library door, two on the other side. At eye-level, recessed into the door, was a square, ten-by-ten-inch window.

Harris moved into position on one side. He reached around a guard and pulled me beside him. "Give me the photograph," he said, holding out a hand, not even looking at me. I handed it to him. Still standing off to the side of the door, his back pressed against the wall, he held it up to the window for a few seconds, then withdrew it. He did this several times, tapping on the glass and showing the photograph to anyone on the inside, then taking it down, and putting it back up for seconds at a time.

"I don't want him to get a long look at this … not yet," he whispered to the guards.

In less than a minute, I heard furniture being tossed around inside the room, making so much noise I slid down the wall farther from the door, my heart thumping, unsure of what was happening. I could smell hot sweat seeping through my blouse.

"Should we go in?" one guard asked.

"No," Harris blurted, agitated at the guard. "They're moving the barricade from the door. He wants a closer look. Let him come to us." The superintendent took a quick peek through the window, then returned with his back and head against the wall, his eyes angled toward the window.

"Come on you sick bastard," he whispered.

After a minute, it became quiet inside. Harris held the photograph up to the window again for a few seconds, then pulled it down again.

From the other side, we heard Sartain's voice. This time there was no harshness, only an understated imperative, "Show me again."

"No," Harris told him. "Not until you release the hostages."

A sinister, measured voice came back. "Slide … it … under … the … door … or … there … won't … be … any … hostages … to … release."

For some odd reason, Harris turned to me, his eyebrows arched while he shrugged his shoulders. He wanted to know if he should, or shouldn't slip it under the door.

Too nervous to speak, I nodded my approval.

As the superintendent bent down to push it under the door, I hustled around him to face the tiny window. I wanted to see Sartain's reaction when he saw the photograph. But there was no Sartain in sight. My view was of a room full of people gathered at the back wall. Then Sartain appeared. He was inches away, staring at me through the window, his oily smile indicating he had won. He had the photograph.

He dropped his head to study it, then turned and shuffled away from the door, his back to me, shoulders hunched, never taking his eyes from the photograph. The pistol hung from one long arm.

The superintendent was now squeezing his face next to mine, to have his own look inside the room.

I saw Oneeda. She was sitting on the floor, legs outstretched, her back against a metal cabinet. The room was a total disaster—books and furniture strewn around like demolished lumber. Then I saw Pastor Davidson. He was walking away from two prisoners, coming toward us—half his face covered in blood, a cut above his eye. The bloody eye was closed and swollen.

Sartain must've hit him, I thought.

The preacher continued walking—he and Sartain on a collision course. The preacher leaned down to lift Oneeda. Sartain was approaching him, but continued to stare at the picture. He suddenly raised his gun and aimed it at the preacher. I jerked backward, thinking he was going to fire. I didn't want to see that.

No gunfire, *thank heavens.*

I turned back to the window. But Harris was already there. I had to squeeze out my own space next to his. We saw Sartain holding the gun point-blank at the preacher's head. Sartain said something. We couldn't hear it.

The superintendent whispered, "Oh, no, Lord, don't let him pull that trigger. Stop him dear God."

I never took my eyes away from the scene unfolding inside. Having gathered Oneeda in his arms, the preacher glanced at the gun, then looked Sartain in the eye, not saying a word. Davidson stepped to the side of Sartain, and walked toward us, holding an arm around Oneeda's waist to help her. She looked like she might faint. Sartain twirled around and pointed his gun at the preacher's back. Sartain never said a word. The inmates inside seemed mesmerized, all of them watching in silence as Sartain held his finger on the trigger.

Ten seconds later, Pastor Davidson and Oneeda were out and on our side of the door.

One of the guards pulled me away, almost breaking my arm. Another guard grabbed Oneeda and moved her down the corridor. A third guard took the preacher and moved him in another direction. The rest was a blur as several guards rushed into the room, weapons drawn. I heard shouting, orders being barked, but no gunfire.

I assumed Sartain had surrendered to the guards, and we'd seen the last of him.

But I knew he'd be staring at that photograph day and night.

—∞—

After Pastor Davidson received several stitches from the prison doctor, he and Oneeda gave their report to Superintendent Harris. I heard the entire story.

The preacher and Oneeda had been in the library. Oneeda held the cookies in her lap while the preacher taught a group of inmates about Jesus. Somehow, Sartain had been given a library pass, came late with a guard escort, and was surprised to find the preacher there. Sartain must've figured he could hold them hostage in return for a chance to see Mary and Michael.

He confiscated the guard's pistol, barricaded the doors, and took command of the room.

The rest of the story, I saw firsthand.

<hr>

Finished with their report, I asked the preacher if Oneeda could drive me back to Solo in my car. He smiled and suggested I see a doctor about my night-vision problem.

Oneeda and I left Parchman at ten o'clock. The Delta darkness had given way to a glorious harvest moon, reflecting its glow across the flatlands, making the millions upon millions of cotton bolls glow like tiny white Christmas lights.

On the ride to Solo I didn't need to ask Oneeda to explain anything. I had heard it all in the superintendent's office. But what I didn't know was why she was there in the first place. So I asked.

"This was my second time to go with Adam to the prison," she said. "I bake the cookies for him now."

"Oh," I murmured, trailing off. My feelings were a little bruised. Not so much because she was going and I wasn't, but because I always enjoyed baking those cookies for the prisoners.

She added: "I asked Adam if I could do the baking. I love doing it for him."

We traveled on in silence for several minutes. Then, as if in a trance, Oneeda said, "Those men were going to kill him, Martha. Adam walked between them like they didn't exist. They didn't lift a finger to stop him. Did you see it? They just let us walk out. I'll never understand how Adam did that."

It was too dark to see her face. But by the tone of her voice, I could sense she was captivated by Pastor Davidson.

Adam. She had called him Adam three times. She'd never called him that before. But I wasn't too concerned about any infatuation. Oneeda had been dating a veterinarian in Bethaven for the past three months.

I ignored her *Adam* references as nothing to get worked up about.

Almost to Solo, Oneeda asked, "Martha, where in the world did all this mud come from?"

"I ran into a ditch." I was too tired to offer details.

Oneeda stopped at her house and we said our goodnights. I drove the two blocks home. I was spent. Not waiting for Pastor Davidson's return, I crawled into bed and slept late the next morning.

All week, Bethel County was ablaze with rumors. Everybody wanted to know whom Sartain had demanded to see.

I was asked a million times. The questions were annoying. "C'mon, Martha, you know who it is. Tell me. Was it Mary?" I wasn't about to divulge anything. And I made Oneeda swear she wouldn't tell either. What a short-lived promise that was.

You can take a person out of the gossip, but it's near impossible to take the gossip out of a person. And Oneeda was addicted to gossip.

Mary couldn't go to work for three days because of the crowd hovering around Calvary. So she stayed with me. A reporter discovered that Mary lived in my boarding house. I watched him pace the street, back and forth, back and forth, waiting for Mary to come out.

Solo had no sidewalks. Five-feet-deep wastewater ditches separated our yards from the street. I peered out my window many a time hoping he would fall into the ditch. Or leave. Either would have been good with me. He stopped cars as they drove by—driver and reporter always pointing toward my house. Of course, Mary never set foot outside.

On the third day, the young man didn't return.

Although everybody had heard it was Mary whom Sartain demanded to see, nobody asked "Why?" or knew about any connection between Sartain and little Michael. Thank goodness.

That Sunday, Pastor Davidson's sermon was about hell. His message was powerful—so strong, there were only a few times my mind wandered to the white bandage above his eye. The preacher never spoke of the incident at Parchman, never even mentioned Sartain by name.

But he did say, "No man or woman is without salvation if God adopts them into eternal life—a new and perfect life;

a new body, no pain, no tears, all sins forgiven. It's God's choice."

I'll never forget his closing words. How could I? I made a plaque that'll be on my kitchen wall 'til the day I die:

None of us is perfect.
But some of us will be.

19

Freddie's Visit

FOR A FEW months after the hostage encounter, the drama faded—until Freddie Carpenter made a surprise visit, coming from Greenlee to see me one afternoon. Oneeda was there, too. It was December, and cold as Satan's heart. Something else, not good, was in the air. I had sensed it since waking at five, uneasy.

We sat around the kitchen table, consuming cheese straws and sweet tea.

Freddie talked about his time in Waterton and how he'd been on the moonshine wagon for three years. Yet, he looked like he'd aged ten. We told him how proud we were for kicking that odorous addiction, and landing the job as Greenlee's assistant postmaster. For five minutes he and I swapped stories about life as a postmaster. Smiling, I asked the obvious ...

"No, ma'am," he said, "I haven't been steaming open any mail."

Then he launched into the real purpose of his visit.

"Miss Martha, you, huh, actually met with Father Cain … in prison … didn't you?" he asked, his sheepish eyebrows locked in the middle, his eyes pleaded for an answer.

"Freddie, why do you still refer to him as Father Cain?" I asked, concerned for his state of mind. I don't believe he expected the question.

"I—I'm not sure," he said, scratching his chest, staring down at the table. "I guess because that's how I remember him."

I thought, *He's haunted by Sartain; maybe still under his spell.* "I did meet with him, Freddie. Once, two years ago, and then this past October. But I wouldn't call my last visit an actual meeting."

Oneeda was long overdue to birth some news. "You heard about it, didn't you?" she asked Freddie. "I mean, Father Davidson and I, being held hostage and all. It was horrifying."

"The whole town of Greenlee knows about it, Mrs. Harpole. Most of us know the woman he wanted to see," Freddie offered.

"But that's not why you came to visit, is it, Freddie?" I asked, steering the conversation away from Mary being the woman Sartain wanted to see.

"No ma'am."

"What did you want to talk about? You know you can trust us." I moved the bowl of cheese straws closer to him. He took one and nibbled, glancing down at his glass of sweet tea.

"You wouldn't happen to have any milk, would you?" he asked.

"Of course. What was I thinking? Cheese straws go better with milk." I fetched a bottle, popped the latch, and began filling a glass. Before my pouring was finished, he looked up at me with a pained stare.

"Miss Martha, there's nobody I trust more. You saved my life. And you kept me from going to prison. I almost lost my mind thinking about Parchman."

"It's an awful place," Oneeda said, wincing. "I know first hand. Just thinking about Parchman gives me the willies."

"They won't go away ..." Freddie trailed off, hesitant to say more.

"What won't go away, Freddie? Tell us," I said.

"These thoughts. About Father Cain and Parchman."

"Have you seen a doctor?" Oneeda asked.

"Ma'am, what could a doctor do?" Freddie asked, shaking his head.

"Not a regular doctor," Oneeda responded. "A fraud. You know, the mind."

I disregarded her comment in order to keep Freddie on track. "Freddie, can you tell us about them, about the thoughts you're having," I asked, hoping not to rattle him.

Oneeda broke in. "That's exactly what a fraud would ask."

No more could I ignore her. "Oneeda, if you'd read more books you'd know they're called psychiatrists. And his name was Freud, not fraud." I was firm, but not harsh.

"Ohhh," she said, still smacking her Juicy Fruit.

"I—I can't tell you about them. They're not something I can say in front of a lady. I wouldn't even tell a man. What he left in my mind is sick. He has men doing unspeakable things to me. It was all I could think about in jail waiting for my trial. And I'm not even sure they weren't real. I don't know. You know I spent time in that loony bin, Waterton? It drove me crazy. That's all I got to say about it."

Freddie hung his head and nibbled on a cheese straw, while Oneeda and I remained transfixed on him. We were too distraught to say a word. After a pregnant pause, he placed the half-eaten nibble on a napkin and lifted his eyes.

"Do you ladies believe Father Cain is the devil?"

His sick obsession with Sartain, layered on top of what must have happened to him in the Waterton Mental Hospital, almost brought me to tears. I had to be honest with him.

"Yes, I do. But I—"

"Well, I certainly do," Oneeda added.

My best friend was officially annoying me.

"But I wouldn't say he's the devil," I said. "I think he's more like one of Satan's minions."

"What's a minion?" Freddie asked.

"A minion is a servant. They carry out the will of their master," I tried to explain.

"Do you think I could visit him?" he asked. I took a step back.

"Why in the world would you want to see him?" Oneeda asked.

"I can't explain it. I just want to … I don't know … hurt him? Somehow. As much as he messed up my mind, maybe I want to do something that'll make him suffer like me."

Oneeda's hands were on her hips. I felt sure she, too, was thinking nothing could be better than seeing Sonny Sartain suffer.

"He hurt me, too, Freddie," Oneeda said.

"You should stay as far away from that demon as you can," I said. "You can't even think about seeing him. The superintendent wouldn't dare let you in anyway."

"Vengeance is the Lord's," Oneeda said. "If you want revenge, it's like you're trying to do God's job. I turned my revenge over to him." She was earnest. And right. It's why I loved her heart, in spite of the flightiness … and Juicy Fruit.

We talked some more with Freddie, and he seemed to understand what Oneeda had said about vengeance being God's responsibility.

Not long after Freddie left, we heard the preacher come in.

"Oh, I was hoping Adam would come home soon," Oneeda said, staring at the swinging kitchen door, where she expected to see him enter.

But when the preacher bounded upstairs, Oneeda frowned and left soon after.

A week later, I was in my first vestry meeting discussing church finances. *Horrid.* What could be worse than hearing our church was on the brink of financial ruin?

"Not enough money to even pay our preacher's full salary," one member said.

We all knew Sartain had spent the money. There was no reason in hashing that over again.

I'll never forget JJ's generosity as he stood and addressed us. "Ladies … gentlemen … I'm willin' to donate ten-percent of JJ Honey sales to Calvary."

I glanced around the room, wondering if anyone was going to ask what that might amount to, money-wise. Nobody asked.

No matter, I was proud of my friend.

JJ must've read our minds. "I can't speculate how much it would mean for the church," he offered, "but I believe it might help pay the preacher's salary." I knew he was a proponent of Adam Davidson and appreciated what the preacher was doing for Calvary and Solo.

"I plan to add somethin' like this to every bottle," he said. "JJ's Honey is donatin' ten-percent of sales to Calvary Episcopal Church, Solo, Mississippi." Then he sat down. I was too stunned to clap. Somebody else did. Soon, all eight of us were slapping our hands together in unison. JJ tried to wave us off, his face, strawberry-red.

Within six months, his little honey operation had turned into a steady employer for Solo. He hired ten more locals to keep up with the demand. From the first month after his pronouncement, a check arrived at Mary's desk, and every month thereafter. Small, the first month, but it grew so fast Mary felt compelled to tell me more than she should have. Church tithes were not, in my opinion, a matter to be tossed around the church's membership.

But, it did turn out to be more than enough to pay for Pastor Davidson's salary, with plenty left over to fix the leaky ceiling, and buy new hymnals. Oneeda was happy about that.

Mary and little Michael continued to live with me. He was three, and a streak of lightning. Mary and I would sit at the kitchen table drinking coffee, or sweet tea in the afternoon, and watch him dart across the backyard to hop on the swing set Andrew Dawkins had built.

One afternoon, Mary asked, "Do people know who Michael's real father is? Do people ask?"

"No, I'm sure of it," I said with no hesitation. "I'm sure everybody thinks he belongs to Capp."

"But Capp's not capable of fathering a child," she said, continuing her quest to protect Michael's future.

There was a long pause as we drank coffee and watched little Michael play.

Mary broke the silence, but continued to keep an eye on Michael. "Are you still pursuing Capp's involvement in Father Baddour's death?"

"Would it bother you if I was?" I asked. (*Sometimes it's best—if you know where someone is headed—to answer a question with a question of your own.*)

"Look at him, Martha. He'll grow up soon. If there's a trial, it'll come out—my past, Sonny Sartain, everything. I think I'd die if he had to grow up knowing all that."

Curious if her worry might involve more than little Michael, I asked, "Would Andrew have anything to do with your concerns?"

"Martha, he's a good friend. Nothing more," she said, her hands cupping a coffee mug, her eyes never leaving Michael in the backyard.

Me? I wasn't so sure. I thought there might be more than mere friendship.

"Besides, he knows everything about me," she said as an after-thought.

I turned to look at her. She reciprocated.

"Friends, Martha," she said. "Andrew is just a friend."

⟞⟝

A week later, I dropped by the butcher shop to pick up some steaks. Annie had been running the place, doing everything Judd used to do—buy the beef, pork, and venison, hang them in the walk-in cooler, and wait for orders; at which time she'd haul the hundred-pound side of whatever species someone had ordered onto the chopping block and carve out the cut. I had ordered four tenderized rounds for country-fried steaks.

The tiny bell above her door tinkled. She was nowhere in sight, but I heard a cleaver in the back, *thwacking* away on her chopping block.

"Annie, are you in the back?" I yelled.

"Yes," she shouted.

When I walked through the swinging door I saw her raise the cleaver and slam it down, *thwack*, one last blow to finish the main cut. Cow blood splattered her apron. "Sorry, I got delayed," she said. "Just take a minute to finish your order."

Taking a carving knife from the table, she pulled the dangling end of a two-inch-wide leather strap taut to her waist and swiped the blade across it, back and forth with several quick strokes until satisfied with the blade's honing.

I watched, as her precision in trimming the excess fat from each cut was more efficient than I'd ever seen Judd perform that same surgery on a piece of meat.

Two minutes passed. Neither of us said a word. I couldn't help but notice how skinny she was. *She's lost thirty pounds, at least*, I thought.

"Annie, you've lost so much weight. Is something wrong?" I asked.

She rolled each cut of meat into brown wax paper, her concentration never leaving the job at hand, and responded, "Nothing's wrong. I just haven't been sleeping much."

A quick thought crossed my mind. "Annie, add one more steak to the order. I want you to come over for supper tonight. There's plenty of food. We haven't talked in ages, and we should catch up."

Catching up wasn't my ulterior motive, though. I was hoping she might reveal something about Capp's involvement. *She has to know something.*

"I suppose so," she said, her eyes blank, her face lifeless.

She took the paper packages to the front counter, wiped bloody hands on her apron, weighed the steaks, and announced, without emotion, "That'll be a dollar-thirty-five."

20

The Delivery Boy

Supper was almost ready when Annie knocked at six o'clock. I opened the door with a smile. "Come on in, Annie. Would you help me put supper on the table?" She nodded. I knew the preacher would have his work cut out for him.

But I had an idea that might help.

Annie agreed to set the table while I whistled and informed my guests that supper was on.

We sat down to country fried steak, mashed potatoes with gravy, snap peas, and sweet tea—all of Pastor Davidson's favorite foods. I had already told the preacher about my analysis of Annie's situation. Depression. I failed to tell him my true motive, though.

He and I told stories during supper to lighten the mood. Annie never said a word.

After eating, everybody helped in the kitchen, while Michael played outside. As we put the last dishtowel away, Mary coaxed a reluctant Michael upstairs for his bath.

The preacher, Annie, and I sat in the parlor, talked, and sipped on my idea—sherry. If Annie would drink two glasses, I figured she'd loosen up and tell the preacher what was bothering her. And hopefully talk about Capp's involvement. As we took our seats, I joked, "Y'all know what they say about Episcopalians don't you?" I grinned and continued, "Where ever you find four, you'll find a fifth."

It was a stupid old joke, but I needed something to lighten the mood. The preacher looked at Annie to see her reaction. She cracked a smile, and sipped away. *Good, she's on her way*, I thought.

Tilting her head to one side and facing the preacher, she said, "But there're only three of us here, not four."

"Actually, Annie, there are four of us here," he responded. "Jesus said, 'Where two or more are gathered in my name, I will be among you.' We always gather in his name."

Annie held my long-stemmed glass up to study it. "I never drink," she said. "But this is good."

He responded in kind, holding his glass up. "I'm sure you remember Jesus' first miracle when he turned water into wine. A little wine is good for the body."

Leaning towards the preacher, she asked, "Was that the wedding?"

"It was," he said. "I see you've been studying your Bible. Annie, do you know why he choose that as his first miracle?"

She shook her head.

"He was using the ceremonial jars of water that were special to the Jewish wedding tradition to put his stamp of approval on God's first institution—marriage between a man and a woman."

Annie listened and sipped more sherry.

"And guess what? Jesus was reluctant at first to perform the miracle," he said.

She glanced at him, puzzled by the preacher's comment. So was I.

"He knew it would set off a firestorm of protests from the Pharisees, and the clock would start ticking toward his own death," he said.

With her glass already hoisted, Annie took it to her lips and swallowed more sherry. Me? I soaked up the preacher's insight.

We made small talk for another half hour. *A little more chitchat and she'll be primed for the preacher.*

I asked if her business was doing okay. "Fline," she slurred, followed by her last swallow of sherry. She had finished her third glass, and being so skinny, I thought the alcohol might be invading her blood stream too fast. I didn't want her drunk. Relaxed, but not intoxicated.

I cut her off when she held the glass out for a refill. "Oh, I am so sorry, Annie, the sherry's all gone." *Lord, please forgive me for lying.*

"Let me make a pot of coffee." I stood and glanced at the preacher. *She's all yours,* I thought.

He didn't hesitate. "Annie, Martha tells me you've been having trouble sleeping. Have you seen a doctor?"

Good. Quick. To the point. Let her do the talking, I thought. I sat down. Coffee could wait. I wanted to hear this.

She closed her eyes for a few seconds, exhaled and said, "No, I've been having bad dreams, that's all."

"Tell me about them," the preacher said with eyes yearning to help.

At first she seemed surprised by the question, so she hesitated. Then she spoke: "I see ... I see Judd's large arms ... whacking a side of venison in two ... then the same scene ... but this time he's whacking Father Baddour in two."

I was stunned. The preacher didn't flinch. "Go on, Annie, it'll do you good to talk it out."

"I wake up ... I want to go back to sleep ... but I can't," her voice so low it was difficult to hear. "There're different versions of the dream," she continued. "Sometimes he uses a butcher—a butcher—" she stopped mid-sentence, not able to finish the word.

"A butcher knife?" the preacher asked.

She nodded and looked out the window with pathetic, lifeless eyes.

"But Annie, that's not how Father Baddour died," he said, trying to comfort her.

Wheeling around to face him, she said, "Don't you think I know that?"

He leaned closer and touched her arm, "What do you think the dreams mean, Annie?"

For the first time, she glanced over at me.

"I don't know …" she trailed off, a bit of frown on her face. Then silence.

It dawned on me that I might be losing my best chance to learn if Capp was involved or not. There were no other informants to implicate Capp in Pastor Baddour's murder. Only Annie. I felt compelled to ask, "Annie, is Capp Grater ever in your nightmares?"

She glanced at me again, but turned back to the preacher and said, "No."

I had pushed too far and Annie was agitated. I should've kept my mouth shut. It was clear, though. The night would end without the whole story. I stood. "I'll make some coffee."

But it was too late. She had shut down.

I believe if the preacher had asked the 'Capp question' she might have talked about his involvement. *Now I may never know.*

After she left, the preacher shook his head. "Annie is carrying a heavy burden," he said, sorrow in his voice.

"You're right. And it's not like she's in mourning. More like something else," I said.

The preacher and I said our "goodnights" and I sat in the kitchen, disappointed that a new revelation of Capp's involvement may have evaporated before my eyes. I was eager to come up with a plan that would get Annie to tell it all. But any ideas would have to wait. I was tired and needed my sleep, which didn't come until two in the morning. In bed, my first thoughts were about Annie and if *she* was sleeping. Then I focused on Mary and what could happen to her and Michael if Capp Grater was ever brought to trial. It was the same conniving conundrum—justice for Capp versus Mary's past life. And a child fathered by a demon. *It'll come out in a trial, for sure*, I thought. She'd be an outcast—a social leper.

That's the way it is in the Delta. Your reputation is your calling card. Most outcasts surrendered to the bottle and never came out. I didn't want Mary going back inside that dark place.

I asked God to put my heart in the right place. *Is my determination to bring a possible killer to justice more important than risking Mary and Michael's future life?*

As if my prayer was answered on the spot, a thought materialized, something Pastor Davidson had said in a recent sermon: "A true preacher is merely the delivery boy for God's word. In fact, we're all delivery boys. Me. You. Every one of us," he said.

That's me. That's who I am. The mailman for Solo. A delivery boy. Maybe I'm meant to deliver Pastor Baddour's murderer and let God fulfill His promise: "For those who love God all things work together for good, for those who are called according to his purpose." He takes care of his children. And Mary was one of them.

After that reassuring thought, I fell asleep.

I should've stayed awake all night.

21

Desires

Lunch was Oneeda's idea. She drove as we traveled to Charlie's Place in Greenlee. A beautiful spring day, tractors were kicking up dust, preparing the rich Delta soil for the season's cotton crop.

Five minutes out of Solo, she dropped the bomb.

"Martha, I'm in love with Adam." There it was again—*Adam*—this time in full bloom. I stifled a laugh—out of pity mostly.

"Whatever happened to that nice veterinarian in Bethaven?" I asked.

"I'm not seeing him any more."

"That's too bad. I heard he was a nice fellow. But Oneeda, do you know if Adam is in love with you?"

"I don't," she said, "but I intend to ask him."

"You're going to ask him if he loves you?"

"What? You don't think he could love *me*?"

"That's not what I meant. I'm just surprised you'd ask, that's all. Are you sure it's love? Maybe you're—"

She cut me off. "Martha, he saved my life that night at Parchman. Not only that, he's everything a woman would want. Or need. Besides, he's single. I'm divorced. Why couldn't we just have a close relationship? So what if he doesn't love me? What diff—"

Then I cut *her* off. "Oneeda, it's called fornica—"

"—Don't use that word," she interrupted, her voice two decibels higher than necessary

"It's in the Bible. You're not married," I said.

She began swerving wildly, crossing the center lane, yanking the heavy Lincoln back to the gravel shoulder, and back again. I was fit to be tied.

"Oneeda! If you can't talk about this and drive at the same time, pull over and I'll take the wheel."

"Just don't use that word again," she said, regaining a temporary sanity.

"Look, Oneeda, you've been chasing priests' pants like they'll be gone in a month. Just slow down. Take it easy. God will provide you with the right man at the right time. And slow this car down."

I leaned over to look at her speedometer. "You've gotten up to eighty miles an hour, woman."

She backed off the accelerator. We settled on a sane pace, and in silence for a while.

"Look, tell you what I'll do. I'll ask Father Davidson if he has any of those feelings for you. Would that help?" I was sincere.

"What if he doesn't?" she asked, gripping the wheel tighter, a stressed look on her face.

"Well, we can grow old together," I offered.

"We're different, Martha. I still have desires," she was quick to say, glancing over at me.

Incensed, I said, "And you don't think I do?"

She ignored me, driving on, looking out the window at the cotton fields every so often, smacking on her gum. I knew she was pondering something.

"God hasn't given me a man in seven years. Not since Bobby Joe ran off to—to who knows where."

I didn't say a word.

A few minutes later her mood changed. She looked over at me, hope in her voice, and said, "Mary is seeing Andrew. Why shouldn't I have a man in my life?" almost begging me to agree with her.

"Oneeda, I doubt anything's going on between them. They both know God's commandments about pre-marital relations."

"Are you sure?" she asked, looking at me.

"No, I'm not. But why don't you just do what I do?"

"And what's that?" she asked, syrupy cynicism in her voice.

"I ignore it."

"Well, dandy for you. But I can't. I think I'm going crazy." She swerved onto the shoulder again. And I swore.

After wrestling the car back under control, she repeated, "I think I'm going crazy."

I had to do something to lighten the mood. I said, "Oneeda, you've been crazy ever since your mama dropped your baby head on the kitchen floor."

Thank goodness she laughed. We both did. "I don't remember it," she said, smiling. She had a harmless absurdity about her, with a measure of innocence that seldom abandoned her—unlike her no-account ex-husband.

In a sincere tone she asked, "Martha, how do you ignore it?"

"How do I ignore my desires?" I asked, not certain what she meant.

"Yea," she said.

"Well, I have a saying: 'While my love for the Lord doesn't cure my human desires, my fear of him keeps me from acting on them.'"

She mulled that one over until we arrived in Greenlee.

After we pulled into Charlie Parker's place, we settled into a booth for some fine barbeque ribs, greens, sweet tea, and *Love Me Tender* on the jukebox.

We talked and laughed for half an hour about men and their awful little habits—commode seats left up, toenail clippings everywhere, those sorts of annoyances. I knew she'd have enough humor to laugh about the man thing.

On ride back to Solo, I kept wondering how I was going to approach the preacher about my promise to Oneeda. *How can I ask him if he loves Oneeda? This is feeling like such a silly thing to do.*

—o‱o—

But I had promised.

The next morning, three scrambled eggs, crisp bacon, fresh fruit, homemade biscuits with JJ's Honey, and orange juice awaited Pastor Davidson.

"Martha, how thoughtful of you. I haven't had a breakfast this big in a while. What got into you?" he asked, unfolding his napkin, casting a happy smile.

"Well …" I said, taking a seat beside him, "if you have a minute, I want to talk with you about Oneeda."

"Oneeda? Is she all right?" he asked, wrinkles etched across his forehead.

"All right" could mean a lot of things when applied to Oneeda, but my first reaction was *Oh my goodness, does he love her?* Before I could answer, the phone rang and my intuition kicked in … *nothing good can come from a call this early in the morning.* I wanted to answer it, but then again, I wanted to keep this conversation with the preacher flowing. Two more rings.

"Should you get that, Martha?" he asked. As I stood, he said, "Just tell me Oneeda's okay."

"She's fine," I said, walking to the phone.

"Hello," I answered, as I watched the preacher dig into his breakfast, hoping this call wouldn't take long—or worse, turn out to be one of my sick intuitions.

"Yes, I'm calling for Martha McRae," a pleasant man's voice said.

"This is Martha McRae."

"Very good. I hope you're doing well today. I just—"

"I'm-fine-how-can-I-help-you?" I asked as fast as I could.

The man said, "I understand you have rooms to rent. I'd like to rent two of them for next week."

"I have one room available."

"Hmmm … would the room happen to have two beds?" he asked in a polite mid-western accent.

"Yes, two twin beds," I said, sneaking a peek at Pastor Davidson diving into his breakfast.

The man said, "Hold one moment, please."

Feds coming to inspect Parchman, I thought. I toe-tapped for longer than I cared and was about to hang up, when he came back on the line. "Very well, we'll take it."

"So it's for two occupants?" I asked, looking over at the preacher.

"Yes, two of us."

"Okay, my rate for double occupancy is twelve dollars a day. I have a pen. Give-me-your-name-your-phone-number-and-the-dates-you'll-be-staying."

I scribbled the man's information on a pad, eager to get back to my discussion with the preacher. He was taking his last bite. I covered the receiver with my hand and told him, "There's more orange juice in the frig."

"Oh, and Mrs. McRae, you wouldn't happen to know the best car rental place in Solo, would you?" the man asked.

I sighed. "Solo doesn't have rental cars or an airport."

"Can you tell me the nearest city with an airport and car rentals?"

"Greenlee, but you'll have to come through Memphis."

"Oh, we won't be flying commercial. We'll be arriving on a company plane."

Rats, there he goes. The preacher had finished breakfast, and hand-signaling a goodbye.

"Uh ... well no, but I suppose you could call the Greenlee Chamber of Commerce. They know all the car rental places," I said, disappointed that I had to wave goodbye to the preacher.

"That's what we'll do. Thank you very much. We look forward to seeing you on the thirtieth," and hung up. He was precise, all business-like. *Must be ... I have no clue. Government workers don't fly around in private planes.*

After cleaning the dishes, I sat at the kitchen table with a cup of coffee to think about Oneeda and the next morning's breakfast with the preacher.

The phone rang. *Now what?*

"Hello," I answered, no longer feeling cheerful.

"It's me. What did he say?" Of course it would be Oneeda calling, as soon as she thought the preacher had left at his normal time. Her enthusiasm reminded me of our teen years, when we giggled over boys, and wondered if they knew we even existed.

"Oneeda," I dreaded telling her, "I didn't have a chance to—"

"You didn't ask him?"

"Oh, I asked him, but the phone rang before he could answer."

"Oh, no. Did I call too soon? You mean he's still there?"

And so it went. Five minutes later I had her calmed down and promised to ask again the next day.

———

Early the next morning I was about to make breakfast when the preacher informed me he was leaving for Salem. "I'll be gone a week," he said. "But tell me about Oneeda before I go."

"She's fine. When you return, let's talk about it then. She just needs some advice and doesn't know how to ask you herself."

He perked up. "Of course, as long as you promise me she's okay."

"I promise. Have a safe trip," I said, smiling.

He was off. And so was I, for a few days of rest and pondering. *Does he really love her?*

———

The afternoon of May 30, as scheduled, two men knocked on my door. They were clean-cut, in their forties (I guessed), dressed in dark suits. *Not suitable for the Delta this time of year,* was my first thought.

"Welcome to Solo. I see you found a rental car," I said, looking over their shoulders at a green Pontiac.

They introduced themselves, but I knew it'd be impossible to remember their names—too many Zs, Ks, and Bradkawskis for me. I decided to think of them as 'Big' and

'Bitty,' as in little bitty. One was big and tall, the other, skinny and short.

"Bring your suitcases in, gentlemen. Your room is at the end of the hall, upstairs. Supper's on at six o'clock."

They came down at five forty-five and nosed around while I finished setting the table for the three of us.

I was thankful Mary and Michael were spending the night out at a friend's pajama party. Supper would be my interview time.

"I hope you like fried chicken," I said, placing everything on the Lazy Susan.

"I do," Big said, spinning the Susan around, picking up a drumstick, then turning it for Bitty.

As soon as I said, "Shall I give thanks?" they both placed their chicken parts back on their plates and lowered their heads. Big dropped all the way down, his nose almost in his plate. I figured this man must've been raised in a fine home.

I gave thanks and dished out some black-eyed peas.

"You seem like nice fellows. Where you from?"

"Minneapolis," Bitty said.

"So what brings you to Solo?" I asked, passing the cornbread.

"We're with Purity Foods, Mrs. McRae. And I'm glad you brought it up," Big said.

Bitty was quick to jump in and do the explaining, "What can you to tell us about JJ's Honey?"

"Well, I can tell you it's good. Darn good on cornbread."

"Sorry, I meant to ask if you would be willing to tell us about Mr. Johnson," Bitty said.

"Whadda you wanna know?" I asked, thinking they should slow they're anxious hearts down or they'd keel over before enjoying dessert—cornbread with JJ's Honey.

Bitty answered. "Well, to tell the truth, Purity Foods is always looking to acquire small companies."

(I'd been raised to believe anybody who said they were ready "to tell the truth" had already been fibbing about something.)

Big added, "We've been researching fast-growing companies."

"Oh, so you want to buy him out?" I asked.

"We're here to talk with Mr. Johnson about it, yes ma'am," Bitty said.

"And he knows you're coming?" I asked, surprised.

"We sent a letter last month, requesting a meeting," Big said. "We offered some dates, and he agreed to this one."

"JJ sent a letter to you?" I was shocked.

"Well, it was signed J. Johnson, yes ma'am," Bitty said.

"JJ has two sons, Jake and Jimmy," I said. "Don't you think—"

Bitty interrupted, "—I spoke with Mr. Johnson, myself, on the phone last week. He even suggested we stay with you."

"That was nice of him. Did he tell you he was willing to sell?" I asked, trying to hide any concern.

"No, he didn't. But he said he'd meet with us. What can you tell us about him?" Bitty asked.

Ahh, fishing for information. Nothing wrong with that.

"Here's what I'll tell you men about JJ. He's unlike any man you've ever met. He's best experienced in person. Not through my opinions."

They turned to each other, puzzled. I put my chicken wing down. "Listen, I'll bet you four bits to a nickel JJ said you'd have to pay Calvary Episcopal Church *ten-percent* of all sales if you bought him out." I looked at Big and then Bitty, waiting for a response.

Stunned, Big started to say, "Well—"

But Bitty interrupted, "Yes, we've seen the charity wording on his bottles, and we've been thinking about that, and ... Purity Foods couldn't possibly give back *ten-percent* of total sales. But we would consider a portion of our profits."

I knew it. *Bitty's the bean counter.*

"We already have top management's approval to work with a charity in the county," Big said. "We're all for giving back to local causes."

And Big, he's the salesman, I concluded.

"What charities have you considered?"

"Well, Calvary church would be at the top of our list," Bitty said.

I smiled. "I've read where big companies like yours always move the manufacturing to their headquarters." I exchanged looks with both of them, waiting for an answer.

Bitty cleared his throat before responding. "Sometimes we do. It all depends on what we find out tomorrow, after we visit his plant."

"Plant?" I laughed. "That'll be interesting. You men wouldn't mind if I tagged along, would you?"

"I think Mr. Johnson would need to okay it," Bitty said.

"Oh, I'm sure he wouldn't mind. I often go out to his place for honey."

"Do you think you might help us talk him into selling?" Big asked.

Bitty chimed in. "You know what, Mrs. McRae, I think we could arrange to ship you, free-of-charge, all the honey you ever wanted. If you can help us, of course."

Bitty seemed pleased with his offer.

Well, there's a bribe if ever heard one. Not worth a hoot, but a bribe nonetheless.

"That's very nice of you," I said. "Now for dessert. Here's JJ's famous honey, and here's some of the best cornbread you'll ever have."

"Never had cornbread, Big said," and then whoofed down half a skillet of it.

After the men retired to their room, I called JJ, filled him in, and asked if he'd mind me coming out with them. He said, "Bothers me none, Martha. Jake and Jimmy wanted me to meet with them. I didn't much care to. So come on."

⚬⚬⚬

What a beautiful day, riding out with two gentlemen whose names I couldn't pronounce or ever remember. And me—excited to learn how the big boys cut business deals.

JJ's hounds surrounded their rental car as we pulled up in a cloud of dust.

I heard Bitty mumble to Big, "I don't see a plant, do you?"

"It's in the back," I said.

"You mean the building behind his house?" Bitty asked.

"Yep," I said, grinning.

JJ waved the dogs off, and we slid out of the dusty Pontiac. Big and Bitty loosened their tie knots to give their necks some breathing room from something they likely had never encountered in their lifetime—"horrible humidity." The Delta beast.

"Welcome to JJ's Honey factory," JJ said to the men, extending a hand. Big and Bitty quickly wiped the sweat off their faces and shook hands with JJ.

"Fellas, why don't y'all come inside where it's cool? We can talk a bit."

Inside, JJ's wife, Peg, brought out a pitcher of sweet tea and glasses, while Jake and Jimmy finished arranging a full display of JJ's Honey jars. The boys introduced themselves and we all walked around the display drinking tea, while JJ explained the various types of honey.

Bitty took a jar from the shelf. "Glass," he muttered.

"Somethin' wrong with glass?" JJ asked.

"Well, at Purity Foods, we've been experimenting with plastic, and I have to say, it's much cheaper than glass."

Studying a bottle, Big had a thought: "And Mr. Johnson, what we could do for your logo and label design would make you—"

"What's wrong with my design?" JJ interrupted, pulling an ear lobe, studying Big.

"Well, it's a little out of date," Big said, wincing.

Bitty changed the subject. "Could we have a look at your plant now?"

JJ smiled at the thought of a plant tour. He led us out the back door. Before entering the building, we all suited up with bee-protection outfits.

JJ's new addition included a forty-by-forty-foot concrete-floored building, walls built with old barn lumber, and two dozen workers, collecting and filling jars on equipment making a deafening noise- Bees enveloped us.

JJ called the equipment his "MIGs."

"What's a MIG?" Big asked.

Cracking a smile, JJ said, "Made-In-Garage."

While JJ and I laughed, Big and Bitty could only smile. Then they started swatting at the bees, careful not to hurt any. JJ walked us around the plant, pointing out this and that, pleased with the operation, and rightfully so. "We've added ten new employees jest in the last month. All of 'em young men and girls from poor Negro neighborhoods. I'm pleased 'bout that, but most of all, gentlemen, I'm thankful to God."

I studied Big and Bitty. They seemed worried about the honeydew attraction to their nice suits, wiping off the nectar with their hankies. After a twenty-minute tour, we stepped outside. Big and Bitty gazed at each other in amazement. We all sparkled. The sun highlighted the golden nectar on our clothes, making us shine like pixie dust. And we carried the sweet smell of honey.

Back inside JJ's house, Bitty said, "Mr. Johnson, I must say, you have quite an operation back there. I'm sure you're proud of what you've accomplished."

"Young man, le' me s'plain somethin' to you," JJ said. "All this has been God's doin'. He made it all possible."

Bitty nodded but carried on with his thought, "You've—I'm sorry—*God* has done a lot here. But I believe he wants you to grow JJ's Honey into a national operation, Mr. Johnson. And Purity Foods can help you do that."

"Boy, if you knew anythang 'bout honey, you'd know local honey is what folks want ... honey from close by. 'Cause local honey is what helps allergies, not honey from New York, or California, or—"

"I get it Mr. Johnson. I apologize, I was thinking too big. We own plenty of successful regional brands."

"That so?" said JJ.

"Yes, sir. And we're prepared to pay you good money for JJ's Honey," Bitty said. "We'll need time for due diligence, of course. We'll need to—"

"Due *what*?" JJ interrupted.

"Your financial information, Mr. Johnson. Before we can make an offer, they're a lot of things we need to know about your operation—sales figures, cost of goods sold, profits, those sorts of things. I'm sure you understand why it's important for us to know this information."

"Son, I don't understand any of that stuff. I just ask God every night to tell me what to do tomorrow."

Big jumped in. "Mr. Johnson, may I suggest we call it a day. And if you would allow us, we'd like to come back tomorrow and continue our discussions. There's a lot more we need to learn. Like how you're able to do this so well," a cajoling Big said.

Turning around to look out the window at his factory, JJ took his hat off and scratched his head. "Well, I'm mighty busy here, as you can see. I don't know. I'll think on it."

"We did come a long way," Bitty said, pinching the skin at his throat.

"Well … I guess you fellas did. I s'pose it'd be rude of me to turn you down for another talk."

The men smiled. Everybody shook hands. Jake and Jimmy never said a word the entire time.

On the ride back, Bitty turned a serious look to me in the back seat. "Mrs. McRae, our sales team has been talking with a lot of stores all through Mississippi, parts of Tennessee, and Arkansas. They can't keep Mr. Johnson's product on their shelves. His business is growing faster than he can manage. And after seeing his operation today, there's no way he can keep up with the growth. Plus, he's wrong about local honey. The Clover Company sells their honey from coast to coast. He needs to sell, Mrs. McRae, or somebody else will start supplying those stores with a different brand of honey."

They seemed to be determined men. Proud, too. I got the impression their management expected them to succeed.

They met with JJ again two more days, cutting their trip a day short. I wasn't there for those meetings, but I'm sure Big and Bitty learned a lot about life. When they checked out and paid, their noses seemed a little out of joint.

"Mr. Johnson drives a hard bargain," Bitty said.

They promised to come back. "Round two," they called it. Me? I wasn't at all impressed with how the big boys cut deals.

⚬⚬⚬

Three days later, Pastor Davidson returned, and woke to one of my "special preacher" breakfasts. We sat and talked about JJ and the Purity boys.

The preacher laughed at my recollection of the plant visit. He said, "JJ is his own man, for sure. There's nobody else like him. He may not be educated, but he has wisdom that points us all in the right direction. I'm glad he's on the vestry."

"I couldn't agree more," I said.

"Martha, you seem a little concerned about these men's determination to buy him out. You don't think they'd do anything underhanded, so to speak, do you?"

I thought for a second and responded, "No, I don't believe so."

There was a pause ... I asked, "Father, whadda you say we pick up where we left off last time?"

"Left off?" he asked, puzzled.

"Remember, we were discussing Oneeda, right before your trip."

"Oh, of course. I'd forgotten," he said, wiping his mouth, placing a folded napkin on the table, ready to talk.

I had spent considerable time planning how to ask him. Somehow, none of it mattered at the time, so I asked him point blank, "Do you love Oneeda?"

"Yes, of course I do," he said matter-of-factly.

I was stunned. "Let me rephrase the question: Are you in love with her, because she's in love with you? There, I said it."

"Oh-my-goodness." He was taken aback. "Martha, I love Oneeda's soul. I'm not *in* love with her like you think. I love her like Jesus loves her. Like a sister." His eyes pleaded with me to believe him. And I did.

"Well, you need to find a way to let her know you're her brother, and not going to be her—well, you know. Just let her know she's like a sister," I said, clasping my hands together.

"I completely understand," he said. "And I'll take care of it." He had the trustworthiest eyes I'd ever seen.

But he didn't take care of it. From then on, the preacher did everything possible to avoid Oneeda. She would stay after church, hoping they could talk, but the preacher invariably disappeared for one reason or another. She dropped by my place many a late afternoon. Always said she was coming to see me. But I knew better.

One night, Mary and Andrew drove into Greenlee to see Alfred Hitchcock's new movie, *Vertigo*, and left me to babysit Michael. I made dinner for the preacher, little Michael, and me.

After I put Michael to bed, the preacher helped me with the dishes. While I washed, he dried. More than anything, he wanted to talk.

"Martha, I need your advice."

"Okay," I said.

"It's about Oneeda."

"Humph, now there's a surprise," I said with sarcasm and a smile. He wasn't in the mood to smile back.

"I can't keep avoiding her like this. It's not right," he said, shaking his head.

"Well, I've sure had fun watching you skirt the issue," I said, casting a broad smile.

"It's not funny, Martha. This is serious. What should I do?"

"Do what you always tell me. Pray about it."

"I've *been* doing that."

There was a knock at the front door.

I put the dishtowel away and got in his face. "Then you need to talk to her," I said. "Let me see who's at the door. Two bits says it's Oneeda," as I walked out of the kitchen.

"I wouldn't take that bet if you gave me odds," he said.

As I pranced to the door, I yelled back to him, "Whadda you know about odds. You're a priest."

He said something, but I couldn't hear it.

"A-ha, it *is* Oneeda," I said to no one in particular when I saw her on the porch.

Opening the door, I said, "Oneeda, what a surprise. Come in. You can help us in the kitchen."

"Who's here?" She asked. "Is Mary here?"

"Nooo. Father Davidson and I are almost finished with the dishes."

I'll admit, she sure looked nice. Fancy new dress, new shoes. New hairdo.

She smiled as we walked through the swinging kitchen door.

"Hi, Adam," she said, greeting him with a bigger smile.

"Hey, Oneeda," he said. "We're almost done here." He looked at me with a *whadda I do now?* look on his face. I smiled and turned away, leaving him to figure it out.

"I haven't seen you in such a long time," Oneeda said, casting another toothy smile.

"I know. I've been busy."

Yeah, busy hiding from her, I thought.

They engaged in more small talk and we finished the drying. I took my apron off and smiled at the preacher, wondering what he would say next.

"Ladies," he announced as if an idea had sprung out of the blue, "we're going to sit down at the table and I'm going to pray for us."

I don't think Oneeda wanted to pray. She looked at me as if I was supposed to say something.

The preacher sat and we followed suit. He bowed his head and said his A.C.T.S. prayer. Adoration for God first. Confession of our sins second. Then thanks to God for everything we have; and lastly, supplication—asking God for his help. Which I think the preacher wanted right then and there.

"… and finally," he continued, "I pray you would find the right man for Oneeda. A man of your choosing. Send a good man into her life …"

While he continued to pray for Oneeda's man, I peeked. A 'look' can speak volumes. And hers said, *What the …?* as the preacher wrapped up his prayer, "… send a man who would cherish her as much as you do. Amen."

We all looked at each other. The preacher cast a wide grin, looking for confirmation of a good prayer. Oneeda's eyes were afire. She pushed her chair back, stood, wiped a tear, and bolted out the front door before the preacher or I could utter a word. I sighed. The preacher hung his head.

"Well, I guess that didn't go as planned," he said.

"The planning was the problem."

"Whadda you mean?"

"Oh, we women, we can smell a 'Dear John' a mile away."

He nodded, and dropped his head again. I don't think the preacher knew much about women.

<hr />

A week passed before Oneeda called me, crying. "He mailed me a letter."

"Who mailed you a letter?" I asked.

"Who do you *think*? Adam."

I felt sorry for her. "Do you want to tell me what it says?"

"He says we're like brother and sister. He thinks I'm his *sister*, Martha."

"Well, I'll bet he said he loves you like a sister."

"How'd you know?"

"Oh, just a gift of mine. Remember, I'm on your side. But, Oneeda, you can't make him love you the way you want."

"I'll never figure this man out," she said, bewildered. There was nothing else to discuss.

—⊶⊷—

But no letter could match the intensity, anger, and heartache of the one that came through the post office that Friday morning.

Sorting the mail, I noticed a letter postmarked from Parchman Farm Penitentiary, addressed to Michael Grater,

Little Michael? What in the world ...?

I couldn't dare open it. But I wasn't about to put it in Mary's postal box for her to retrieve who-knows-when. I put out the TEMPORARILY CLOSED sign and headed straight for Calvary and Mary.

Mary was behind her desk, typing Sunday's Order of Service bulletin, which I printed on my press every Friday. She was happy to see me. "Martha, you're on time, but I'm not. Running a tad behind. Give me a few more minutes."

"I didn't come for the bulletin. I came to see you." Handing her the letter, I said, "This came an hour ago. I don't like the looks of it, Mary."

"Let me see," she said, taking it from my hand.

Using a letter opener, she slit it open and pulled out a piece of paper. Glancing down to read the sender's name, she dropped it on her desk, pushed her chair back, and shrieked, "Oh my God, Martha."

Staring at the letter, her face turned pale. I bent over to see the sender's name. It was signed, *Daddy.*

A lump formed in my throat.

"I can't—" she said. Not able to complete the thought, her head fell back, her eyes opened wide, staring at what we both knew was the devil's handwriting … "—you'll have to read it. I—I can't."

22

Fear

WHEN I PICKED it up, I noticed my hand trembling. I glanced down at Mary. She was clutching and pulling on her necklace. "This can't be happening," she said, terrified. There was no going back. I had to read it to her.

My dear little Michael,

How I have longed to see you. To be with you. You are mine, and I want to spend time with you. You are my favorite child, you know that, don't you? Whatever you want, I want to give you. If you'll come visit me, I'll give candy to you! Please show this to your mother, and she'll bring you. It'll be the best thing for her and you!

Your Daddy loves you,

Daddy

Father Thomas Cain

Fear changed to anger as I struggled to finish.

Mary was sobbing, shaking her head, muttering, "No, no."

"Mary, I'm going to report this to the superintendent. You do not have to stand for this nonsense." I felt the red heat of rage flow through my face.

She stammered, "Martha, every … sentence … ends … with … *you*."

"What?" *What's she talking about?* I wondered.

I studied the letter. "Oh, no. He's insane," I said. "Mary, listen to me, there's no way he can get to Michael. Or you."

"He's broken out before," she blurted, as if his next escape was imminent.

"No, Mary, no. He's in maximum security. He's on death row. I've been there, remember? There's no way—"

"—He has a power," she interrupted, dazed, not hearing me. She pushed her chair away from the desk, drew her knees into her chest, and folded into a fetal position. "I can't explain it. He has a power that gets him whatever he wants. Martha, he's coming for Michael. I just know it." She cried, while holding her palms out, separating herself form the letter.

"Get it away from me," she yelled.

She turned sideways to the wall. I came around behind the desk and covered her with my arms. While she wept, I looked to the ceiling and begged, "Lord, don't let this man do any more harm to Mary. Protect her. And Michael. We ask you to bring justice now, before this man does any more evil."

While I never had children, I could only imagine how a mother must feel when it comes to protecting her only child—regardless of who fathered the baby.

And I didn't have enough faith to believe we'd seen the last of this father's evil.

———

On Monday morning, I rode with Pastor Davidson to Parchman, where I presented the letter to Superintendent Harris.

"How could this happen?" I asked, pointing at the letter, but wanting to point at him.

"Mrs. McRae, I'm as appalled as you are. This prisoner, Sartain, must have somebody inside our post office who let this get out. I promise to fix this. Please, give my apologies to Mrs. Grater. I'll write a letter and assure her it won't happen again," he said.

———

A few days later, I called JJ. I'd run out of honey. I could've purchased JJ's Honey in any store from Greenlee to Greenback. But JJ made me promise long ago if I ever needed honey, I should come to him.

His wife, Peg, and I talked a while, until she needed to start supper. Then JJ and I spent time on his porch, in rocking chairs, talking about Mary and the letter from Sonny Sartain.

JJ's conclusion about Sartain was simple and direct: "He's evil, Martha. Don't let him git near 'em."

"I won't. Don't worry."

It was time to change the subject. "Now, tell me what you thought of those men from Purity Foods," I said, rocking in unison with him.

"Whadda you think I should do, Martha? You think I should sell?"

"It's not for me to say, JJ. All you can do is pray about it."

"I been doin' that. I ain't convinced they'd keep up the support to Calvary. Are you?" he asked.

"Truthfully, no, I'm not."

JJ turned to study his factory workers, knocking off for the day. "And these good young men and women ... they'd prob'ly be without a job."

"Probably," I said.

We rocked a bit more and it was time to call it a day.

I settled on one light and two dark ambers.

"It's on me, Martha."

"What? Why?" I asked.

"Like I've always told ya, you're my friend. No need to say nothin'. Go on. Git outta here 'fore it gits dark."

That was JJ. Direct, but not to a fault.

<hr />

I preached my first sermon that next Sunday night, while the preacher was at Parchman, teaching the inmates. But this time, Oneeda wasn't with him. He had told her she shouldn't be going to "such a dangerous place."

I spoke on discernment, and even acknowledged JJ as God's example of someone with the gift of discernment, knowing right from wrong, good from evil.

I added, "Solo has seen more than her fair share of evil. Friends, we need to pray Satan will leave us alone." And we did pray.

Yet ...

23

Advice & Confessions

COULDN'T SHAKE THE dark cloud of dilemma. *Should I try to deliver Capp to justice? Or forget about it and keep Mary's past from public scrutiny?*

I decided to seek Pastor Davidson's advice. We had a brief discussion over breakfast.

"Hypothetically speaking," I said, "let's say you believe someone you know was involved in a murder. But bringing that person to justice could ruin someone else's life. What would you do?"

Pastor Davidson's answer appealed to me as Biblical wisdom: "When justice on this earth is possible, God expects it to be done. He will take care of Mary."

"But I never said it was Mary."

"You didn't need to," he said, smiling. Then, putting a soft hand on my shoulder, he said, "Don't be afraid, Martha. You won't be doing this alone."

It was a hot July night. I lay awake thinking, getting down on my knees and praying, then back in bed … more thinking, getting back on the floor, my hands on the bed, clasped and clammy … praying for guidance.

Sometime in the morning, I realized the preacher was right. *My task is to deliver the truth about Pastor Baddour's death. Mary? Well, Jesus would take care of her.* I felt confident it was time for the "delivery boy" to deliver. But I would need help. I couldn't leave the post office at the drop of a hat. And there was my newspaper job.

I hired a young girl as my full time assistant. I was thrilled to have her. Especially knowing I'd soon be taking a secret trip to Phillipsburg.

But first, I needed to compose an important letter.

I had a new plan.

With coffee as my companion, and my typewriter as a weapon, I pecked out an anonymous note to Annie.

I know Capp Grater was involved with your husband in poisoning Father Baddour. I have the evidence. If you won't confess that you also know, I will turn you in for obstruction of justice, and you will go to prison. I will be in Solo on Thursday, July 16. Meet me at Calvary Church, ten o'clock in the morning, in the back pew. We need to talk.

It would take a day and a half to make this Phillipsburg trip. But it had to be done—for the plan to work. I tucked the note in an envelope and addressed it to Annie Insner, Solo, Mississippi. I drove to the first post office in Phillipsburg I could find. I bought a Liberty Bell stamp, affixed it to the envelope, dropped it in the mail slot, and spent the night in a cheap motel. The next morning I headed back to Solo.

It would take at least five days for the letter to reach Solo, so I waited an extra day to visit the crotchety sheriff in Greenlee.

I wasted no time in explaining my plan. I asked him to hide on the floor of Calvary's nave, between pews, three rows from the rear so he could be there in case Annie admitted to Capp's involvement. But he laughed so hard he rocked backward in his swivel chair and banged his head against the wall, which made for a loud *thud*.

Ouch! I thought, *that must've hurt*. He reached down to retrieve his hat, still laughing. That was the first time I'd seen him without a hat.

Everybody's name means something, and like his flattop haircut and bulldog face, his name fit him to a tee—*Butch*. Sheriff Butch Turnbull.

He didn't much like my plan, so I asked, "How humiliated would you be, sheriff, if I—singlehandedly—put another murderer right in your lap? This is your chance to be the hero. A legend. Plus, it wouldn't hurt your re-election chances."

His laughter turned to interest as he stretched his large mass forward and placed his hands on the desk. He stared at me. Pondering.

Every law officer lives and dies by their reputation. And more than anything, Butch Turnbull wanted to stay on as sheriff of Bethel County.

Sitting in Calvary's last pew at nine-forty-five that Thursday, I could hear the sheriff's heavy breathing, from the floor, two pews ahead. I told him to cover his mouth with a handkerchief. It seemed to work.

Ten minutes later, Annie walked through the church's side door—instead of the rear. *Oh, no, she'll walk right by the sheriff. I should have told her to enter from the narthex.* I jumped up and walked past the sheriff toward her, but she stopped and pointed at me.

"You," she shouted, her eyes wide and angry.

I put a finger to my lips, "Shhh, be quiet."

I had to get control or she'd turn and run.

"Come here, Annie," I said. I walked closer and stopped, hoping she'd come to me. Step by step, she came. I wanted to hug her and calm her, but …

She was upset, to say the least. She said, "The letter … it was mailed from Phillipsburg. I thought he sent someone to kill me. But, *you?*"

"Annie, sit, please, I'll explain everything. Just please sit."

"Why am I here?" She looked around, probably thinking she should run. When she turned back to me, I could see mist in her eyes. She was clutching a large object in her arms.

She walked closer, all the while looking to her right and left. As she approached, I saw the huge yellow purse she'd been holding.

My mind flashed back to her with a cleaver, chopping a slab of cow in half. *Surely she wouldn't. Not here. Not in church.*

I was too nervous to speak. I motioned with my arm for her to sit. We sat three rows in front of the sheriff. I could hear his soft breathing, and prayed Annie couldn't. She tucked her purse tight to her side, on the pew. I was thankful the sheriff was there to save me, but wondered if he'd be able to get his big body off the floor in time.

There was no sense in beating around the bush with her. But I was gentle. "Look, Annie, I'm sure Capp was involved with Judd when Father Baddour was poisoned. Tell me how *you* know, because I'm sure you do."

"What makes you think I know anything?" she blurted, still angry, still avoiding eye contact.

"The nightmares …" I said with compassion. "They won't go away, will they?"

She looked pitiful, even thinner than before. She looked me square in the eye. "No, they won't go away." A tear rolled down her cheek. I hugged her. But she pushed me away.

"My nightmares … they're worse. Now they're about him …"

She stopped, not wanting to say more. Her eyes were damp and large with fright.

"Annie, they're about Capp Grater, aren't they? You thought he was sending someone here to get rid of you, didn't you?" I tried to be compassionate.

She nodded.

"You were so close to telling Father Davidson at my house that night, weren't you? Tell me, Annie. Capp was involved, wasn't he?"

"He's a man who can do whatever he wants, and get away with it. Don't you understand?" she asked, breathy, looking around, as if searching for boogeyman.

"Tell me who you're afraid of. Just say it, Annie."

She grabbed her purse with both arms. I reached over to cover her hands with mine. We were face-to-face, six inches apart. She shook her head, and tried to stand. I gently pulled her down.

"Annie, please sit. You can't keep harboring a nightmare. Capp had something to do with it, didn't he?

"Yes," she whimpered, looking down at the floor. "Mr. Grater … Him and Judd, they—". She shook her head again. After a pause, she gathered herself and let the rest of the story spill out like an unclogged faucet. "Mr. Grater and Judd, they planned the whole thing. Judd wanted money to expand our business. I shouldn't be telling you this, Martha." She blew her nose with a hankie.

"No, you should. Now go on."

She sighed and released some pent-up air. "That's how we doubled the size of the butcher shop. Judd always wanted to be a big man in town."

Annie's sad eyes looked up at the church ceiling again, as if an answer could be found there. It was as if I wasn't even there for one moment in her ordeal. Her chin drifted to her chest. Her nose was red. She blew again.

"You don't understand," she said. "Nobody does. Judd ... he came from a successful family in Little Rock. He was just a young boy in high school when he stole that car. They sent him to jail. His good-for-nothing, self-righteous parents disowned him." Annie was angry.

"Annie, that's terrible," I said. "What happened?"

"His parents never forgave him ... so he ran away. He wanted to make something of himself," she said, glancing at me for a split second.

I put an arm around her shoulders, trying to console her. "He did, Annie, he did," I said. "He made something of himself. But we all make mistakes."

"His last mistake cost him his life," she said, as more tears streamed down her gaunt cheeks.

"Annie, it's not right for Judd to get the whole blame for trying to make Father Baddour sick," I said.

She nodded, still not looking at me.

"Tell me how they planned it. I promise you'll be protected from Capp Grater. You have to trust me." (I knew I'd have to pray about this later.)

She whispered, "They were talking ... in the back of the store ..." She stopped. I waited.

"Annie, tell me. What did they talk about? What was said?"

She held her chin up, closed her eyes, and let out another breath.

"Poison," she whispered.

"They talked about poison?"

"Yes. Judd had gone to Mr. Grater before, asking to borrow money to expand. That day, in the store, Mr. Grater offered Judd the money. With one condition. Judd had to put something in Father Baddour's food to make him sick. Not to kill him, Martha, just to make him sick."

"Why would Capp want to make him sick?"

"So he'd leave Solo. I heard Mr. Grater was going to pay some doctor in Greenlee."

"I don't understand," I said, confused.

"It was Father Baddour's doctor. The doctor was supposed to tell him that the farm chemicals were making him sick. Mr. Grater thought it would get Father Baddour to leave the Delta."

Interesting, I thought. "And do you know why he wanted him to leave?" (*I* knew. I wanted to know if she did.)

"Mr. Grater had something against Father Baddour. I heard him telling Judd about it. I think Mary was having an affair with the rector."

"What's the doctor's name in Greenlee?"

She shook her head. "I can't remember."

"Why didn't you tell the sheriff all this?"

"I couldn't. He's not a man to trifle with, Martha. You know that," she said.

"You mean Capp Grater?"

"Yes. Martha, listen to me. Judd didn't kill him. He swore to me. He said that much potassum cloride, or whatever it's called, wasn't enough to kill him."

Annie had regained her composure and her voice. I thought maybe it was because her confession had cleared out a closet full of guilt.

"He told me Father Baddour ate the whole rack of ribs. Enough for two people," she said. "Judd told me he must have had an awful big appetite that day." She snickered at the ludicrousness of her own comment. "I guess it turned out to be awful after all," she said, looking up at the ceiling.

"Wait. You're saying Father Baddour died because he ate more than Judd and Capp expected?" I was totally confused.

"Yes, that's what Judd told me," she said.

Ate more than Judd expected? I'll need to think more on that. But later.

Annie was in that spiritual state of euphoria, same as when someone confesses an awful secret they've been harboring far too long. Release it and it goes on somebody else's plate.

She sighed and looked at me with relieved eyes. She had reached the spiritual bottom and was on her way up the other side. It was all out in the open—the guilt, the fear of Capp. There was nothing else to hide. She bowed her head and asked for forgiveness. That's when her guilt and fear were transferred to Jesus' plate.

As we left arm-in-arm, I imagined Turnbull had all the evidence he needed.

And Annie didn't know the sheriff had been there—not until the trial.

Capp was arrested in Phillipsburg on August 27, 1959. I have no idea how he reacted. He was transported to Greenlee's County jail.

The District Attorney and his prosecutor didn't think he could get a murder conviction, so they settled on a charge of manslaughter. A grand jury would decide if Capp should be tried in criminal court.

I guess Annie's comment about "making Father Baddour sick, not kill him," was their reason for a manslaughter charge instead of murder.

Me? I was just glad justice would be served. Yet, I had that nagging feeling about Mary and little Michael.

An awful lot of half-truths come out in every trial. And sometimes, even truths people have no business knowing.

Part III

Trials & Tribulations

*There will be tribulation and distress for
all those who do evil.*

Romans 2:9

24

The Grand Jury

MARY, ANNIE, SHERIFF Turnbull and I were subpoenaed to testify before the Grand Jury.

The subpoena's instructions were clear. "No discussion whatsoever with anyone involved in the proceedings—before, during, or after." It was the law.

I wasn't surprised when Oneeda dropped by. I figured she'd heard about the subpoenas.

We sat in the parlor. She seemed anxious.

"Martha, I thought you wanted to keep Mary's past a secret," she said, her eyebrows pressed together in concern.

Oh, how the tables have turned, I thought. My best friend, the queen of gossip, was chastising *me* about un-kept secrets.

"How did you know it was Mary?" I asked.

"Martha, I have a little sense. I hear things."

"Well, Mary and Michael's well-being is in God's hands. Always has been," I said. "Besides, there's nothing I could do to prevent Capp's arrest. Justice can be better served if I do my part. That's Father Davidson's advice, too." I hoped she would drop the matter.

But Oneeda was persistent. "You won't be able to keep Mary's past from coming out in a trial. She's my friend, too, you know."

"It's not a trial, Oneeda. Not yet anyway. This is a grand jury proceeding."

"But her past will—"

"Stop, Oneeda. I'm not allowed to discuss it."

"It's just us two talking," she said, louder than necessary.

"No, there's someone else here." I pointed upwards, moving my finger up and down, up and down. She got the picture and stormed out, mumbling something I couldn't understand.

Truth is, I didn't want to discuss it anymore. I had already settled on leaving Mary's reputation in God's hands.

I had become the "delivery boy" for Capp Grater's guilt or innocence.

September 21, 1959, the Greenlee Court house

This grand jury business was the strangest legal proceeding I'd ever seen. No judge was present, no defendant or his attorney—only a jury of eighteen men and women, the prosecutor, and a few witnesses.

I had researched the history of grand juries. The concept has survived since early Greece. In America, the first grand jury was impaneled in 1635 "to consider cases of murder, robbery, and wife beating." Nice to know somebody back then was protecting us women from the boogeyman.

The prosecutor's job was to present just enough evidence for the jurors to obtain an indictment. In this case, for manslaughter.

But the tricky part was knowing what "just enough evidence" meant. I learned that prosecutors never wanted to give away more evidence than necessary. They didn't want the defense knowing *all* of the prosecutor's tactics. Better to keep the defense on their toes in the criminal trial.

But first, the grand jury would decide if there was sufficient evidence, or probable cause, to warrant an indictment. If they couldn't, the accused would walk.

If the grand jury decided there was probable cause, then a criminal trial jury would decide the ultimate guilt or innocence of Capp Grater.

⚬⚬⚬

Mary, Oneeda, and I sat together in the Greenlee courtroom. We were shocked to see Betty Crain walk in. None of us knew she had been subpoenaed. It'd been three years since she divorced her husband and left Solo. Oneeda promptly informed me that Betty had caught her scoundrel husband with another woman.

Thinking out loud I muttered, "What's happened to Solo?"

It was a rhetorical question but Oneeda answered anyway. "There's something in the water," she said without batting an eye.

Maybe there is, I thought. *It's called evil.*

For a brief moment, I turned around to see what an empty courtroom looked like. It was strange, seeing all those bare pews and only us witnesses on the front row, and a jury box of eighteen men and women.

Frank Acuff, the prosecutor, strutted in from a side door and walked straight to the jury box. He informed the jury and us: "The witnesses will give evidence of facts known only to them in respect of the matter with which the accused stands charged," he said.

Awfully stiff language, I thought. *He should talk like a real person.*

Acuff was a tall, lanky, mid-forties man, wearing a dark suit, white shirt, and thin black tie. And shiny black shoes. He looked like an FBI agent, not a prosecutor. I had read about him—an ambitious up-and-comer in state politics. A graduate of the Ole Miss Law School.

Sheriff Turnbull was the first witness called to the stand. The clerk instructed him to raise his right hand and place his left on a Bible. "Do-you-swear-to-tell-the-truth-the-whole-truth-and-nothing-but-the-truth-so-help-you-God?"

"I do."

"Please state your name and occupation."

"Butch Turnbull, Sheriff of Bethel County."

"You may be seated."

Prosecutor Acuff stepped to the witness box. "Now, tell the jury, if you would, Sheriff Turnbull, why you had the defendant, Mr. Grater, arrested."

The sheriff's face turned red—*embarrassed*, I thought, having to talk about hiding on the church floor and all. But he managed to get through the whole story.

To my amazement, Acuff turned to the panel of jurors and asked if any of them had a question. I jerked my head toward them. None of them made a move or a sound. I hadn't realized the jury could also ask questions of a witness, which only added to my nervousness about my turn in the witness box.

The sheriff was excused and the prosecutor called Annie to the stand.

"I'm Annie Insner. I run the meat market in Solo."

"Mrs. Insner, are you referring to the same meat market your husband owned, before his unfortunate death?"

"Yes."

"Now, please describe for the jury what your husband and the defendant, Mr. Grater, were discussing in the back of the butcher shop."

Annie recounted all of what she had heard—the poison to be used, how Judd would do it, the money Capp was going to give Judd ... she told it all.

"And why didn't you report this to the authorities?" Acuff asked.

"I was afraid."

"Afraid of what?"

"Of Mr. Grater. What he might do," she said, staring at the floor.

"Explain to the jury what you mean."

Annie turned to face the jury. "He's rich. He's able to get whatever he wants. That's all I want say."

There were no more questions from Acuff and none from the jury.

Acuff called Mary to the stand.

Mary's testimony was brief. When asked by the prosecutor if she had indeed had an affair with Baddour, she lowered her head and replied, "Yes, I did."

"To your knowledge, did your husband know of the affair?"

She raised her head to answer. "I'm not sure. I suppose he did," she said, dabbing her eyes.

"You *suppose* he did? Explain to the jury why you suppose he was aware of the affair."

Mary told of Capp's sermon on adultery and his dark-chocolate attitude toward her.

"I have no further questions, Mrs. Grater," Acuff said. "Oh, before you go, I must ask the jury if there is anything they'd like to ask you." He studied the jury. No one said a word.

Acuff called Betty Crain to the stand.

"My name is Betty Crain. I'm a former nurse, which I intend to pursue again when this is—"

"—Thank you Mrs. Crain, that's more than we need to know," Acuff interrupted.

A former nurse? I'd forgotten that. It was a long time ago. As I recalled, she'd done some nursing for a year or so.

"Tell the jury, Mrs. Crain, what you know about Father Baddour's death."

"Well, I don't know anything about his death, except what was in Martha's newspaper," she said, pointing at me. "But I know he was having an affair with Mary Grater."

Witch, I thought. *Don't you dare go into her past.*

Prosecutor Acuff was grinning when he said, "Please tell the jury what brought you to that conclusion."

"I saw them in a car in Greenlee on Saturday, November 6, and watched them park at the Alamo Motel. I then saw them go inside a room together," she said, as if it meant nothing for her to let the world know what she had seen her Bible study "friend" do.

I sensed the jury was thinking *jealous husband, motive for murder.*

"And when did you become aware Father Baddour was having an affair with Mrs. Grater?"

Without hesitation she said, "Oh, I'd say several weeks before."

Acuff stepped away from the witness stand and addressed the jury. "Those are all my questions for Mrs. Crain. Do any of you wish to ask Mrs. Crain a question?"

One little prim and proper lady raised her hand.

"Ma'am," Acuff said, "Please stand and state your question."

The lady stood, and said, "Mrs. Crain, you say you followed them. At what point did you start?"

Acuff turned to Betty, waiting for an answer.

Betty stared at the lady. Finally, Betty spoke: "Well, I –I suspected they had been seeing each other for some time, like I said earlier."

The lady raised her hand again. "So, did you follow them from Solo into Greenlee, or were you already in Greenlee?"

Betty's eyes bore down on the lady as if none of this was any of her business. Acuff's strong voice brought Betty out of her trance. "Answer the question, Mrs. Crain."

"Sorry, I don't understand the question." Betty's sudden nervousness was apparent. I saw it in her rapid eye-blinks and subtle head twitching.

Acuff clarified the juror's question. "Quite simply, Mrs. Crain, when did you start following them? Was it from Solo, or were you already in Greenlee at the time?"

Betty hesitated, and shifted positions in the witness chair.

She doesn't want to answer. Why?

"Solo. No, Greenlee," she blurted, changing her mind. "I'm sorry. I can't remember." At that moment, I knew there was more dirt under Betty's skirt than I had realized.

"Can't remember …" Acuff said, trailing off. "I suppose that's understandable. But tell the jury why you didn't report this earlier, after Father Baddour's death."

Betty's breathy voice was like a shy fifth-grader in their first school recital: "After Judd Insner's suicide, well, we all assumed he had killed the rector." She shook her head. "There just didn't seem to be any reason to tell anybody after Judd hung himself."

She straightened her back into a proper lady-like posture and regained her confidence. "Something else," she said, smiling, "we wanted to protect Mary's reputation. She was in our Bible study group."

Hypocrite lying witch, I thought.

"I see," Acuff said, returning to his desk. "That'll be all, Mrs. Crain. You may be excused."

Betty had told me four years ago how she *happened* to be in Greenlee when she saw David Baddour and Mary go into that motel room. I wouldn't have caught this new revelation if she hadn't flubbed her answer. *She had followed them all the way from Solo, for goodness sake. Why?*

My mind was racing as I began taking notes of her testimony.

Suddenly, my name was called. "The State of Mississippi calls Martha McRae to the stand."

The dreaded witness box. I needed to gather my wits—try to get Betty off my mind. I was a tad nervous, walking up the two steps into the box with the creaky little swinging gate and the hard oak chair with no cushion.

The clerk asked, "Do-you-swear-to-tell-the-truth-the-whole-truth-and-nothing-but-the-truth-so-help-you-God?"

"I do. I swear to tell the truth, the whole—"

"—Thank you, a simple 'I do' will suffice," Acuff interrupted. "You may be seated. Please state your name and for the court."

"Martha McRae. Newspaper and boarding house owner."

I shifted in my chair, let out a breath, and tried to get ready for his next question.

He turned his back to me, moved a stack of papers to one side of his table, and gathered up another file. He walked to the witness stand, file in hand, shuffling through some papers, and said—without even looking up at me—"Mrs. McRae, I understand you played a rather large role in Mrs. Insner's story. The story of how she overheard her husband and the defendant discussing the poisoning of Father Baddour. Tell this court how you came to the conclusion Mr. Grater might be involved in the murder of Father Baddour."

Frank Acuff made me feel comfortable and at ease. I corroborated Turnbull's, Annie's, and Mary's testimony. I told the truth about Mary's affair and how she had confessed it to me. (I didn't have a choice. Betty had already brought it up anyway.) But I never mentioned Mary's former life.

No one on the jury had any questions.

And that was the end of it. Prosecutor Acuff rested his case and asked the jury to make a determination.

Would Capp Grater be dismissed, or indicted on a charge of manslaughter? We witnesses weren't allowed to stay and wait for the decision, but I figured Annie's testimony would be the deciding factor. She'd heard Judd and Capp talk about poisoning Father Baddour. Surely that would be enough to convince the jury that the case should go to criminal court.

I heard the next day it took the jury one hour to report back. Capp Grater was found to have "probable cause." There would indeed be a criminal trial for manslaughter.

I wasn't surprised. I had read that ninety-nine out of a hundred grand jury proceedings result in indictments.

The trial was set for November 16, 1959.

Why would Betty have followed them from Solo to Greenlee? It doesn't make sense. My mind was a cauldron of thoughts about Betty's possible involvement, and Capp's upcoming trial.

In my kitchen, and at the post office, I pondered for days, determined—before his trial—to find the dirt under Betty's hem and haw skirt. But every idea had a flaw. I was clueless.

Two weeks later, the answer came out of the blue. Or was it from above? Anyway, I was confident I'd found a way. Tricky, but doable.

My intuition was at work again. I could sense the lid popping open and the undoing of Betty Crain. (There was no revenge involved. I merely wanted justice to prevail.)

I wondered if Annie might hold the key to Betty's involvement as she had for Capp's. So I decided to pay her another visit.

Annie and I had been through a lot together (the church confession, her time in my parlor with Pastor Davidson, plus Bible study). We'd become pretty close friends. I wasn't expecting any problems.

The familiar bell tinkled above her door as I walked in. She was kneeling in front of a large refrigerator, counting packaged meat. She looked up and asked if I was there to pick up some steaks.

"Oh, yes, of course," I said. "But Annie, I need to ask a question first, if you don't mind."

She closed the cooler door and walked behind the counter. I stood across from her.

"Something about the steaks?" she asked.

"No, not that," I said.

"Oh, more questions about Father Baddour," she guessed, exasperated.

"Just one. Can you recall the last time Betty Crain was in here?" I could detect Annie's tension easing—maybe because I was asking about Betty.

"I don't know. It's been a long time. You know she's been in Oxford with her daughter for what, three years now?" she said, brushing her apron.

"I believe that's right. Now think back to the last time she was here."

"Let me see …" she paused, wiping her hands, thinking. "Yes, I believe it was close to three years ago. Or was it four? That's right. She was in here right before Father Baddour's autopsy …" she said, trailing off. She turned away to take on some other chores, ignoring me.

I guessed she shut down because the rector's autopsy brought back bad memories of Judd's suicide.

"Were you here when she came by?"

"Yes. But, I'm sorry, I don't remember what she bought," she said, moving down the counter to retrieve something. Annie was no longer interested in discussing the matter. I was patient, and waited for her to talk.

"Why are you asking all this, Martha?"

"I'm just trying to piece a puzzle together, Annie."

"*Another* puzzle? You already did that with Mr. Grater. And now you think *Betty Crain* is involved?" She chuckled.

I leaned in closer, "Look, if you'd show me the storage room I'd appreciate it."

"Why would you want to go in there?" she asked.

"I have a hunch. It might clear Judd's name."

Annie's attitude changed completely after I said Judd's name might be cleared.

"I don't go back there much," she said sadly. "Judd and all, you know? It was pretty much his room."

"I understand. But what if I can find something that might help clear Judd's name?"

"Well, I suppose it's all right if I let you in there. But I'm not goin' in."

We walked to the back. She unlocked a door that I'd never seen before. She stayed behind as I walked in to find a light switch. Two ceiling lights came on. Annie turned and left.

Against the far wall was one tall metal cabinet with open shelves, all of them jam-packed with bottles. Most had labels with some designation, a chemical name or a number.

I knew what I was searching for, and found it: a canister of potassium chloride. I studied the label. A skull with cross-bones was printed in the middle. I grabbed one of Judd's knives and popped the lid off. As expected, some of the contents were missing. It was a twelve-ounce container. I found a measuring scale and poured the remaining contents onto it. The scale measured eight ounces. *Huh, four ounces missing.*

After pouring the contents back into the container I left, thanking Annie on the way out.

"I hope you found what you're looking for," she said in a sincere tone.

"I believe I did, Annie. I believe so. But may I ask if you or Judd ever used potassium chloride in your business?"

She paused and thought. "No, I'd never heard of it before that day Judd and Mr. Grater talked about it."

"Thank you, Annie."

"Will this get Judd's name cleared?"

"Possibly. Oh, I almost forgot. Would you like to come for supper next week? Maybe Thursday? I promise there won't be any inquisition this time," I said with a genuine smile.

"I'd like that," she said. "I've been wanting to ask the preacher some questions about the material he gave me to study."

"Terrific," I said, opening the door to leave.

"Martha, your steaks?"

"Oh, right. Can I pick'em up later? I have an errand to run."

"But you never told me what you wanted."

"Let me think. Yes, make it four rib eyes. And thank you," I added as the doorbell tinkled.

—◦◦◦—

I needed to find a chemistry book on potassium chloride. I wanted to know how much it would take to stop a heart.

It was a thirty-minute drive to the Greenlee library. The librarian escorted me to the chemistry section. I searched the chapter headings of the library's four chemistry books. Nothing could answer my question. I would have to go to the state library in Salem to find the answer.

Before leaving Greenlee, I had one more stop to make—the Alamo Motel.

I asked the resident manager if I could have a look at the registration book for November, 1954.

"I ain't so sure I should do that," she said.

She was the typical gruff, beehive-bleach-blond, gum-smacker, wanting me to beg for a chance to look at the register. I was too tired to try flattery. I glanced at her name badge.

"Julie, if you don't give me the register within five seconds, I'll call Sheriff Turnbull and have this motel shut down by tomorrow morning for prostitution. Now spit the gum out and hand me the register."

She didn't spit the gum out, but she said, "When are you people gonna give this up? You been here annoying me for two months. *Here*." She shoved the register at me, and turned to walk away. I shook my head as she strutted her little hiney back to the motel's private office.

"Redneck," I muttered under my breath.

Taking the register, I thumbed back to November 6, 1954, the Saturday Betty had seen them. There were no names for

"Mary Grater" or "Baddour." But I did notice a "David Barton" had signed the register. *Could this be Pastor Baddour's way of signing the book?* I grabbed a piece of paper and traced the signature. I was about to leave, but something occurred to me. I flipped forward two weeks in the book to November 20, the date of his death. Moving my finger down the page I couldn't believe my eyes when I came to the name, "Mary Grater." *What the .... ?*

I traced it, too.

I left the front office and walked to #10, the same room Betty Crain had seem them walk into on November 6, two weeks before that fateful Saturday. I had no key to the room, so I stood at the door and imagined where Betty and her car might have been in order to see them. There's no way she could've seen them from the street. *She must've been inside the motel lot, not more than twenty or thirty feet away.*

There was nothing special about the surroundings—only a newspaper dispenser next to a Coca-Cola machine with a rack of empty bottles.

⚬⚬⚬

Back in Solo, I stopped by the church office and asked Mary if she would show me some of Father Baddour's documents.

"Anything with his signature on it," I said.

"Whatever for, Martha?" Mary asked.

"I'll explain later. But it's important." I had already decided to ask Mary about her name being in the register *after* I checked on David Baddour's signature.

Mary found several documents with his signature.

They matched the "David Barton" tracing paper to a tee. *So he did use a fictitious name*, I thought, enjoying a surge of energy. I turned to confront Mary.

"Mary, I have something very important to ask you."

"Okay," she said, her eyes squished together in puzzlement.

"Were you with Father Baddour at any time on November 20?"

"Martha, why would you ask such a question? I've told you before, I had no idea he was even in Greenlee that day."

I showed her the signature with her name. "Mary, I traced this from the Alamo register. Tell me this is not your handwriting."

She looked at it for a second and said, "It surely is not. What's going on, Martha?" she demanded.

I explained everything to her. She was as flabbergasted as I. And I felt confident she was telling the truth. Then, again, people can fool me sometimes.

"I believe you, Mary. Someone else was with him at the Alamo that day," I said.

"Who?" she asked, leaning forward.

"Can't say for certain. But I know how to find out."

At home, I searched through my Bible study material and found what I needed—notes from Betty Crain. I compared her writing with the "Mary Grater" handwriting. The similarities were unmistakable. *Betty Crain was at the Alamo Motel the same day Pastor Baddour died.*

It didn't take a genius to figure out what she was doing at the Alamo with him. But if I could prove Betty's involvement in his death, the digging and prodding for information during the trial would shift from Mary's past to Betty's. I trusted Annie's story—Capp and Judd were just trying to make him sick. I thought Betty might have gotten hold of some extra potassium chloride, and somehow given it to him at the Alamo. The extra poison must have caused Pastor Baddour's heart to stop.

I wondered, *Would Judd need more than two ounces just to make him sick?* Four ounces were missing from the canister.

The next day, leaving for the main library in Salem, I told Mary not to expect me for supper.

The Salem librarian led me to the chemistry section. I found a book that might help: *How to Use Potassium Chloride for Prison Executions.* Before the end of the first chapter, I learned potassium chloride must be injected intravenously in order to render death. *So, taken orally, it shouldn't kill you,* I thought. The article stated it would take large amounts of it to cause cardiac arrest. How could Betty have contributed to Baddour's death with only two extra ounces of potassium chloride?

It doesn't make sense. What if the poison had come in contact with another ingredient—maybe it was the Coca-Cola? Could syrup, or carbonation change the chemical structure, making it lethal?

More books, another half-hour, and I finally came across an article about PC's inability to change structure. A chemist had written: *"No reaction to testing various known substances can change the chemical make-up of potassium chloride."*

I drove back to Solo, tired, the highway busy with car lights blinding me, reminding me these potassium rabbit holes were getting me nowhere with Betty. I missed supper that night. The kitchen was clean. The preacher, Mary, and Michael had gone to bed. Exhausted, I thought sleep would come quickly. But it didn't. My mind kept grinding, coming up empty. I was at a loss for what to do next.

In a few weeks the attention would be focused on the trial. *If I can't dig out Betty's involvement before then, she'll sit up on that witness stand and bring up Mary's awful past.*

And I'd be a failure for not digging the dirt out of Betty's skirt.

Annie came for supper on Thursday. She was quiet, not saying a word during the meal. Afterwards, we sat in the parlor—Annie, the preacher, and I. We sipped on sherry, but only one glass that night.

This was the night Annie wanted to ask the preacher more questions. She looked at the preacher with searching eyes and opened her mouth, but nothing came out.

"What is it, Annie?" he asked with a tender voice. "Tell me."

"Back in May, when we talked," she began, "I've been wondering. If God is all knowing and created all things ..."

"Yes?" the preacher said, his eyes searching Annie's.

"Then where does evil come from?" she asked.

Even I wanted to hear this answer.

"Well, that's a fine question, Annie. Let me explain it this way: When God created the angels in heaven he gave some of them freewill," the preacher said. "God didn't create puppets. They were free to make choices. And so are we. Anyway, Lucifer—the chief angel—decided he wanted to be worshiped like God. Lucifer's pride led him to revolt against God. One-third of the angels sided with Lucifer. They were ejected from heaven."

"So Lucifer and Satan are one and the same?" she asked.

"Yes, he's also known as the devil, the deceiver, and the 'father of all lies.' He's been battling God ever since."

The preacher made an arc in the air with both arms. "There's this huge spiritual warfare going on around us," he said, letting his arms down. "We just can't see it."

"And God created Adam and Eve with this same freewill?" she asked.

"He did. He never forced us to love him. He loved us first, and has always desired our love in return. In fact, we can't love him until he changes our hearts."

Wanting more, Annie continued. "In Genesis, it says Satan tempted Adam and Eve into doing something God had warned against. But they did it anyway. Why does their sin have anything to do with all the evil in the world now? I don't understand it."

"It's called original sin," he said. "Adam and Eve allowed sin to come into a perfect paradise. Their sin tainted God's whole creation. God is not only merciful, he's just, Annie. He had to judge their sin. He cursed the ground they stood on, and we've been under that curse ever since. But Annie, one day this earth will be restored to its original paradise. God promised it. Those who've given their lives to Jesus will live in a new paradise, right here, on a restored earth. Perfect in all ways. No tears. No pain. No sin."

"It all sounds like a fairy tale. So hard for me to believe," she said, rubbing an arm.

"Annie, it takes as much faith to believe it's *not* true as it does to believe it is. Let me say it this way: Suppose, just suppose, Christ's followers have it all wrong. Suppose Jesus was a liar, or maybe he was insane ... after all, he made claims no other man has made before or since. He claimed to be God. Now, if we're wrong and non-believers are *right*, what's the worst, Annie, that would have happened to any Christian here on earth?" The preacher didn't wait for a response. "At the very least, they would have lived a moral life, with a few hiccups here and there, of course. None of us is perfect." The preacher paused. "*But*, if we're right, and non-believers are wrong, what's the worst that will happen to non-believers?" This time he waited for a response.

"I don't know. What?" she asked.

"God says those who don't believe in his Son will spend eternity in hell, the worst place imaginable. Forever. And believers will have Jesus as their advocate. Non-believers will have the accuser, Satan."

"It's just so unbelievable," she said, shaking her head. "I'm supposed to trust in someone I can't see, and something I can't imagine?"

"Isn't that what faith is? Being sure of what you hope for, and certain of what you can't see," he said. "Atheists have as much faith as believers, Annie. But there's something else, too."

"What?"

"No one, including me, can ever convince you of this truth. Only Holy Spirit can convince you."

"I suppose so," she said, yawning.

It was late, so we called it a night.

But I loved every minute of these theological interludes. They were as much a part of my life as my search for the guilty.

25

7 Men and 5 Women

Oneeda told me Capp's attorney had been in Greenlee for two weeks—even spent a few days in Solo.

"His name's Benston, or something like that. I can't re-member," she said. "He's a hot-shot trial lawyer and senior partner with McLean & Adams in Phillipsburg."

"The name means nothing to me," I said.

"I checked 'em out. They're the largest firm in Phillipsburg—two-hundred lawyers," she said. "He's one slick, three-piece-suit lawyer. I got a good look at him last week."

"You've seen him? Where?"

"Charlie's Place."

"Charlie Parker?" I asked, surprised.

"He and Charlie talked for thirty minutes."

"Did you hear any of it?" My curiosity had risen.

"Too far away. They were in the kitchen most of the time. But they kept pointing through the serving window toward the counter. Then I did what you've always taught me, Martha: *Be patient and see what happens.*"

"And so ... ?" I asked, ready to know more.

"Here's where it got interesting. I watched them come out of the kitchen and go behind the lunch counter. Charlie pointed at the stool."

"The stool where Father Baddour died?"

"Yep. And Benston, or whatever his name is, went back in the kitchen and took photographs. Of the whole place. He must've used an entire role of film. Then he left. That's when I talked to Charlie. He said the lawyer had wanted to know where Judd was standing in the kitchen and where Father Baddour was sitting. Charlie told me he also asked what the rector had eaten that day. Interesting, huh?"

"What he'd eaten? Yes, that's very interesting."

I stared out my kitchen window, wondering what Capp's defense was up to.

—◦◦◦—

A week later, the reporters came pouring into Greenlee, Bethaven, and Solo. For Solo, two sleeper buses parked next to the old train depot. Other than the Emmitt Till murder trial four years ago in nearby Sumner, this would be the largest gathering of reporters the Delta had entertained. Bigger than Freddie's trial. Since many of them had been to the

Delta for one trial or another, most of the repeaters hung out in Greenlee. The fresh ones, though, came to Solo for background interviews and photographs.

I read the newspapers being dropped off at the post office every day. It didn't take long before these newer reporters discovered Oneeda. She was quoted twelve, maybe fifteen times in the newspapers. She became the reporters' poster child for Solo, telling them all about Capp's house, and how rich he was; and about Father Baddour, how kind he was. She even gave reporters a tour of Judd's Meat Market. Naturally, they swarmed Annie, wanting to know what she would say on the witness stand.

"Annie refused to talk about it and kept selling them meat for their bus kitchens," Oneeda said.

Thank goodness Oneeda didn't talk about Mary.

November 16, 1959, the Greenlee Court House

It was cold. Outside and in. Heaters strained to generate any warmth. Everybody bundled up, crammed together like sardines in a cold can. The stranger behind us? He may have actually *eaten* sardines and onions for breakfast. He stunk. If the courtroom hadn't been so packed, Oneeda and I would've picked up and moved to another seat. It was the first time I ever asked Oneeda for a stick of her Juicy Fruit. I considered offering it to "smelly breath" behind me, but he looked a tad scruffy. So did the courtroom.

Built in 1898, it had seen better days. The windows were tall and leaked air; the walls, old wood paneled. Four ceiling fans remained motionless. *Thank goodness.*

In the jury box were seven men and five women.

Arthur Bernstein sat at the defense table, next to Capp and two other lawyers. The prosecutor, Frank Acuff, sat across the aisle with his two assistants.

Bernstein was a five-foot-seven bantam rooster with a barrel chest and thinning grey hair combed straight back. His round eyeglasses and three-piece suit added to his spick-and-span Ivy League persona. He appeared to be in his seventies, confident in his own skin—pink skin that'd never tasted the sun.

Frank Acuff was the prosecutor. Of course, I already knew him from the Grand Jury proceedings.

The bailiff shouted, "All rise!" We stood and watched as Judge Clarence Chapman, wearing a long black robe, entered the courtroom from a side door. As he sat in the high-back judge's chair, the bailiff yelled, "Hear ye, hear ye, hear ye, all persons having business before the Honorable Clarence Chapman, Judge for The Circuit Court of Bethel County Mississippi, draw near, give your attention and you shall be heard. God save the great State of Mississippi. Be seated."

Everybody sat. The court clerk stood and read: "The State of Mississippi versus Capp Grater, on the count of manslaughter. Court is now in session."

Judge Chapman opened with a few remarks addressed to the courtroom. "Ladies and gentlemen, this will likely be a lengthy trial. I want to remind all of you to remain quiet during these proceedings. There will be no outbursts or unnecessary noise in my courtroom. I hope you have comprehended my warning."

Addressing Bernstein, Judge Chapman asked, "How does the defendant plead?"

Bernstein stood. "Not guilty, Your Honor."

"Is the prosecution ready?" the judge asked Acuff.

"We are, Your Honor."

"And the defense?"

Bernstein said, "Yes, Your Honor."

Opening a notebook, the judge addressed Acuff, "The prosecution may begin with an opening statement, and call its first witness."

Prosecutor Acuff outlined his case, stating he would establish a motive for manslaughter, and call a witness who overheard the plot that led to Baddour's death.

Acuff called his first witness—Betty Crain.

She was sworn in, gave her name and occupation (this time not mentioning she was a former nurse), and took her seat in the witness chair. My adrenaline was active and my mind on alert.

"Mrs. Crain, is it true you witnessed the defendant's wife, Mrs. Mary Grater, and the deceased, Father Baddour, drive into the Greenlee Alamo Motel parking lot, register at the front desk, and enter room number ten, on November 6, 1954, exactly two weeks before his death?"

"Yes."

"Had you ever seen Father Baddour and Mrs. Grater exhibiting any act of affection toward one another?"

"Well, I would see them together after church, talking, and it seemed to be more than just casual conversa—"

"Objection, Your Honor. The witness is speculating," Bernstein said.

Right then I figured Bernstein objected because he didn't want Acuff to establish a motive for his client, Capp Grater. *The jealous husband motive.*

"Sustained," the judge said matter-of-factly.

The prosecutor continued. "Mrs. Crain, since the defense will argue that you never actually saw Mrs. Grater and Father Baddour *inside* the motel room, can you tell us anything about Mrs. Grater or Father Baddour that would lead you to believe they were having an affair?"

Oh, no, please no. Don't lead her into Mary's past.

"No, but I do know she had … how should I say it? A checkered—"

"—Objection, Your Honor. Mrs. Grater's past has no relevance in this case," Bernstein said.

The judge pondered. "Sustained," he finally said.

I whispered a "Thank you" to Mr. Arthur Bernstein for not allowing Betty to go any farther into Mary's background.

"Tell the court, Mrs. Crain, how you know the defendant and his ex-wife," Acuff said.

"We're members of the same church, and she's in a Bible study with me."

"How long have you known the defendant, Mr. Grater?"

"My whole life," she said.

"Had you ever seen Mr. and Mrs. Grater affectionate toward each other?"

"No, truthfully, I can't say I have," Betty said.

Acuff turned to Bernstein. "I have no further questions. Your witness."

Bernstein stood, and for the first time, I could clearly hear his high-pitched, raspy voice. "Mrs. Crain, the prosecutor stated I would ask if you actually saw them in the motel room together; but that won't be necessary. We all realize you weren't in the room with them. Instead, you're merely speculating as to what took place in that motel room aren't you? You can't say with certainty what they were doing there can you?"

It was obvious to me at this point that Bernstein was trying to dismiss any "jealous husband" motive ... make the jury doubt they were having an affair and Capp's motive might disappear.

Betty was flustered and wanted to say the obvious, but she was smart. She smiled, and said, "No. I can't say with certainty what they were doing in the room."

"So it's possible Father Baddour was merely counseling Mrs. Grater?"

Acuff used his hands to push his lanky body up from the table. "Objection, Your Honor, the defense is trying to mislead the jury. When a man and a woman enter a motel at ten in the morning, they're not there for counseling ... or tiddlywinks."

Giggles spilled through the courtroom.

"Sustained," the judge said. "I'm sure the jury knows what they were doing in the motel."

I knew enough about the law to know that a judge shouldn't render opinions like that. But I suppose stranger things have happened in courtrooms.

"No further questions, Your Honor," Bernstein said.

Prosecutor Acuff called Mary Grater to the stand.

"Mrs. Grater, I just have a few questions," Acuff said with politeness. "Did you in fact have intimate relations with Father Baddour on November 6, 1954, at the Alamo Motel in Greenlee?"

Mary lowered her head and said, "Yes."

"Louder, Mrs. Grater, we can't hear you."

"*Yes.*"

"And was that the only time you and Father Baddour met to have intimate relations?"

Mary pulled a handkerchief from her purse, blew her nose, and shook her head.

"No."

The packed courtroom squirmed and shifted in their pews. The jury didn't flinch. But I did. I knew Acuff was establishing a motive for Capp—*the jealous husband motive, exactly what Bernstein had tried to avoid.*

"How many times, Mrs. Grater, did you and Father Baddour have these intimate relations?"

Mary wouldn't answer.

Oh, no, this is awful. Say twice. Say two times. Not five or six.

"Two other times," she blurted. "I was lonely." Mary looked at the jury, pleading for sympathy.

"Why were you lonely, Mrs. Grater?"

"My husband is impotent."

Murmurs cascaded through the room. Judge Chapman gave a light tap with his gavel.

When it was quiet again, Acuff asked, "And how long has he been impotent?"

"Since before I married him."

"I see. Did your husband, the defendant know about your affair with Father Baddour?" Acuff asked gently.

"I don't know, I guess he did," she said, raising her eyes at Capp. "I just don't know."

Mary had given up. Shaking her head, she looked around the courtroom, but I doubted she could see us for the tears in her eyes.

"The defendant—your former husband—preached a vestry sermon about adultery on March 6, 1955, is that correct?" Acuff asked.

"Yes, but I'm not sure of the exact date," Mary said, still whimpering.

"Do you know why he chose that topic, Mrs. Grater?"

"I think so. I suppose he thought I was having an affair."

"And were you upset about that sermon, afterwards?"

"I guess so …" she trailed off.

"No more questions, Your Honor," Acuff said, and retreated to his desk.

Bernstein remained seated and stared at Mary. The judge asked him, "Does the defense wish to cross-examine?"

"Yes, Your Honor." Bernstein walked to the witness box. Mary was dabbing her eyes.

"Mrs. Grater, since you've testified that you were indeed having an affair with Pastor Baddour, were you with him on November 20, the day he died?"

"No, sir."

Bernstein approached the bench and Acuff followed. Bernstein presented some paper to the judge. From my vantage point I couldn't make out what it was. The three of them discussed it, and Judge Chapman allowed it to be entered as Exhibit A.

Bernstein turned his attention back to Mary. "I have here, Mrs. Grater, a Xerox copy of the Alamo Motel registration book. It shows that you, Mary Grater, signed the register on November 20. You are under oath, and you know the penalty for perjury. You were there with Father Baddour on November 20, weren't you, Mrs. Grater?"

"No. I wasn't, I swear," Mary said, pleading with the jury.

"But your signature is right here in the register."

"It's not my signature," she said, shaking her head.

Oh, no. Bernstein is pointing the finger of guilt at Mary, away from Capp, I thought.

"Mrs. Grater, I'm going to do something I don't recall ever doing in my legal career. I'm going to name the murderer. I'm going to claim that you murdered Father Baddour. What poison did you give him on November 20, 1958?"

Mary shook her head back and forth, back and forth. She was trying to speak but the courtroom burst into a cacophony of conversations. Judge Chapman banged his gavel to bring order.

I might have been the only person in the packed court-room who believed Mary wasn't with Baddour the day he died.

I reached both ways and grabbed Oneeda's and Annie's thighs. I squeezed them in horror as Mary was now being blamed for murder. She had suddenly become the guilty party.

This can't be happening.

It was close to noon, so Judge Chapman called for a recess. Court was adjourned until one-thirty.

I had the 'Mary Grater' signature copy along with a sample of Betty's signature in my purse. I approached Acuff in the courtroom hallway. I presented them to him and explained that it was Betty's signature in the register, not Mary's. He studied it for a while, and said, "Thank you. But it's not sufficient proof. The defense will tear it apart."

Looking at it again, he said, "I'm not even positive these were written by the same person. Neither will the jury."

I was disappointed that he wasn't going to rebut Bernstein's accusation.

I thought Charlie's Place would be packed with reporters and courtroom curiosity-seekers, so Oneeda, Mary, and I walked to a downtown Greenlee cafe. It was busy, too, but at least nobody approached our table to talk about the trial.

And Mary? All she could do was keep whispering, "I wasn't there ... I wasn't there ... What's going to happen to me, Martha? I could go to jail. I could lose Michael."

Mary was about to have a breakdown. And in an hour she would be back in the witness box. *I need to calm her down before she falls apart.*

"Mary, we're going to trust in Jesus. Let's not worry about your tryst with Father Baddour ... that's water under the bridge. People in Solo will forget about it. They'll forgive you. We need to pray that Acuff does his job and gets Capp convicted. And we need to pray that Michael never finds out about his biological father. We all know how important that is."

Mary placed her hand over mine. "Thank you, Martha. Let's don't wait, let's pray now."

So we did.

Back in the courtroom, we waited for 'Mr. Sardines-and-Onions.' We settled on the opposite side.

At one-thirty-five, Mary was back on the stand, looking more frightened than ever, as bantam rooster Bernstein confronted her.

"Mrs. Grater, I'm going to pick up where we left off," he said, then retrieved a copy of the motel registration page from November 20th. He turned back to Mary.

"Mary Magden Grater, I believe you murdered Father Baddour. I believe you were with Father Baddour in the Alamo Motel in Greenlee that day. So why don't you give your conscience a rest, and tell this court why ... why you poisoned Father Baddour?"

"I wasn't there. I told you. I'll swear to it on God's Bible."

"But your signature, it's right here in the—"

"—That's not my handwriting, I swear," she shouted.

"No further questions, Your Honor," Bernstein said, shaking his head in disbelief.

The judge turned to Acuff, "Does the prosecution wish to re-direct?"

"We do, Your Honor."

Acuff approached the court clerk and borrowed her Bible. He walked to the witness box. "Mrs. Grater, you've said you would swear on a Bible that you were not with Father Baddour on the day he died. I have a Bible right here. Are you prepared to put your hand on this Bible and swear to God that you had nothing whatsoever to do with Father Baddour's death?"

"Yes I am," Mary said, without hesitation.

"Objection, Your Honor. The witness has already sworn to tell the truth," Bernstein said.

"Overruled," Chapman said. "I'm going to allow this."

Acuff turned back to Mary, still holding the Bible by his side. "Mrs. Grater, I've heard that you're a Christian woman. Is that true?"

"It's true. With all my heart."

"Do you believe you will be punished much more severely by God if you are lying?"

"Yes, I understand the consequences."

"Now, place your hand on this Bible, and swear before God that you had nothing to do with his death."

Mary placed her hand on the Bible and said, "I swear before God, I had nothing to do with Father Baddour's death."

I studied the jury to see if they had any reaction. A few of them closed and slowly opened their eyes. That was enough for me.

I let out a long, overdue sigh.

"Your Honor, I have no more questions of this witness," Acuff said. "I now call Dr. Samuel Mays to the stand."

From the back of the courtroom appeared a dapper man in his fifties. Oneeda leaned into my ear and whispered, "This is who Capp paid to tell Father Baddour his sickness was being caused by the farm chemicals."

Sure enough, Acuff asked all the right questions. The doctor was embarrassed to admit it, but said Capp had personally called him and offered the bribe.

"Mr. Grater said if I examined Father Baddour, and told him it was the cotton poison making him sick, he would pay me a good deal of money."

"How much money?" Acuff asked.

Mays lowered his head. "Five-thousand dollars," he whispered.

"Louder, Dr. Mays. We didn't hear you," Acuff said.

"Five-thousand dollars," he said.

The courtroom chatter was palpable. Dr. Mays straightened and said, "But I never received any of it because Pastor Baddour never made an appointment."

"No more questions, Your Honor."

Acuff had extracted the vital information. I was feeling better.

And the defense? Bernstein wasn't about to cross-examine a witness who'd just sold his client down the river. Thank goodness the finger of guilt pointed back toward Capp, away from Mary.

Acuff is plenty smart, I thought. He remained focused on Capp's guilt, heaping as much evidence as possible on his head, instead of wasting time defending Mary from Bernstein's accusations.

Acuff announced, "The prosecution calls Sheriff Butch Turnbull to the stand."

After taking the oath and stating his name, the sheriff squeezed his big frame into the witness chair. I thought Acuff might have called me first, but I figured he knew what he was doing. *Sheriffs make better witnesses than part-time reporters.*

All of Acuff's questions pointed to that day inside Calvary when Turnbull overheard Annie tell me about Judd and Capp discussing their plan to poison the rector. Turnbull gave an account of the entire conversation. Then Acuff turned the sheriff over to Bernstein, "Your witness."

But Bernstein declined to cross-examine.

Acuff said, "The prosecution calls Martha McRae to the stand."

I figured all he wanted from me was to corroborate the sheriff's story. And I did. I repeated everything Annie had told me.

But what I hadn't expected was Bernstein's cross-examination.

He stood directly in front of me, holding a piece of paper, his chest stuck out.

"Mrs. McRae, did you write an anonymous letter to Annie Insner requesting she meet you inside Calvary Church on July 16 of this year?"

I was taken aback. "An ... anonymous ... letter?" I stammered.

Bernstein walked a few feet to face the judge. Acuff joined him. Bernstein handed a piece of paper to the judge. I was close enough to hear every word.

"Your Honor, I have here a letter written by Mrs. McRae to Mrs. Insner. I request that it be entered into the court as Exhibit A."

How'd he get that? I wondered. *Annie. She must've given it to him.* The judge studied the note and handed it to Acuff, who nodded and gave it back.

The judge said, "I'll allow it."

Bernstein held the letter directly in front of my face. "Mrs. McRae, allow me to refresh your memory." He read the note aloud. "*I know Capp Grater was involved with your husband in the poisoning of Father Baddour. I have the evidence. If you won't testify that you also know, I will turn you in for obstruction of justice, and you will go to prison. I will be in Solo on Thursday, July 16. Meet me at Calvary Church, ten o'clock in the morning, in the back pew. We need to talk.*"

"Did you write this note, Mrs. McRae?"

Shocked, embarrassed, I hesitated ... "Yes."

He presented both envelope and letter to the jury.

"First, why don't you tell the jury how you managed to have it mailed from Phillipsburg, because you see, it shows right here—it has a Phillipsburg indicia, and there's even a

Liberty Bell stamp affixed to the envelope," he said, looking pleased.

My mouth was dry. *Why don't they have water up here?*

"Answer the question," Judge Chapman said, peering down at me.

"I—I drove to Phillipsburg—" I paused to catch my breath—"and mailed it from there."

Bernstein asked, "And why would you do that, Mrs. McRae?"

"I didn't think Annie would meet with me if she thought the note came from someone in Solo, so I used a Phillipsburg address."

"Ahh, I see," he began, gradually raising his voice as he continued. "So you fabricated this anonymous, *threatening* letter, coercing her into meeting you, in hopes she might be intimidated enough to tell you what you wanted to hear, isn't that correct, Mrs. McRae?" His raspy voice was shrill enough to make me cringe.

Acuff jumped up, "Objection, Your Honor. Leading the witness."

"Sustained," Judge Chapman said. Turning to Bien-stein, he said, "Counselor, you might pull these shenanigans where you come from, but I won't allow it in my courtroom."

I tried to respond to his accusation. "That's not what I—"

"—No more questions, Your Honor," Bernstein interrupt-ed. He turned and walked back to his desk.

So, that was it. I wasn't allowed to respond. From then on I had a real *dis*-like for Mr. Bernstein.

"Does the prosecution wish to re-direct?" the judge asked Acuff.

"No, Your Honor. But the prosecution does call Mrs. Annie Insner to the stand."

I continued to fume as Annie was sworn in. Acuff led her through a calm, convincing, and detailed account of the Judd and Capp poisoning conversation she had overheard.

Finished, Acuff told the judge he had no more questions.

Bernstein approached Annie to cross-examine.

"Tell the jury, Mrs. Insner, how it's possible that you could hear your husband and the defendant's conversation from where you were standing behind the counter while they were in the back room?" Bernstein didn't wait for an answer. "I have here a diagram showing the distance between your counter and the back room where they were talking. Isn't it possible that you misunderstood their exact words? Isn't it possible, Mrs. Insner, they were discussing Father Baddour's own sickness ... his heart problems?"

I hoped the jury didn't fall for something so lame as this.

Annie didn't flinch. "No, I heard them say they wanted to make him sick."

Then Bernstein changed tactics. "Mrs. Insner, I hope you'll indulge me for one minute while I read again the anonymous letter you received from Mrs. McRae."

Annie nodded.

I cringed.

Bernstein read my note again.

"Mrs. Insner, I have to say ... even *I* would be frightened by such a note. Anonymous, threatening, and from Phillipsburg—the very city where Mr. Grater often visited on business. Did you wonder who might have sent the letter?"

"Yes," she said. "I thought it might be one of Mr. Grater's men. I thought Mr. Grater might be trying to get rid of me, so I couldn't testify. That's why I carried the meat cleaver in my purse."

"You carried a meat cleaver in your purse?" he asked, surprised.

"Yessir," Annie said.

"So, when you received this letter, did you feel *threatened*?"

She thought about the question for a second, and said, "Yes. I suppose I did."

"Then why did you go?"

"Since we were to meet inside Calvary, I just didn't think he would try to harm me, not there, not in church."

"Mrs. Insner, do you know what coercion means?"

"I'm not sure," Annie said.

"Coercion means being forced to do something against your will," Bernstein said. "Now Mrs. Insner, when you received the letter, did you feel you *had* to meet this anonymous person at Calvary?"

"Well, when you put it like that, I would have to say, yes, I felt I had go."

"And is it fair to say when you discovered it was *Mrs. McRae*, you were still scared and willing to tell her what she *wanted* to hear? You felt threatened and coerced into telling her a story, didn't you, Mrs. Insner?"

Annie paused, her eyebrows melded in the middle, confused.

"Mrs. Insner, you've testified you felt threatened by this letter purporting you could go to prison if you didn't meet with this anonymous person. So, I'm asking … did you feel threatened into telling Mrs. McRae that story?"

"I suppose I did," she said, her eyebrows wrinkled in confusion.

Bernstein had masterfully led Annie and the jury down a path of damaging innuendo.

The attorneys at Acuff's table were whispering to each another—their faces confused and puzzled.

Bernstein continued to pour it on: "And did you feel, in any way, trapped into going?"

"I guess I felt like I didn't have a choice. I sort of had to go, like I told you before."

Bernstein had jammed Annie's mind into a state of confusion. "Your Honor, the defense is compelled to ask for a recess so the prosecution and I might meet with you in chambers."

Judge Chapman agreed and called for a one-hour recess. The judge, the prosecution team and the defense team slipped into the judge's chambers.

Oneeda turned to me, "What's going on?"

"I think Bernstein is going to ask for a mistrial."

"A mistrial? How's that possible?"

"He'll say Annie was coerced and trapped into making those statements to me."

⸻

They returned to the courtroom within thirty minutes. Acuff was exhibiting a slight grin; Bernstein's lips were sealed tight.

"No mistrial," I whispered to Oneeda.

The judge sat, banged his gavel, and announced that Bernstein could continue with his witness.

Annie was back on the stand. Bernstein approached.

Bernstein said, "No further questions of this witness, Your Honor," and returned to his chair.

I thought Bernstein had deposited some strong doubt in the jury's mind.

Acuff stood. "The state wishes to re-direct, your Honor."

Acuff walked to the stand. "Tell the court, Mrs. Insner, *why* they wanted to give him potassium chloride."

She fidgeted in the witness chair, but managed a soft answer: "It was my belief Mr. Grater wanted Father Baddour to leave town in order to break up an affair between Mrs. Grater and the preacher."

"And tell the jury how you came to that conclusion," Acuff said.

"I began going out with a doctor in Greenlee who told me he had a friend who was Father Baddour's doctor." Annie paused and asked, "But hasn't Dr. Mays already testified?"

"The jury is well aware of his testimony, Mrs. Insner. The jury needs to hear *your* answer to why Mr. Grater wanted Pastor Baddour to leave Solo, *and* they need to hear how you learned about that information. You've answered the first question—you said he wanted to break up an affair between them, correct?"

"Yes, to stop the affair," she said without hesitation.

"Now, if you would, please finish what you were saying about Dr. Mays. You've told us that he was Father Baddour's physician, but you haven't told us what you learned."

"Well, my friend told me Dr. Mays was going to be paid a large sum of money if he would convince Pastor Baddour that some illness he had was being caused by the farm chemicals."

"Thank you, Mrs. Insner, that was perfect. Now I'd like to ask you a few questions about the letter you received from Mrs. McRae. When you arrived that Thursday at Calvary Church to meet this anonymous person who'd sent you the letter, and you saw it was Martha McRae, your friend, did you feel *she* posed a threat to you?"

"No."

"And in those discussions inside Calvary Church, did you tell her anything that was not factual? Anything at all."

"No."

"So, to make sure the jury isn't confused about what you told Martha McRae, did you, or did you not, tell her that you had overheard your husband and Mr. Grater talk about poisoning Father Baddour?"

"I did."

"And did you feel coerced in any way to tell her?"

"I did not," she said, looking at me with a tiny smile on her lips.

"No further questions, Your Honor," Acuff said, walking back to his table.

The judge excused Annie, and asked Acuff to call his next witness.

Instead, Acuff said, "The State of Mississippi rests, Your Honor."

Judge Chapman tapped his gavel and said, "Court is adjourned until Monday morning, nine-thirty, at which time the defense will call its first witness.

26

Barbeque Ribs

Monday morning, November 23

Dozens of people milled around the courthouse lawn. Walking in, we followed our routine.

"Where's 'Mr. Sardines-and-Onions'?"

We staked out another location.

———

Bernstein called at least a dozen witnesses to the stand. Most were from Phillipsburg. Two were his yardmen. All gave glowing testimonies about Capp Grater's fine character. That took up the entire morning and lasted until after lunch.

Then, Bernstein got to the real meat of his defense. "The defense calls Mr. Charlie Parker to the stand."

After being sworn in, Bernstein started in on him. "Mr. Parker, before that day Father Baddour died in your restaurant, you had served him lunch several other times, is that correct?"

"Yessir. He liked my pork ribs."

"And what had been his usual, or let's say his typical, order of ribs? Had it been a half rack, or a full rack of ribs?"

"Your Honor," Acuff said, a sour look on his face, "could the defense explain why this court would be interested to know whether Father Baddour ate a half or a whole order of ribs?"

Bernstein addressed the judge. "Your Honor, I'm establishing an important point in my client's defense."

Judge Chapman nodded and Bernstein continued. "Mr. Parker, answer the question, please."

"Oh, he had always ordered a half rack of ribs."

"But, on November 20, he ordered a full rack. Is that correct?" Bernstein asked.

"Yessir, I remember it like it was yesterday."

"And why is that?"

"Because he died," Parker answered.

Bernstein started to smile, but cut it short.

Reaching back to his desk, Bernstein retrieved a large chart with photographs taped around the margins. He took it to the judge. "I have a chart and photographs showing the interior of Mr. Parker's restaurant," Bernstein said, "which I request be entered as Exhibit B, Your Honor."

The judge and Acuff studied it; the judge waved a hand to approve it, while Acuff looked baffled, but allowed it.

Then Judge Chapman glanced at his watch and banged his gavel. "We'll continue this tomorrow. Court is adjourned until nine-thirty tomorrow morning."

———

As witnesses, we were not allowed to discuss anything pertaining to the trial, so none of us met that night. Only tuna fish and coffee for me. No sherry.

———

At nine-thirty the next morning, it felt like eighty degrees in the courtroom. *The heater must've been on all night.* We followed our routine to avoid "smelly breath."

Resuming from the day before, Bernstein took the large chart and placed it on the jury rail. It was a detailed diagram with photos of Charlie Parker's restaurant.

"Father Baddour sat at the lunch counter, right here," he said to the jury, pointing to a spot marked X. "See this dotted line? It shows you that Father Baddour had a clear line of sight into the kitchen, at the very location where Mr. Insner always prepared his ribs on Saturdays. What I'm showing you is evidence. Evidence which shows Father Baddour witnessed Mr. Insner rub a white substance into the meat."

"Objection, Your Honor," the prosecutor said. "The defense has no idea if Father Baddour saw anything in the kitchen."

"Sustained." Turning to Bernstein, the judge said, "Counselor, you'd best keep your comments to facts, and not conjecture."

Bernstein turned back to Charlie Parker: "Mr. Parker, at any time, did you see Father Baddour looking back into the kitchen while Mr. Insner prepared those ribs?"

"I—I remember him sitting at the counter, yes, looking around, like he usually did. I suppose he looked into the kitchen."

"And when did Father Baddour change his order from his *usual* half rack of ribs to a full order, Mr. Parker?"

"Right before I brought it out of the kitchen. I remember. He said something like, 'Charlie, today, I think I'm in the mood for a full rack.'"

Turning to the jury, Bernstein said, "So, it was after Father Baddour *could have seen* Judd Insner in the kitchen sprinkle and rub a white powder into his ribs, just before he changed his order from a half rack to a whole rack of ribs. I know Mr. Parker's ribs are good, but I want this court to understand that Father Baddour had never eaten a full rack of ribs."

"Your Honor," Acuff said, his long body stretched out over the table, "could the defense explain where he's going with this?"

Bernstein said, "Your Honor, I'm establishing grounds for *why* Father Baddour died."

"Proceed," the judge said. "I'd like to hear this."

Bernstein turned back to the jury. "Ladies and gentlemen, we all know white powder of any substance is never used as a dry rub on cooked ribs. It's my contention Father Baddour saw Judd Insner rubbing something white into that rack of ribs, moments before it came out of the kitchen. The color white was absorbed by—"

"Objection, Your Honor, the defense has no idea if Father Baddour saw Mr. Insner rubbing anything into a rack of ribs," Acuff said.

"Sustained. Counselor Bernstein, you'd best keep your comments to facts."

Bernstein grinned broadly and turned to face the jury again. "Folks, I don't know about you, but all this talk of barbeque ribs is making me hungry."

Laughter erupted in the courtroom. Even the jury managed to chuckle.

Me? I thought the discussion of barbeque ribs in a manslaughter trial was bizarre, yet plenty entertaining. But I couldn't figure out where Bernstein was taking this line of questioning.

The judge's gavel came down several times. "Order in the courtroom," he said, not smiling.

I wondered why the defense hadn't mentioned that potassium chloride could only kill a person if it's injected intravenously.

I would soon find out.

Bernstein turned to the jury. "Ladies and gentlemen, Father Baddour was a man of small stature. Eating enough potassium chloride might indeed have stopped his heart," Bernstein said with conviction.

Wrong, I thought. *He's misleading the jury. But why?* I thought he was either senile, or brilliant. I wasn't sure which. He could have continued to go down the road of "just making him sick—not trying to kill him," like he had established with Annie. Of course, "making him sick" would likely still get Capp ten years in prison for wrongful death. I figured Bernstein must be shooting for the moon. Trying to get Capp off all together—no prison sentence whatsoever.

But how? I wondered.

"I have a picture of him," Bernstein said to the jury. He took an oversized photograph and held it up to the seven men and five women. "Here is Father Baddour standing next to a man of average size. As you can see, Father Baddour was a slight man. Records indicate he weighed 150 pounds."

Wrong, I thought. *He weighed more than that.*

Staring down at the defense from his high-backed chair, Judge Chapman looked restless and impatient, rocking back and forth in a steady rhythm. "Counselor, counselor, where is all this leading? I'd like to see this trial to its conclusion while I'm still alive."

The judge's remark produced a few chuckles from the crowd, but nothing rowdy enough to rile him.

"Your Honor, thank you for your patience. I'm about to make my point now," Bernstein said, turning to face the jury again. "Ladies and gentlemen, just for a moment, place yourself in Father Baddour's situation. Here's a man, a priest, who might indeed have fallen from grace. Maybe he did commit adultery. Now, I have here ..." He walked to his table, retrieved a file and held it up high … "I have here, a list of twenty-six clergy who took their own lives in the last three years. Now I can't prove they all committed suicide because of some indiscretion, but I'm sure you can imagine the guilt Father Baddour must have felt if he did indeed commit adultery. Here's a respected priest who crossed the line and would likely face ex-communication from the church. I believe he was a tormented man, don't you?"

Bernstein had obviously changed his strategy from "no jealous husband," to "tormented priest." *What a tricky little man, that Bernstein.*

Judge Chapman seemed baffled, too. I wondered if he was bemused, or frustrated by Bernstein's new direction. I wasn't sure.

The judge gathered himself and spoke in a calm, deliberate manner. "Counselor, are you trying to insinuate that Father Baddour committed suicide?"

"Your Honor, I contend Father Baddour saw Judd Insner putting poison on his ribs, and subsequently ordered a full rack of ribs to make sure his death was quick as possible."

The courtroom turned into a beehive of chatter. Chapman banged his gavel three times and ordered, "Quiet. Quiet. I'll have quiet in my courtroom or I'll have this entire gallery cleared out," he said, flushed and cheek-red.

Nobody moved a muscle. *Who would want to be removed from this entertainment?*

The packed courtroom was generating so much heat the judge ran a finger between his neck and bow tie, trying to loosen it.

Bernstein kept pouring it on. "Ladies and gentlemen of the jury, Judd Insner's intentions may have been to make Father Baddour sick—nothing more, just sick. But it's obvious to me—and I hope to this jury—that Father Baddour *wanted* to end his life."

I wondered, *Did Bernstein's jury selection process convince him we're all a bunch of country bumpkins to fall for such a ludicrous argument?*

Down South, we all know barbeque ribs are to die "for," not "from."

Even Judge Chapman shook his head in disbelief.

An excited Acuff jumped to his feet, yelling, "Objection, Your Honor, speculation. The defense has no way of knowing what was on Father Baddour's mind. Then, or any other time."

"Sus-*tained*," an exasperated judge said.

Bernstein didn't bat an eye. "I have no further questions for this witness." He sat beside his client, Capp, and patted him on the knee, as if they had won a major battle.

Me? I didn't think the jury would fall for it.

"Do you wish to cross-examine?" the judge asked Acuff.

"No, Your Honor, I believe the jury has heard enough fantasy for one day."

Turning back to Bernstein, the judge said, "Counselor, it would be most helpful if you could call a witness who can provide substantive testimony in this trial." After wiping the sweat from his forehead, he looked down at Bernstein. "Do you have any other witnesses to call?"

Bernstein stood erect, stuck his chest out and announced, "We do, Your Honor. The defense calls Capp Grater to the stand."

The courtroom murmurs and shuffling were loud enough for Judge Chapman to give his gavel a soft tap, and ask for "Quiet." This was the moment everybody had been waiting for—to hear Capp Grater defend himself.

After taking the oath, he sat and swung one leg over a knee, brushing off imaginary dust from the side of his cowboy boot, waiting for his attorney's first question.

Bernstein spent thirty minutes asking questions designed solely to make Capp Grater look like Solo's savior—his community philanthropy, warden of the church, money he had given to Calvary ... all sorts of polished sympathy, same as his character witnesses had done.

Then it became interesting.

"Mr. Grater, tell the jury how you knew the amount of potassium chloride needed to make Father Baddour sick," Bernstein said, looking at the jury, casting a sly smile.

"I didn't," Capp answered.

Bernstein asked, "Then who did? Was it Mr. Insner who knew?"

"Yes. He had the potass—potassi—"

Bernstein turned to the witness stand. "Potassium chloride, Mr. Grater? Is that what you're trying to say?"

"Yes."

"You're not familiar with potassium chloride, are you?"

"No, I'm not."

"So, is it your contention Judd Insner acted on his own when he put the potassium chloride on Father Baddour's ribs?"

"Yes."

"And did you ask Dr. Mays to tell Father Baddour it was the farm chemicals making him sick?"

"Yes, I did. But I later changed my mind, and told Judd not to go through with it."

Liar, I thought.

"Now, Mr. Grater, I have to ask you a sensitive question. Your answer is important. Did you ever suspect your wife, Mary Grater, of having an affair with Father Baddour?"

"I did not," he said with a straight face.

Liar.

Looking up at the judge, Bernstein said, "I have no more questions for Mr. Grater, Your Honor."

"Your witness," Judge Chapman said to Acuff.

To my mind, that was Bernstein's best argument. But would the jury buy it?

Acuff leaned out over the table and locked eyes with Capp for several seconds. I couldn't decide if Acuff felt like the cat that'd cornered a mouse, or if he was pondering his first question. One thing was certain. The courtroom was quiet as a mouse.

Acuff walked to the witness box, never taking his glare from Capp. "Mr. Grater, is it true you paid Judd Insner money to expand his meat market if he would help you poison Father Baddour?"

"Objection, Your Honor," screamed Bernstein, jumping from his chair.

"On what grounds?" asked Judge Chapman.

"I object to the prosecutor's use of the term 'poison,' Your Honor."

"Defense counselor, do I really need to remind you what the cause of death was in this case? Over-ruled. Answer the question, Mr. Grater."

"Yes, it's true, I did. But I—"

"No need to elaborate, Mr. Grater, you've answered my question. Now I have another question." Capp swung his boot off his knee and brushed his trousers. He arched his back into a stiff posture. His bushy eyebrows almost covered his eyes as he glared at Acuff, daring him to ask any more questions.

"Mr. Grater, is it true that Sonny Sartain, otherwise known to Solo as Father Thomas Cain, spent his last night in Solo with you, at your home?"

Bernstein jumped and screamed, "Your Honor, I must object on the grounds that Sonny Sartain had nothing to do with this case."

"Overruled. I'd like to hear this."

Acuff turned back to Capp. "Let me get right to the point, Mr. Grater. Were you and Sonny Sartain involved in any way in the death of Father David Baddour?" Acuff didn't give Capp a chance to answer, "and did Sonny Sartain come to you months before he appeared in Solo with the idea to do harm to Father Baddour, so that he, Sonny Sartain, could pose as Solo's rector?"

The courtroom became a beehive of chatter and shuffling bodies.

Bam! The judge's gavel came down again. "Order in the courtroom."

"No. It's not true," Capp said. "Sonny Sartain was an evil man. But he didn't have anything to do with Father Baddour's death. In fact, he got to Solo four, maybe five months after Father Baddour's death."

"But Mr. Grater, if Sonny Sartain was so evil—as you say—why were you such good friends with him?"

Aha, I thought. *Well done, Acuff, well done.*

Capp didn't answer. He closed his eyes for two or three seconds. I looked at Bernstein. His head dropped. He knew the implication: *We're known by the company we keep.*

Everybody knew Sartain had escaped months after Pastor Baddour's murder. But Acuff had used the ruse to trap Capp into admitting Sartain was evil, and was his friend. All those glowing character witness testimonies were now dubious.

Well done, Acuff. Again.

"Mr. Grater, I'm sorry to ask you this question, but it's important," Acuff said. "Your wife has testified you've been impotent for quite some time. Is it true?"

Capp knocked more imaginary dust from his boot and said, "Not any more. I had an operation to repair things."

Mary and I turned to each other. She whispered, "It's not true. I don't think."

Acuff continued. "Well, this court still doesn't understand why you offered Dr. Mays five-thousand dollars to tell Father Baddour the farm chemicals were making him sick. You say you changed your mind. You say you didn't suspect your wife of having an affair, so why would you ask such a thing in the *first place*? Tell the court why you wanted to poison Father Baddour. What other possible reason did you have? These jury members aren't illiterate, you know."

Jumping to his feet, Bernstein said, "Objection. Badgering the witness. Mr. Grater has already testified he changed his mind, and there is no one who can refute that fact."

"Overruled. Answer the question Mr. Grater," Judge Chapman said.

Capp hesitated, shifted in his chair, and blurted, "Because I changed my mind. I've already told you. Judd did it by himself." Capp's cheeks had turned crimson.

Several of us in the courtroom shook our heads in disbelief at Capp's answer.

Acuff walked to his desk. "And you expect us to believe that. *Tsk-tsk.* You had an initial intention to drive him away, and you still haven't answered the question."

Capp lost his temper. He came out of his crossed boot stance and placed both feet in front of him and gripped the chair arms. "Because I changed my mind about any affair. I told you," he shouted.

"But at one point in time, you wanted to drive Father Baddour out of town, out of the Delta. You must have had a reason, and you're not being honest. I have no further questions for this witness, Your Honor," Acuff said, his mouth twisted in disgust as he paraded past the jury box.

Judge Chapman asked Bernstein if he wished to re-direct, but Bernstein declined.

"You may call your next witness," the judge said.

"The defense rests, Your Honor," Bernstein said, taking his seat. He tried to disguise it, but I saw him wipe his forehead with a handkerchief.

"Very well. Summations next Tuesday morning at nine-thirty," Chapman said.

Court was adjourned.

I thought Acuff had done a masterful job of coaxing Capp's guilt back to the surface for the jury's benefit. But I was concerned about Capp's story of changing his mind. I thought it might get him off because there was no way for anyone to know if he had, or hadn't changed his mind.

His reputation, and Bernstein's tactics, appeared to be his only avenues of escaping prison.

I was happy about something else, too. Capp's lie about his impotency allowed folks to believe he had fathered little Michael.

On the final trial day, Prosecutor Acuff presented his closing arguments, explaining why the jury should "search their hearts and separate fact from fiction ... facts from made-up-stories by the defense."

Then it was the defense's turn. Bernstein spent two hours trying to convince the jury Capp had changed his mind and

Judd had poisoned Baddour on his own. Then he reminded the jury of the suicide theory.

Bernstein even repeated his account of the clergy who had committed suicide because of some infidelity. "It's all in the records," he said, holding the file high in the air, wanting people to believe he committed suicide.

Bernstein must've figured he had dumped so much doubt in the jury's minds there wouldn't be sufficient evidence to convict Capp "beyond a reasonable doubt."

Me? I was pretty sure the jury's heads were spinning, not knowing what to believe.

Finished, Bernstein sat, patted Capp on the thigh, and smiled like a winner.

Judge Chapman announced, "The jury will meet in chambers, determine a verdict, and report to the bailiff with its decision. This court is adjourned."

———

The jury deliberated for an entire day, while Oneeda and I did some shopping and hung out at Charlie's Place. Every time the restaurant wall phone rang, every conversation froze and all eyes gaped at Charlie, the receiver to his ear, all of us wondering if it was a call from the courthouse.

At four in the afternoon, Charlie took a call, replaced the phone and announced to his patrons, "The jury is about to return." Nobody waited for a check. More than enough cash was left, and everybody rushed to the courthouse.

It was packed again, buzzing with chatter. The jury marched in, single file, and sat.

"Has the jury reached a verdict?" Judge Chapman asked.

The jury foreman stood. "We have, Your Honor."

"Please read the verdict."

"We, the jury, find the defendant guilty."

Judge Chapman announced Capp Grater would be sent to Salem's prison to await sentencing. As the bailiff was about to escort Capp from the courtroom, Bernstein stopped them and said something to Capp. I don't know what was said, but Capp didn't look happy. Bernstein packed his briefcase. When he passed by me his chest was stuck out. So was the scowl on his face.

<hr />

Bernstein soon filed an appeal based on venue prejudice, and requested a new trial be held in Salem, "where none of the parties are known."

It took months, but the Federal District Court denied the appeal.

Capp's outcome wouldn't have been any different. The Bethel County jurors had kinfolk by the dozens in Salem. And *The Salem Clarion* newspaper had covered every aspect of the trial, so everybody knew all the details anyway.

Bernstein had gambled with his client's life, and lost. I thought he should have stuck with the "make him sick" argument, but he chose to make Pastor Baddour's death appear to be a suicide and try to keep Capp out of jail all together. And Capp's "reputation" in the community did nothing to save him.

———

Three months later, a sentence of fifteen years was handed down, but it was to be Parchman, not the Salem prison. At fifty-eight, Capp would likely never make it out alive. He'd hired the wrong lawyer. He'd be making his own bed now, for the rest of his life.

But I felt sure he'd find a way to survive, even in that hellacious place.

27

Dead Ends

AFTER THE TRIAL, Solo was at peace again. But not for me. I was determined to bring Betty Crain to justice. *She has to be involved. Too much smoke for no fire.* But I couldn't come up with a motive for her wanting him dead.

I was certain she was at the Alamo Motel the day Pastor Baddour died, but there was nothing to connect her with any wrongdoing; other than her likely infidelity. *Maybe she just signed into the Alamo under Mary's name, had a tryst with the rector, and nothing more. Maybe the poison Judd and Capp had used somehow did kill Pastor Baddour. Maybe he had a bad heart to begin with, like Shorty.* I didn't know what to think anymore.

In late March, something terrible happened.

On a Saturday morning, JJ's two boys, Jake and Jimmy, left the house to help their daddy in the honey factory. Although the plant was closed on weekends, JJ spent Saturdays working on his machinery. He had always worked six days a week and rested on the seventh.

Jake and Jimmy found JJ on the factory floor in a pool of blood. Dead.

The sheriff appeared an hour later. He interviewed the family. There were no witnesses. Nothing. He sent his deputies into Solo to ask if anyone had seen a stranger in town. I, of course, told them about Big and Bitty.

What I heard from the Greenlee coroner the next afternoon was enough to make me sick. JJ had been stabbed multiple times. And his head was missing.

Of course, none of those details were mentioned in his obituary—an obituary I struggled to finish—a single typewritten page with tears on it. It took forever to say goodbye. I felt drained. Sapped in the sense I couldn't go on anymore. *What's the use? There's so much evil in the world. Where's God in all this?* I was beginning to lose my faith.

Then came the funeral. April 2, 1960. What else could I expect but a cold and wet day. The cotton fields lay fallow, as did Solo and I. Calvary Episcopal Church's nave was filled. I couldn't tell if people cried or not; I was too busy with my own grief.

A thought crossed my mind: *It's ironic how all the evil and mayhem had made Solo infamous, yet JJ's Honey had made us famous. He left a legacy for generations to come. He has a special place in heaven. We'll all miss him.*

Glancing at Mary, I noticed she wasn't gazing down at her feet like she had at Pastor Baddour's funeral. She was free of all scrutiny and standing proud next to Andrew Dawkins.

The preacher's eulogy was straight out of the book of Matthew. "Johnny 'JJ' Johnson was a Christian herald," Preacher Davidson began. "A man who pointed us toward good, away from evil. Yet people reviled him—even wrongfully removed him from this very church. But he came back, redeemed and loved. Then the schemes of the evil one took JJ from us—by violent force. But Jesus says, 'Do not fear him who can kill the body, but fear him who can kill both body *and* soul.' JJ Johnson's soul is now with his creator. He could be looking down on us right now, wondering how Solo remains unable to discern good from evil. So I ask, why can't we see the evil before us?"

That's all the preacher had to say about JJ.

As JJ would have wanted, Pastor Davidson then preached a sermon on Christ's redemption of our souls, of how we should glorify God, instead of the man we had known as Johnny "JJ" Johnson.

Afterward, we filed into Calvary's basement fellowship hall.

When old people die, these *after-funeral* occasions can take on an atmosphere of celebration—'the deceased lived a full life. Now he's up there in heaven … let's eat.'

But with JJ, it wasn't like that. He still had a lot of living to do. Somehow, JJ's departure would bring glory to God. I just didn't understand how.

I sat by myself in a corner—a plate of untouched food in my lap.

It was common knowledge JJ and I were good friends. Various *good-intentioners* wandered by to talk. I half-heartedly listened and nodded. Most asked rhetorical questions about JJ's killer. *Why would anyone even ask?* Nobody had a clue. Except Sheriff Turnbull. He told me the two Purity Foods men had been apprehended. I never suspected them anyway, but I nodded.

Oneeda came and sat beside me. She wanted to talk about JJ's Honey.

"Do you think the Johnson family will sell, Martha?"

"Who knows," I said, not able to make eye contact.

She continued, "I think they'll sell. *Then* what'll we do for church funds?"

I didn't answer.

Annie joined the conversation: "Somebody said they'd seen a stranger in town for a couple of days. Did y'all notice anybody?"

I shook my head, knowing the hallmark of small towns—'all strangers are conspicuous.' I wasn't interested in hearing any of this.

Oneeda said, "I saw a strange person. I assumed he was a reporter, still hanging around."

"What'd he look like?" Annie asked.

"He was taller than Bobby Joe, I'm sure of it. Six feet maybe. He wore a hat and overcoat. I didn't get a good look at his face, though."

"I got a good look at him," said Pastor Davidson, joining the conversation. "I stopped him on the street and we talked for a while. I'd never seen him before. He wasn't a reporter, I know that. I invited him to visit Calvary while he was in town."

Oneeda asked, "Who was he?"

"I don't know," the preacher said. "He never told me his name. Said he was looking to buy some property out in the county."

"Was there anything unusual about him?" Oneeda asked.

"He had a Northern accent, and a pock-marked face," Pastor Davidson said. "Oh, and terrible breath. Like onions."

I perked up. "Humph, a man like that sat behind us the first day of the trial, didn't he, Oneeda?"

Before she could answer, the Johnson clan walked by and I stood to hug and cry with them. Fifteen minutes later, exhausted, I walked home and crawled into bed.

The next morning, the preacher asked me to give the sermon on Sunday night. I told him I couldn't. I was too weak to think about being in the pulpit a second time.

"I'll help you write it," he said, his eyes as sorrowful as mine. How could I turn him down?

"What would the topic be?" I asked, not really caring.

"Vengeance is God's domain," he said.

Annoyed with the preacher, I said, "And what, you think I want revenge for JJ's murder?"

"No, Martha, I think the congregation needs to hear it." His eyes convinced me he was right. He missed JJ, too, and I should have realized it. He must've known I was hurting because he said, "I'll try to visit with Sonny Sartain on Sunday night. Would you like me to ask him if he was involved in JJ's murder?" Pastor Davidson's question was gentle and sincere.

"No, please don't. I might ask him myself."

⁓

The Saturday after JJ's funeral—with the preacher's notes in one hand, and coffee in the other—I sat in the kitchen, praying for God to remove all vengeance from my heart so I could focus on the sermon.

I don't remember giving any sermon the next night. I read it and put as much emphasis as possible on those parts the preacher had underlined. But even *I* wasn't convinced of my own words. My prayers to avoid hatred for Sonny Sartain had failed.

Monday morning I woke knowing nothing could stop me from seeing Sartain again, to look him in the eye and ask him about JJ's murder. I wasn't sure if I felt revenge or not. I just wanted to know the truth. And the *why*—if he indeed had a hand in it.

I lay in bed and visualized a meeting with Sartain. I could see myself on a stool in front of his cell. I must have had the best intentions on my heart, because I imagined him saying, "You and JJ ... y'all were good friends, weren't you?" In my imagination, Sartain seemed genuinely concerned. *"No, Martha, I can't say that I killed John Johnson. I'm not gonna lie anymore. I feel like whoever did should be punished."* In my daydream, he was so conciliatory I thought he might have changed.

Maybe he wasn't involved. After all, he was behind bars when JJ was brutally murdered.

Coming back to reality, I remembered how he'd been the master of human disguise. How when he first arrived in Solo he could be the genuine, concerned pastor—when it served his purpose. And how evil he could be when it served the desires of his true nature.

So I wrote a letter requesting to see him. Two weeks later I was turned down. "Inmate Sonny Sartain declines to grant your request." That was the gist of the prison superintendent's letter. I felt denied.

But I would soon learn firsthand Sonny Sartain's true nature.

28

Closure?

ONE WEEK LATER, I emptied another mail bag on the sorting table. One letter grabbed my attention. It was addressed to me, *Mrs. Martha McRae*. The return address, *Parchman*.

Is this from Superintendent Harris? Probably writing to let me know he's cracked down on out-going mail. I studied my name on the envelope.

God forbid.

I had seen the handwriting before.

How could he possibly get another letter out of that prison? I sat and read. Half way through, I felt sick to my stomach.

Dear Martha,   May 3, 1960

I prayed about this before writing. You won't know how John Johnson died, don't you? Well, I'm going to tell you. When Capp came to Parchman I was thrilled. My disciples brought him to me in the yard. He was so frightened by me he peed in his new prison trousers. I enjoyed seeing his face. I asked him about Mary and my son. I was disappointed to hear that he didn't know anything about them. He wasn't able to speak. Nothing at all. But he did do what I kindly asked him to do. I knew he must have some "friends" on the outside that could do what I needed done.

You know, Mr. Johnson never should have questioned my priesthood that day in church. I never forgot that. Send me a picture of Mr. Johnson's head. Would you do that? It must have been a sight to see, was it not! I will be seeing you, Mary, and my little boy if you don't send me that picture real soon.

Father Thomas Cain

PS: There is nothing anybody can do to me now.

I became angry at all the evil in this world.

Sonny Sartain was right about one thing, though. There was nothing anybody could do to him now. He would be executed soon. Surely. And likely Capp Grater, too, given the news of his part in it.

I took the letter to Sheriff Turnbull in Greenlee. He cussed up a storm. Not at me but for having to deal with the Phillipsburg police. "I wish it'd been those two men from Purity Foods," he said, his mouth in a frown. "They were easy to track down. Now I gotta go and dig around for Capp Grater's connections in Phillipsburg."

I had no reaction to his concerns. I asked for two copies of Sartain's note. He kept the original. The sheriff raised a hand to thank me for my help. I was on my way out when I heard him pick up the phone, telling the operator to call the Phillipsburg police.

I stopped and turned back. "Put the phone down," I said.

The sheriff stared at me like *what the?* as he hung up the receiver.

"Sheriff, you should look for a six-foot-tall man, greasy black hair, with a noticeable pock-marked face. Oh, and he likes sardines and onions."

The sheriff spent a good five seconds staring at me, his mouth open, his eyes expressionless.

"Oookaay ... and why is that? What do you know that I don't?"

I explained it all to him ...

"Yesss," he said, gazing out the window, scratching his chin, "it would make sense, wouldn't it? Capp had used his cronies in Phillipsburg to have Johnson murdered. And Sonny Sartain must've sent the man to relay updates on Capp's trial."

"Will you be needing anything else, Sheriff?" I asked.

He continued to stare out the window.

"*Sheriff.*"

He jerked around, out of a daze. "Oh ... no thank you, Martha. You've been very helpful. I'll take it from here."

Back in Solo, I took the copies of Sartain's letter to Pastor Davidson. It was after five so Mary had gone home.

"Martha, what a surprise. Please, have a seat."

"I don't have time to sit," I said. "Look at this."

As he read Sartain's letter, he kept shaking his head. "The man is demon-possessed. If he's not the devil incarnate, he's one of his disciples."

He tried to hand the letter back to me.

"No, please give it to the superintendent. I'm sure he'd like to see it."

"I will," he said.

As I turned to leave, he asked, "Martha, are you all right?"

I stopped and turned back. "No. I feel like crying. But what good would it do? Besides, I don't have time to bellyache over spilt milk. Or blood, or whatever you wanna call it. There's a lot to do."

After going straight to my *Gazette* office, I wrote a story about the evil that had murdered JJ Johnson. Inside the story was a picture of Sartain's letter.

The day after the *Gazette* came out, several people stopped by to express their sympathy.

Annie Insner asked, "What'll happen to Mr. Grater, now that Sonny Sartain claims he arranged it?"

"There'll be another trial. This time for murder."

She asked if I had found closure.

"Closure?" I asked.

"I mean now that you know it was Sonny Sartain who murdered JJ. I found closure that day in court when everybody learned Judd didn't poison Pastor Baddour by himself."

"I suppose knowing who killed JJ does bring a certain amount of closure. Thank you, Annie, for reminding me. Have your nightmares gone away? "I added.

"They have," she said, smiling.

I had no idea I'd be having a weird dream of my own.

29

Discovery

ALWAYS KEPT PENCIL and paper by my bed. Even dreams can reveal hidden puzzle pieces.

At two o'clock in the morning I came out of a strange one: *A crazed doctor in a full-length white lab coat was injecting an enormous needle into a dragon. Or was it an elephant? Not sure.* It meant nothing to me.

The next morning I rolled out of bed to read the dream note. Still, it made no sense. At the kitchen table, warming my hands on a cup of coffee, I began to ponder the dream. But not for long. I relaxed and tried to think about *nothing*. A quiet mind can sometimes produce more results than dwelling on a problem—maybe even conjure up extraordinary solutions.

But it didn't happen. Not that day.

Later in the week, Mary, little Michael, the preacher and I gathered to eat breakfast. After the blessing, Mary asked, "Has Oneeda told y'all she's back to seeing that man in Bethaven?"

"No," said a surprised and smiling Davidson.

"Good, I'm glad she's seeing someone," I added. "I can't remember … what's he do?"

Mary said, "I think he's a vet."

I put my fork down. "A vet?"

It was a gift from above—my *A-ha!* moment about the long needle and dragon.

"I need a veterinarian," I bellowed, jumping from the table and hustling to the telephone book.

"What in the world?" Mary asked. "What's wrong, Martha?"

They all stared at me like I'd lost my mind.

"I need a veterinarian," I said again, excited.

"Call Annie's friend," Mary said.

"What's his name?"

"Jeremy Green," she said.

I found his number in the phone book and called. One, two, three rings.

"Green's Animal Clinic," a female voice answered.

I asked to speak with Dr. Green.

"Dr. Green, this is Martha McRae, I'm Oneeda's friend. May I ask if you had a blond woman by the name of Betty Crain working for you three years ago?"

"No, we didn't."

"You're certain?"

"Yes. What's this about?"

"I don't have time to explain right now. I'm sorry I bothered you." I hung up.

Thumbing through the Greenlee phone book, I called the first vet listed in the Yellow Pages.

"Ma'am, you'll need to come to my office with some sort of written authorization before I can give out any information about our employees."

My second call produced the same results, as did the next half dozen: "Ma'am, I can't give out information about our employees over the phone."

The preacher and Mary finished breakfast and were shaking their heads at me as they left the house with Michael.

Deciding to change my approach, I created a new identity—the first ever *Mississippi Criminal Investigation Unit*. I made it up. I would be the sole investigator. I called the rest of the vets in Greenlee, two in Bethaven, and was making a dent in Salem. I announced to each of them, "I'm with the *Mississippi Criminal Investigation Unit* and need to know if you had a blond woman by the name of Betty Crain on your staff four years ago."

All of my calls produced the same results. "No one by that name," they all said. At least they were talking and not putting me off. I gave each of them my name and phone number in case their memory improved.

Two days later, I answered the phone with an uncaring "Hello."

"Sorry. I must have the wrong number," a man on the other end said.

I was about to hang up when I asked, "Who are you trying to reach, if you don't mind me asking?"

"The Mississippi Criminal Investiga—"

"—Oh, I am so sorry," I said. "I'm new here. I should have answered the phone more properly. This is the *Mississippi Criminal Investigation Unit*. How may we help you?"

"I'm Harvey Gwin, a veterinarian here in Greenlee. Someone in your unit called a few days ago asking about an assistant who worked here four years ago. I'm calling to let you know I asked my staff about your question. There was this one woman … she worked here for, oh, a week or so. The staff remembers her, but I'd forgotten about her."

Yes, Yes, I thought, clenching the phone with delight.

He continued, "They can't remember her name, though, but she was blond. And she—"

I interrupted him again. "Dr. Gwin, I'd rather not talk about this on the phone, if you don't mind. May we meet in your office? Say, tomorrow?" I tried to sound nonchalant, more like a real investigator.

"That's fine," he said.

—⦿⦿⦿—

When we met the next morning, I said, "Dr. Gwin, there's no such thing as the *Mississippi Criminal Investigation Unit*. I made it up, but I *am* trying to solve a murder, and I need your help."

He frowned. "Then you're a lawyer?"

"No. Our rector in Solo was murdered. I'm searching for the person who poisoned him." I hoped my pleading eyes were enough to convince him.

He agreed to talk. We sat in his tiny ten-by-ten office, as I breathed in the noxious cleaning fumes—a vet clinic smell I'd always detested.

It didn't take long to realize Dr. Gwin was a nice man. And wanted to help.

"My staff remembered her as a hard worker," he told me. "They said she was dedicated. Worked late at night, helped with everything around here. Then, after a week or so, she never showed up again. The staff wanted me to contact her and see if I could get her back. But I had no way of reaching her. We can't even remember her name. It's been four years. We have some turnover, you know, so well …"

"Do you remember if she was a nurse?" I asked.

"Yes, in fact, that's why my assistant, Ginger, hired her. The woman said she was a registered nurse. She even showed Ginger a nursing certificate. Wasn't familiar with animal husbandry, though, according to Ginger. But Ginger thought the woman was more qualified than any others she interviewed."

While he was talking, I fished out a photograph of Betty Crain from my purse.

"Is this her?"

"I think so, but I'm not sure," he said, shaking his head.

"May I show this to your assistant?"

"Sure." He pushed an intercom button and asked for Ginger.

———

"Yes," that's her, Ginger said, holding the photograph. After Ginger left I turned to Dr. Gwin.

"May I take a look at Betty Crain's employee file?"

"I suppose so. But you'll need to give me a day or so to find it."

"Of course. You'll call me?"

"What's your number?" He wrote it on a prescription pad then looked up at me. "I apologize, what did you say your name is?"

"Martha McRae. I live in Solo. Oh, one more question. What drug would you use to put an animal down? A large animal."

"Pentobarbital," he said without hesitation.

"And you keep it in stock?"

"Yes, in the drug closet."

"May I see what it looks like?"

He nodded and we walked down a hall where he unlocked a door. From a small wall cabinet, he handed me a tiny, sealed bottle of clear liquid.

"Can it kill a human?"

"Of course. I've never tried it, though," he said, smiling. "By the way, it would need to be mixed with sugar syrup and sodium."

"Really? Colas contain those ingredients," I said with enthusiasm.

"Yes, I believe they do," he said.

"How much of this would it take to kill an adult male who weighted 170 pounds?"

"Oh, nine grams I suppose."

"Do you remember if any of this—this—"

"Pentobarbital," he said.

"When you conducted your inventory three years ago, was any of it missing? Unaccounted for?"

"I don't recall. You want me to check those records, too?" he asked, raising an eyebrow and slipping his hands into his white lab coat.

"Yes, please. Oh, one last thing … I may need you to testify in court."

"You said you weren't a lawyer."

"I'm not. I'm just a delivery boy."

His raised an eyebrow again and pulled on an ear lobe. "I've never testified in court before."

"Don't worry. The prosecutor will prep you."

Driving back to Solo, I was on cloud nine, but needed a plan—some way to produce a confession from Betty. I knew it wouldn't be easy.

The plan had to be perfect.

Deciding there was no chance Betty would ever confess something of this magnitude to me, I called on Annie once more.

After I told her what I learned from Dr. Gwin, she asked, more agitated than curious, "What makes you think Betty would confess something like that to me? You used me to get Capp convicted. Now you want to use me against Betty?"

"Yes, but there's a difference. In this case you could clear Judd's name entirely. Don't you see, Annie? If Betty put this stuff in Pastor Baddour's cola Judd *couldn't* have killed him. Potassium chloride is not supposed to kill a person unless it's injected intravenously. Annie, that attorney was right. Judd and Capp were just trying to make him *sick*. It was Betty who killed him." I pleaded with her. "Wouldn't you rest easier knowing it wasn't Judd who actually murdered him? And you know Father Davidson wants you to help me."

"He does? He said it was okay?"

"He did." And I was telling the truth.

"Okay, I guess. I never cared much for Betty anyway," Annie said with a crooked half-smile.

"Good," I said. "Let's sit down and work out a plan. How can we get Betty to confess this to you?"

—◦≋◦—

By the next day Annie and I had worked out a pre-determined date and time she would call Betty. I would be on the party line to corroborate the conversation. It was only the first step, but a crucial one if our plan was to work.

"Hello."

"Betty, this is Annie. How are you?"

"I'm fine, Annie. Why do you ask?"

"Oh, I just want you to know that *I know*."

"Know what?" Betty asked, annoyed.

"We need to talk," Annie said.

"We're talking now."

This is not how we planned the conversation to go, I thought. *Annie, you need to put her on the defense straight away.*

"No, I mean we need to *meet* and talk," Annie said.

"Talk about *what*?" Betty's tone was rude.

"Doctor Gwin, the veterinarian in Greenlee. You remember Harvey Gwin, don't you? Well, I know things."

"You know things? I have no idea what you're talking about. I'm going to hang up now, Annie. Goodbye."

"Wait. The missing pen-o-bar-bi-tall. That's what I'm talking about, Betty."

There was a long pause on the line.

Then Betty responded. "Where? Meet where?"

Oh my goodness, Betty's voice was like Sonny Sartain's when his true nature took over.

"The old train depot. Thursday. Two o'clock," Annie said, her voice stronger, steadier.

"Oookaay. Two o'clock Thursday afternoon. I'll—"

"—No," Annie interrupted. "Two o'clock Thursday *morning*."

Betty paused for a few seconds. "Fine. I'll be there." She hung up. So did I. I rushed over to Annie's house. She was a nervous wreck.

"What am I doing, Martha? I—I can't do this. It's too dangerous."

"Don't be afraid. We'll have Sheriff Turnbull there."

"This is all so bizarre. I feel like I'm reliving an awful moment in my own life." She was visibly shaken. "And at the depot?" Annie asked. "There's no place for the sheriff to hide."

"We'll work it out. Just stay calm."

"Do you have any sherry here?" I asked.

"I bought a bottle just last week."

By ten o'clock we were laughing like schoolgirls. I think it did her good. She had been way too wound up and I was afraid she'd back out at the last minute. It *was* dangerous. Betty would be cornered, and if I knew anything about caged women like her, she'd fight hard before giving up. It was time to see the sheriff.

⸺∘∞∘⸺

At first I wasn't sure if the big man was pleased to see me, or just agitated. "Martha, don't come in here asking me to squeeze my fat rear-end between some church pews again," he said, laughing as if it was his big joke of the day. "Oh, I been meanin' to tell you," he continued. "You remember that man you described? Six-foot, black hair, onion breath? The Phillipsburg police have a lead on him, thanks to you."

I stood there, staring down at the sheriff with sheepish, pitiful eyes. He pulled his big body from the chair. Deep wrinkles spread across his forehead.

"Oh, no. You're up to something, aren't you, Martha?" he asked.

"Are you interested in catching the real murderer, sheriff?"

"How on God's green earth do you keep coming up with these—these—"

"Murderers?" I offered, smiling.

"No. These *concoctions* of yours. Whatever it is, I wish you'd consulted me first. Okay, so what is it you want me to do this time?" he asked, resigned to a plan he hadn't even heard yet. (I sorta liked him for that.)

"Do you have any plans for this Thursday morning?" I asked.

"What time?"

"Two o'clock."

"Two o'clock in the morning? Holy cow, woman, what have you cooked up now?" he asked, hitching up his khaki pants and yelling to his assistant, "Susie, bring me a cup of coffee. Make it two coffees." Then he looked at me and lowered his voice, "Miz McRae and me are gonna need some caffeine."

⸻

On Wednesday afternoon, the sheriff placed several tall metal cabinets not far from the bench where Annie and Betty would sit.

At one o'clock Thursday morning, June 9, Sheriff Turnbull and I were standing behind the cabinets, close enough to hear and close enough for the sheriff to intervene if he thought Betty would harm Annie. Thank goodness there was some light from a full moon.

At two o'clock, a flashlight beam spread across the floor. It was Annie. She took a seat on the bench.

Betty appeared a few minutes later. I could hear her sit. And sigh. "Have you told anyone else about this?" she asked Annie.

"Nope."

"What is you want, Annie? Is it money? I'll give you whatever you want," Betty said.

"I want to hear you say you did it. That you poisoned Father Baddour. That's all."

Betty let out a long sigh, the unmistakable sign of resignation. *She has no way out and she knows it.*

"Well, I had to," she said. "Don't you see, Annie? David was going to break it off between us. He was even going to make a public confession and resign his priesthood. I couldn't let him ruin my reputation like that. Then, when the second autopsy report came out I left town. I was so scared, Annie. I couldn't stay here in Solo. Somebody would have noticed my nervousness. I'm sure you understand. So I moved to Oxford, to be with my daughter. And Annie, I was so sorry to hear about Judd. Well, I realized he had done the same thing to David I did."

"No," Annie yelled. "Judd and Capp only wanted to make him sick so he'd leave Solo. You killed him. Not Judd."

"He was going to leave, Annie. To resign and confess everything."

There was a moment when neither said anything.

"But you know what," Betty said. "I had to make sure he would leave. For good. You see why, don't you, Annie?"

"So Betty, you're confessing to the murder of Father Baddour, aren't you?" Annie asked.

Betty sighed. "Yes, isn't it a relief to get stuff like this off your chest? You know what it feels like, don't you, Annie? But you know what? You don't know the other half of it, sister," Betty said, venom cresting in her voice.

"What do you mean, '*other half of it*?'" Annie asked.

"Ohhh, I mean this is the half where it's your turn to leave for good," Betty said matter-of-factly.

Then we heard scuffling. Turnbull raced around the cabinets. I was behind him. Betty had Annie pinned to the concrete floor. The moonlight revealed Betty atop Annie, a knife in Betty's hand. Annie was struggling to hold it off.

For a split second it reminded me of those old black and white movie scenes where two people are fighting and you see only glimpses of them because there's that single shaft of moonlight flickering over them, like a light turning off and on, off and on.

The sheriff caught Betty's arm on a leaping dive, pulling her off Annie and tumbling to the floor.

Betty was no match for the big man. Sheriff Turnbull cuffed her.

Betty didn't cry or complain.

Annie and I hugged. I thanked her with all my heart. Annie opened her purse and shined her flashlight on our back-up plan. The meat cleaver. We hugged again, joyful this episode was over.

The sheriff phoned me a few days later. He said Betty had a nervous breakdown and was being transferred to the Waterton Mental Hospital, same as where Freddie had gone.

Then Sheriff Turnbull said he could use me on his team. Said I was "a natural dog catcher." I think he was joking.

But it was the nicest compliment the big fella could've paid me. I was sort of proud, but replied, "Sheriff, I'm just a delivery boy. Nothing more."

30

Justice

July 25, 1960—The Greenlee Courthouse

A FTER BETTY MADE a confession, her life turned into a full-scale murder trial—no grand jury needed.

Judge Clarence Chapman was presiding again. "How does the defendant plead?" he asked defense counsel.

"The defendant pleads not guilty by reason of insanity," her Salem lawyer said.

What? She can't get off on something that flimsy.

But she did look insane in those prison stripes. No make-up. Yellow, scraggly hair exposed two inches of new brown growth. Pathetic. But I'll never believe she was insane when she murdered Father Baddour.

Frank Acuff was the prosecutor again. The trial lasted only two days. I was in a daze most of the time. The sheriff testified to Betty's confession and I testified to corroborate, as did Annie. But Dr. Gwin was the best.

He said after Betty worked in his vet clinic, his inventory report showed five grams of missing pentobarbital. He added, "Nine grams would cause heart failure within thirty minutes, and five grams might take longer; but since Pastor Baddour also had potassium chloride in his system, he probably died soon after the barbeque reached his stomach."

Acuff summed it up in his closing argument: "Betty Crain used her nursing license to land a job at Dr. Gwin's clinic. She was there for a week. That's all the time she needed to steal five grams of pentobarbital. Ladies and gentlemen, I'm going to guess that she wanted to poison her husband back then. But he left her. So what did she do? She just held onto it. Until Father Baddour said he was going to resign his priesthood and come clean with his affairs. That's when she decided to use the pentobarbital on Father Baddour. You see, ladies and gentlemen of the jury, Betty Crain's reputation was more important to her than the life of Father David Baddour.

"She checked into the Alamo Motel that Saturday, November 20. She signed the register as 'Mary Grater.' She was even willing to implicate her friend if the register was ever checked. She wasn't insane. She was devious. The timing would have been perfect for her to purchase a cola from outside the motel room, pour in the poison, give it to Father Baddour, and leave for Solo—about eleven-thirty that morning—while he stayed in Greenlee and ate lunch at Charlie's Place. Ladies and gentlemen, the defendant has confessed. This is the clearest case of pre-meditated murder I've seen in my career. I implore the jury to return a guilty verdict of first degree murder."

I looked at the jury. *I wish I could read minds.*

The best thing about the trial? Nothing was ever mentioned about Mary. Her bad past had escaped public scrutiny. *Thank you, Lord. Again. You protected her, as the preacher had promised.*

On the third day, the jury returned a verdict of "Guilty." None of us ever spoke with or saw Betty again.

The courthouse grounds were covered with reporters asking Oneeda and me what we thought about the verdict. But we strolled through the onslaught of questions, not saying a word.

Oneeda came by that night. We all had supper, sat in the parlor, and sipped on sherry. I asked Oneeda how she was able to walk through those reporters without stopping to answer a single question.

She explained: "Jeremy Green, the veterinarian I'm going out with again … he told me, in a nice way, I have a 'motor mouth.' That I gossip too much. I don't want to lose him, so I'm on the gossip wagon."

She smiled and I smiled back.

The sheriff called me the following week to say they had "Mr. Sardines-and-Onions" in custody. With a confession. A confession that pointed the finger of guilt squarely on Capp Grater for ordering JJ's murder on behalf of Sonny Sartain. The sheriff said I'd be called as a witness for Capp's next trial.

Great. Another hour in the witness chair with no cushion and no water.

31

Behind Bars

In August, a month before Sartain's scheduled execution, the Delta was swarming with boll weevils and all sorts of evil. They seemed destined to live here forever.

It's difficult to explain how much I yearned to look evil in the eye, and ask *why*. *Why did you kill JJ?* Maybe, somewhere in the recesses of my soul, I wanted to either try and save Sartain's soul, or give him a last farewell to hell. I wasn't sure which. I just I needed to see him one more time.

"I want to go with you," I told the preacher. "Can you arrange it with the superintendent?"

"Why, Martha? Why would you want to see him again?"

"I want to look him in the eye and ask him *why* ... why he had JJ murdered. I want to tell him he's on his way to hell. Or, like you, maybe I want to save his soul ... I don't know why, Father. All I know is that I have this deep need to see him again."

"Martha, it's a bad idea to speak with him. I don't even think the superintendent will allow it, given Sartain's past conduct. Besides, Sartain would have to approve any visit." The preacher's eyes searched mine. He wanted to dissuade me from seeing evil one more time.

"He'll be behind bars. I'll be safe," I said. "And I have this intuition he'll see me now. He already sent the letter about JJ. He'll want to tell me how he planned it. The gory details. He wants an audience. And he knows he'll be executed in a month. If you'd just ask the superintendent, he can ask Sartain. Maybe I can even save his soul. Please."

On August 27, Oneeda and I baked twelve dozen cookies.

"You're going with Adam to Parchman tomorrow, aren't you?" she said.

"I am. I want to see him."

"You're *not*. Why in heaven's name would you?"

"Because, I want to give him a proper send-off."

"What's that mean?"

"It means I want to tell him he's on his way to hell. Maybe that's what I'll say. I don't know, Oneeda."

I didn't feel like exploring it with her. There was too much confusion in my mind about needing to see him again.

"I wish I could go with you," she said, pleading. "I want to be there when you tell Sartain where he's going."

I put a hand on her shoulder. "I know you do, Oneeda. But I need to face this alone."

Finished with the cookies, we wrapped twelve dozen in aluminum foil.

⋘⋙

The next afternoon I rode with the preacher to Parchman. On the drive there, he handed me a book.

"Turn to page seventy-four and read what I've underlined," he said. "Read it out loud, if you don't mind."

I looked at the book's cover. *Mere Christianity*, by C.S. Lewis. I turned to page seventy-four and read: "'When a man is getting better he understands more and more clearly the evil that is still left in him. When a man is getting worse, he understands his own badness less and less. A moderately bad man knows he is not very good; a thoroughly bad man thinks he is all right.'"

"What does that say to you about Sonny Sartain?" the preacher asked.

I turned to face him and said, "He thinks he's all right; he thinks he's good."

"Exactly. So do you think telling him he's on his way to hell will hurt him, and satisfy you?" he asked.

"Maybe not."

As the preacher drove on, I began to wonder about all the evil in the world. "Father, I don't understand where evil comes from. I remember you told Annie about it. But I'm not getting it. How could God allow it? I thought he was completely sovereign."

"He is. Let me explain it this way: God cannot do evil and he did not create evil; but he did allow evil to exist."

"What's that mean?"

"Look at it this way," Pastor Davidson said, "if God allowed evil to enter into this world, it would be His sovereign decision to do so. Since He is always right and perfect, we have to conclude that His allowing evil to exist is a good decision. That's not the same as saying 'evil is good.' We should never say that. However, we can say, 'It is good that there is evil,' solely based on the fact God allowed it. I know this is a difficult doctrine to understand, but there would be no evil if God didn't allow there to be evil. The outcome of evil is always turned into His glory; we just can't see how it's being done. But He can. One day, Martha, those of us who know and love His Son, will return to earth in perfect bodies … with no sin, no tears, only work and worship. Perhaps then we'll know the answers to our perplexing questions."

I couldn't respond. As he drove on to Parchman, I gazed at the cotton fields and pondered what I would say to Sartain—my epitome of evil. *Will I tell him that he's evil, but God allowed it? Will I ask about JJ? Will I tell him he's on his way to hell and deserves it? Or should I plead for his soul?*

I don't remember going through security, or visiting the superintendent. It was only after we walked into Unit 29 that I have vivid memories. I tried to calm my nerves, stop the shakes. *Put one foot in front of the other* I kept telling myself, still not knowing what I would say.

A young man stood guard by the Unit door.

As the preacher and I walked by the cells, carrying our small stools, several prisoners jumped from their bunks.

"Preacher, you come to heal me, right?" one said.

"I need to talk, preacher, about salvation."

"I need to know what's next, preacher," one begged, as we kept walking.

Half way down the corridor, the preacher stopped and put his stool down. He turned and motioned for me to go on to Sartain's cell. In a soft voice, he said, "There's nothing to fear, Martha. I'll be right here."

He turned his attention to the prisoner and pulled his stool close to the cell bars. As I moved away I heard the preacher say, "Carlos, are you ready to talk some more about Jesus?"

Carlos said, "My boy, he's sick … will you heal him?"

I was taken aback by the inmate's question.

"What's his name?" the preacher asked.

"Pablo."

"Only the Lord is able to save him from his sins," the preacher said. "Do you believe?"

"I believe," the man said.

I didn't have time to think about what I'd just heard. I needed to move on. Not only could I feel my heart pumping, I could hear its thumping beat. Worst of all was the same ol' hot, putrid smell.

———

Nearing Sartain's cell, I noticed he was lying on his bunk. *Asleep?* I placed the stool in front of his cell and sat. I faked a cough. He didn't budge.

Inching closer, I said in a weak, nervous tone, "Let's talk."

Then I spotted a lone photograph on his wall. It was my Polaroid of Mary and Michael—the one he'd taken in the hostage incident. The wall was blank except for that photograph.

I heard him whimper. I couldn't believe it. Was my fantasizing about saving his soul going to become reality? *Is he going to repent?*

Suddenly, he bolted out of bed and rushed me. He grabbed the bars and crammed his head halfway through. I glimpsed his swollen eyes as I fell backward off the stool onto the concrete floor.

I heard Pastor Davidson shout, "Are you all right?"

I nodded and picked up my stool, thankful Sartain was in that cell and I wasn't. He rammed some paper at me through the bars. "This is why I let you in here." He was so angry the veins on his neck bulged, his face so contorted, he was unrecognizable.

"Is - it - true?" he demanded.

I took the paper from his hand and sat, not aware I had moved the stool closer to hell. As I read, my heart pounded like a jackhammer.

The Greenlee Herald

THE GR~~~~~~~~~~~~~~~~~~~~~~~~~~~~~ AUGUST 26, 1960

MOTHER AND SON MURDERED

Mrs. Mary Magden Grater of Solo, and her three-year old son, Michael, were shot and killed in a Greenlee parking lot on August 20. The assailant fled, but was captured under a river bridge.

According to police reports, Mr. Capp Grater, former husband of Mary Grater, and father of the child, was implicated in the murders. The assailant claimed that Mr. Grater, who remains incarcerated in Parchman Penitentiary, paid him two-thousand dollars to commit the murders.

There are no further details to report at this time, but a full investigation is under way according to police. This newspaper will carry an extensive story next week on these tragic murders.

Funeral services for Mrs. Grater and her son are planned for August 29, eleven o'clock in the morning at Calvary Episcopal Church.

"Is it true?" he barked.

Confused by the article, I couldn't look up.

"No," I said, in shock, still studying the news clip.

"You're lying," he screamed.

I heard the preacher yell, but couldn't make out what he said. I thought he might be concerned about Sartain's screaming.

"Believe what you want, Sonny, but I don't know anything about this," I said.

He didn't believe me—probably because I hadn't made eye contact. I was too focused on that news article. I heard Pastor Davidson yell again. I turned toward him. This time I heard the words, "too close!" But it was too late.

Sartain had reached through the bars and grabbed my blouse, yanking so hard my head hit the cell bars at his waist. I yelled in panic. And pain.

The preacher was the first to reach me. The guard was behind, his pistol out and pointed at Sartain. Sartain twisted me around. He had dropped to the floor inside his cell, his hands around my throat. I could barely breathe. I was sitting on the concrete floor with my back against the bars.

"I'll snap her neck like a stick if you so much as try to touch her," he said, his hot sour breath saturating my face.

The guard was young and scared. I glanced up to see his hand and gun shaking.

But in an instant, Sartain's tone changed from viper to victim. "Oh, what have I done? What - have - I - done? Please forgive me. *Please* come get her before I do something terrible. Please help me, officer."

The guard inched a little closer.

In a calm tone the preacher told the guard, "Don't go any closer."

Ignoring him, the guard reached down to pull me away. Sartain released his left hand from my throat and grabbed the pistol. *Bang!* The gun fired into the ceiling. It happened in an instant.

The next thing I felt was a hot barrel pressed against my temple. I smelled the gunpowder wafting in the air.

"I swear, I'll kill her if you don't unlock this door right this second," he said to the guard.

"You won't … able … ten feet … door," the guard stammered, stepping backward.

Sartain pointed the gun at the guard and said, "Open the door you stupid fatso."

Davidson said, "No, Sonny, you don't want to do this."

"Open the door *now* or I will kill her, you, and this preacher. Do it. *Now.*"

The guard stepped toward the door, fumbled for the key, and unlocked the door to hell. I heard the other inmates shouting. I had no idea what they were saying.

Sartain didn't hesitate. He shot the guard. I was in shock. The ringing of the gunfire reverberated in my ears while my eyes couldn't stop staring at the dead guard four feet away.

Pastor Davidson was firm with Sartain: "In Jesus' name I command you to stop this instant."

The maniac might have killed us both if the preacher hadn't said that.

But Sartain had other plans. He opened the cell door and stepped out, pushing the barrel into my temple. He shoved us into his cell, and using the guard's keys locked us inside. We were in Sartain's cell about to watch hell unfold.

As Sartain moved down the cellblock I snatched the photograph of Mary and Michael off the wall and stuffed it in my purse.

"He may get me but he's not gonna see them again," I said, looking over at the preacher. His reaction to my impulsive outburst was not what I expected. He nodded his approval.

An alarm sounded, blistering my ears. Red lights flashed along the perimeter walls. Another prison guard came barreling through the door at the end of the corridor. Sartain fired at him. The guard retreated. The death-row inmates were howling. I saw Sartain opening their cell doors. I heard him yell, "Who's your savior now, huh? Say it, or I ain't openin' your door."

"You are. You're my savior," the first one shouted. Then others.

"And what's my name, you ingrates? Say it," Sartain yelled.

"Father Cain."

"Father Cain."

"Father Cain," they all shouted.

The riot was in full force. Sartain had taken control of the entire floor. I glanced at the preacher. He was kneeling beside Sartain's bunk, praying.

Sartain came back and retrieved the preacher and me. He shoved us in front of him, moving the gun barrel from my head to the preacher's, back and forth, back and forth, constantly pushing us toward the main door. One of the prisoners opened it. In the corridor, we faced two-dozen guards with shotguns leveled on us. Sartain kept shoving, using us as human shields, while the guards could only inch backward. The superintendent was there, pleading with Sartain to surrender. The sirens continued to shriek.

Sartain shouted to one of the inmates, "Open the door ahead on the right." He held us at the doorway while the prisoners hustled through. I could hear their boots pounding against the metal treads as they scurried down the stairs. Sartain backed into the doorway, pulling us with him, the pistol at my head. I looked at the frightened guards, their shotguns aimed at us, as we stumbled through the door, and down, backward. Sartain kept pulling us, grabbing the preacher, then me, and the preacher again—one flight of metal stairs, until we reached the bottom.

We were in the mess hall, and then the kitchen before he turned us around. The cooks' hands were already high above their heads, surrendering. Sartain didn't kill them. They were also inmates. Inmates did the cooking. Instead, he shouted, "What's for supper, you scumbags?"

They barricaded themselves in the kitchen. A Sartain disciple found the pantry. "We got plenty to eat," he yelled.

Another shouted, "Come get it, boys, we could live here for weeks."

Sartain circled the kitchen, waving his pistol, telling his disciples to barricade the doors.

One of the prison cooks said, "No, man. This ain't no good. We all's gonna be dead." He obviously wasn't one of Sartain's disciples. He was an inmate in the wrong place at the wrong time.

When Sartain heard the cook, he stopped, stared at the big man and said, "I don't know you, do I?" Sartain raised his pistol so fast it was hard to see. *Bang!* He shot the man between the eyes. I had to look away.

Sartain didn't hesitate. He knocked Pastor Davidson to the floor. Sartain wasted no time pulling the newsprint article from his pocket and shoving it in the preacher's face.

"Now, I'll ask *you*, preacher—'cause Martha here won't tell me. Is this true? Are they dead? Capp had 'em killed, didn't he? And now everybody thinks the boy is Capp's … not mine," he screamed.

"It's not true," Pastor Davidson said in a calm voice.

"I don't believe you," Sartain shouted, punching the newsprint with his finger. "It says so right here in this newspaper." Sartain hit the preacher with his pistol in the same place as before, gouging out another two-inch wound. Davidson fell to the floor. Sartain cursed and spit on him.

The preacher's face and shirt were quickly covered in blood. He pulled himself up against a cabinet next to me. His jaw had gone slack, his mouth open. Again, I had to look away.

I heard heavy equipment outside, then loud bullhorns with men demanding that the prisoners surrender. *National Guard,* I thought. *Thank heavens.*

The bullhorns bellowed for hours, late into the night. The prisoners grabbed and ate everything they could find.

The cook lay dead where he was shot.

Sartain sat on the floor, leaning against one of the steel cabinets opposite Pastor Davidson and me, no more than fifteen feet away, both arms out-stretched on the concrete floor, the pistol in one hand, the news article in the other. He looked tired. He let out a loud sigh. He looked as if he might fall asleep.

Does Satan sleep? I wondered. I decided to stay awake. I wanted to know.

Pastor Davidson passed out about midnight, according to the wall clock. I couldn't sleep. Neither could Sartain. The bullhorns never stopped. And Sartain never acknowledged them.

⸺◦⸎◦⸺

I watched the morning light cast a golden hue across the kitchen floor. There was a moment of peace. It made me wonder if I was in some sort of nightmare. *This can't be real.*

But Sartain startled me, scrambling to his feet with renewed vigor, as if he had a new idea.

"Get me something to eat, boys. And strip the clothes off our preacher here."

Sartain ate an apple and watched his disciples rip off the rector's clothes. I looked away. Sartain slapped me. "Watch this," he said. "You're gonna be my witness at his trial."

They tied his hands and feet and dragged him nearly naked into the middle of the floor. Sartain tossed the apple away, then took turns with another inmate bludgeoning the preacher with broom handles. Finished, they tossed him against the cabinet like a rag doll, three feet from me. I closed my eyes. I heard one of the prisoners spit on him. I couldn't believe this was happening. I prayed for the National Guard to do something.

"Preacher, you are accused of heresy against the almighty. That would be *me*," Sartain shouted, tossing his head back. "Now, how do you plead?"

I turned to see what the preacher might say. Pastor Davidson said nothing. His head was resting against his chest. He continued to stare at the concrete floor. Sartain said, "Well, since the accused preacher here ain't gonna speak for himself, what are we to do, men? If you won't speak up, preacher, this jury is gonna vote anyway. Surely you got something to say … are you with us here, preach? You got nothing to say in your defense? *Tsk-Tsk.*"

Adam Davidson continued to stare at the floor.

"So be it," Sartain said. He turned to the men and shouted, "How do you vote, men of freedom?"

They shouted, "Guilty."

Looking down at Davidson, Sartain said, "And so shall it be. You will be executed by hanging." Sartain laughed. "Find some rope," he yelled to the men.

The bullhorn outside kept threatening Sartain to surrender. But Sartain ignored it.

His men returned with a bundle of aprons. They fashioned a rope. One of the men made a hangman's noose.

Oh, God, no, they're really going to hang him. I was sweating profusely, and felt like jumping out of my skin. But I was too shocked to move a muscle.

Pastor Davidson never appeared afraid, nor said a word. I was astounded. He prayed for them as they draped the knotted aprons over a ceiling pipe.

"Father, save them from everlasting damnation. Forgive them. They don't know what they're doing," he said.

They hoisted him onto a chair and tightened the noose around his neck. Sartain kicked the chair away. Pastor Davidson was hanging, and not moving; but the aprons were stretching. *Thank heavens.*

Two canisters came rolling across the floor, bouncing like grenades. Sartain shouted something I don't care to repeat.

Boom! Boom! Tear gas enveloped the room. The prisoners dropped to the floor. My face was on fire. Chemically induced tears gushed from my eyes. I was useless. The room was in chaos. Uniformed men wearing black gas masks rushed in. A man in a green military uniform bent down, trying to lift me. The tear-gas-filled room made it almost impossible to see. But I spotted Sartain over the man's shoulder, fifteen feet away, crouched down, one hand covering his eyes. He was peering through his fingers, waving the gun around through the thick vapor. He turned and pointed at the soldier's back.

Bang!

The guard fell.

Bang! I saw Sartain shoot Pastor Davidson in the back.

Bang! A soldier shot Sartain. He crumpled to the floor. The soldier moved toward him, continuing to point his pistol at Sartain. More uniformed men swarmed the room, shouting what, I don't know. It was all so loud and scary. I remember a man putting a rubber mask on my face. The horrible burning sensation didn't go away.

—❦—

Sonny Sartain's wound was not mortal. He'd been shot in his left collarbone. He was handcuffed and taken away.

I was outside when they loaded Pastor Davidson's body into the ambulance. The prison doctor placed a stethoscope on his neck. He was pronounced dead. He was taken to the Greenlee morgue.

Yes, I was in shock. And yes, I wept like a baby.

It was August 28, 1960, three years after Rector Adam Davidson first set foot in Solo.

—❦—

Mary and I moped and mourned the whole next day. We did our best to prepare food for the funeral but we had no idea when it might be. We called the diocese in Salem, but the lines remained busy.

—❦—

The following day, I received a call from Bishop Plunk.

"Mrs. McRae?"

"Yes ..."

"This is Bishop Plunk. Mrs. McRae, I know that Father Davidson was a resident of your boarding house so I thought you should know—in case you haven't heard. Father Davidson is alive. However, the doctors are not able to remove the bullet. It's too close to his heart."

"But the doctor … at Parchman … pronounced him …"

"Mrs. McRae, it's called a miracle. I have no other explanation at this time—other than to let you know he's now at the Salem Catholic Hospital and under good care. This is good news, indeed," the bishop said.

I could hardly speak. "Thank you, thank you, Bishop Plunk."

We disconnected, and my tears became a waterfall of joy. And disbelief! I had to see for myself.

I grabbed Mary, then called Oneeda and Annie. We raced to Salem. To see him.

We hesitated before walking into his hospital room. But a pleasant nurse told us he had been expecting us.

"Expecting us?" I asked, my throat thick with more disbelief.

"How is he?" Annie asked the nurse.

"He's doing better," she said. "But the bullet can't be removed. It's too close to his heart."

"We heard," Oneeda said.

We walked in, not surprised by what we saw. His bed was raised, his eyes closed. He was praying to his Father. We quietly moved to one side of the bed.

Opening one compassionate eye, he asked, "Did you think I would leave you? Didn't I tell you I would never desert you? I will always be here for you."

We could only stare at him.

He looked at me. "And Martha, did I not promise I would send a comforter to replace me?"

I felt a tear roll down my cheek. "Yes, you did, Father."

"Don't be anxious. I'm sending an advocate who will be a light revealing all our Father has done for those who believe."

Mary spoke: "But, Father, you need to come back ... you're our pastor."

His voice was weak, but soothing. "Mary, you know I love you. The one that comes after me ... he will be your comforter and your advocate. I will not be with you many more days," he said, looking at each of us.

"But why can't the bullet be removed?" Oneeda asked.

"Too close to my heart. I will soon return to my Father."

He saw our tears.

"Stop your crying. Be joyful," he said.

Then he told us to go and tell others in Calvary that we all need to be joyful, and strong. "Now go, be disciples for Christ. Tell others that good will prevail in the end."

Driving back to Solo, we told stories about him—so many that one book couldn't contain all the special memories.

32

Revenge

ANOTHER TWO WEEKS passed and Freddie came to visit. I wasn't in the mood. Even so, I pulled a tin of cheese straws from the pantry. Oneeda and Mary were here. We sat around the kitchen table. Mary kept a watchful eye on Michael in the backyard.

I didn't know it at first but Freddie had come to gloat.

I asked, "Freddie, what brings you to Solo?"

With a bright face he turned to Mary and said, "When I heard the rumors that the woman Father Cain had demanded to see was you, Mrs. Grater, my friend from the *Greenlee Herald* helped me figure out how I could hurt him."

Mary had been watching Michael, but turned and focused on Freddie, as he continued his story.

"I wanted to mess with his mind so bad … the way he had done to mine. I knew Father Cain must've had some strong feelings for you and the boy, Mrs. Grater."

Freddie cast a broad smile. "So my friend from the newspaper came up with this idea." Freddie pulled from his trouser pocket a copy of the fake article he had fabricated about Mary and Michael's death.

We were stunned.

"You did this, Freddie?" Mary demanded.

"Freddie, what you did led to the riot at Parchman," I said, adrenaline and anger producing a harsh reaction. "Don't you realize Father Davidson was tortured and shot by Sonny Sartain because of that story?"

Freddie's expression changed from pride to perplexity. He couldn't speak for several seconds. We waited for his response.

"I didn't think about that. Was it not right, what I did?" he asked, his expression, flustered with confusion.

Oneeda chimed in. "Freddie, what you did was wrong."

"But you don't realize what he did to me," he snapped, pleading with each of us.

"Freddie, revenge is God's job, not ours," Oneeda said.

Freddie hung his head. There was a long pause as he pondered this. He fidgeted in his chair, but said nothing. He tried to leave, but Mary gently pushed him down.

"I'm sorry," he said. "I don't know what to say. I am so sorry. I didn't—I just didn't think about Father Davidson."

He looked around the kitchen, not able to make eye contact with any of us. He smothered his face in his hands. "None of you know. You don't know what he did to me."

"We do know, Freddie," Oneeda said. "You told us when you were here before."

Freddie stretched his upper body across the table and sobbed. "I see it. I see it now. I'm so sorry. So ashamed. I shouldn't have done it."

Deep down, Freddie was a sensitive young man. He realized what he'd done was wrong.

Mary was the first to hug him. Then Oneeda and I wrapped our arms around him, while he shook and sobbed.

Michael burst through the door like any three-year-old, but stopped when he saw us hugging Freddie. "What's wrong, Mommy?"

"Honey, go back outside and play some more … for Mommy, please. Just a little while longer," Mary said.

With concern in his eyes, Michael looked up at Freddie, but did as his mother had asked.

After we released Freddie, he wiped tears on both shirtsleeves.

"What should I do now?" he asked, pleading for an answer.

We looked at each other, none of us knowing how to respond. Then Oneeda placed a hand on Freddie's shoulder. "Freddie, we'll keep this a secret. Between the four of us. Tonight, though, you better get down on your knees and ask God for forgiveness. Will you promise me you'll—"

"—I will, I will," he said, his bottom lip quivering. "May I leave now? I don't feel so good."

We all nodded. Freddie walked out the back door, his shoulders slumped like a boy who'd lost his mother.

Little Michael ran to Freddie and hugged him around the knees. Freddie stiffened. His hollow eyes stared at us. He stood there, erect, never bending down to return Michael's hug.

Then he was gone.

———

After Oneeda left, Mary and I cooked supper.

We had finished our discussion about Freddie when—without even looking at me—Mary said, "Did you hear Andrew's going out with a woman up in Memphis?"

"What? Why didn't you tell me?" I said, sad for her.

"It's okay, Martha. It's for the best."

"What happened between you two?"

"Oh, he broke it off a month or so ago. It's no big deal."

"It *is* a big deal," I said, reaching to put an arm around her, but she stopped me.

"It's okay. I wouldn't—well, let's just say I refused to go all the way with him."

"You mean …?"

"Yes. But it doesn't matter. Besides, I don't think he wanted to help raise a three-year-old boy," she said, observing Michael in the backyard.

She didn't shed a tear about Andrew. But she did when she looked back at me and said, "Martha, I want to thank you for trusting in Jesus. For letting him protect Michael and me."

We hugged.

We finished cooking, in silence, while little Michael munched on cheese straws and drank his milk.

I attended a vestry meeting a couple of weeks later. We were down to four members. We had no rector, and no clue what would happen to JJ's Honey donations.

We were in a dire state of spirit when the two Johnson boys, Jake and Jimmy, walked in the room on a surprise visit. Tagging along behind were the three Johnson sisters, all dressed in their Sunday best. We watched as they strode down the aisle and planted themselves in front of us, like we were some important audience.

These boys couldn't be more than twenty, I thought.

Jake and Jimmy looked at each other. Both were smiling. I thought they were about to tell us they'd sold out to Purity Foods. I waited for the inevitable.

"Ladies, gentlemen," Jake said, fidgeting, clearing his nervous throat. "We want you to know we're taking over Pop's honey operation."

We turned and looked at each other.

Jimmy added, "And we're not selling," he was proud to say.

They stood motionless, not saying another word. We didn't know what to say.

"Oh, and we've made a decision," the oldest girl said. "We're going to continue making our bottles with the same label."

"You know … the label with the ten-percent donation to Calvary," Jake said.

The four of us stood and clapped. The Johnson children blushed so red their cheeks glowed like a strawberry patch.

When the clapping stopped, nobody said a word. So I did. "Jake … Jimmy … girls … if you ever need help out there, I expect you to call me, because I'll be racing up that dusty road to help with whatever you need."

"Oh, Miz McRae," one of the girls said, "we paved that road. There's no more dust anymore."

She pointed to the back of the room. There was Peg, their mother, standing proud, smiling.

We all hugged, praised God, and gave thanks.

Then JJ's legacy proceeded to leave.

Jabbing each other in the side, one of the girls squealed, "Stop it, Jimmy. Pop would bust your tail for that."

The four of us prayed for them. Then we thanked God and JJ for leaving Calvary and Solo in such good hands.

Afterward, the other members elected me to replace JJ as Calvary's delegate. Keeping my plate full of God's things needing to be done was not a problem for me.

Father Davidson remained in the hospital for over a month. We visited two more times. The doctors confirmed he would die if moved. X-Rays on the light box in his room showed the bullet lodged less than an inch from the back of his heart. We could see it.

"Because his heart is working harder and harder to pump blood through his body, it's growing larger and larger," the doctor told us. "He's developing an enlarged heart."

He received many visitors during that time, and kept encouraging everyone to spread God's word. So we did. We invited more folks to join Calvary, gave talks in the school gymnasium, and raised money for missionaries. Calvary grew in the process. Some men even started their own Bible study group.

On the fortieth day, Adam Davidson ascended to his Father, and our Father.

Bishop Theo Plunk presided over Rector Davidson's services at Calvary. Attending were six priests from diocese headquarters, all in long white flowing vestments.

I can't remember what was said. I kept trying to hold back tears. We sat together—Oneeda, Mary, Annie, Butch, and I. Occasionally, I would break into a slight smile, thinking about Adam Davidson and how he'd promised to send a comforter to Solo some day in the future, "when my Father brings me home," he had said. I smiled because I knew he wouldn't let us down. *Not now*, I thought.

Then my demeanor would change from resigned smile to disappointed sulk. *How could you leave us like this? You were the best thing that ever happened to Solo. Why, God?*

Walking out of the church, I saw a group of prisoners in the back corner, in a special roped-off section. Guards with shotguns were stationed around them. I looked closer at the inmates. They were weeping with me. Some were praying out loud.

I will always believe they were giving thanks for the one who had saved them from eternal damnation.

I smiled again, and thought, *Yes, y'all miss him now, but one day you'll be with him again. None of us is perfect. But some of us will be.*

———

Three weeks later, I traveled to Salem for my brief vestry training and meeting with Bishop Plunk. His secretary told me I'd need to see Father Compañero instead. "The Bishop is in a meeting," she added.

"Father Comp—Compan—" I couldn't get it out.

"Compañero," she said, stressing the '*yero*' in his name. "Paul Compañero. You'll like him. Here, I'll take you to his office."

On the way, I asked the obvious. "Is he …"

"Yes. He was born in New Mexico. Son of immigrants. Graduated top of his seminary class in St. Louis. Wonderful man."

We met in Pastor Compañero's meager office, exchanged the usual pleasantries, and then I asked the same question JJ had asked when he met with Bishop Plunk four years before: "Would it be possible, Father, to request a rector with a family?"

Pastor Compañero was indeed a pleasant man, and in many ways reminded me of Pastor Davidson—especially his eyes, resonating the same compassion.

"Well, Mrs. McRae," he said in a Latino accent, "we're in need of Episcopal rectors in many churches—not only here in Mississippi, but everywhere. However, I would like to offer *my* services. No, I don't have a family yet, but it would be an honor for me to come to Solo and preach as many times as you'd have me. It's what I do. I travel to churches that need me, and preach the gospel. I'm between churches right now. When would you like me to come?"

"I don't know," I said, surprised not only by his eager desire, but his eloquence and sincerity.

"Would you allow me to report back to our vestry, and contact you then?" I asked, embarrassed he might take my response the wrong way.

"Of course. Don't be afraid, Mrs. McRae, I'm harmless. I may have dark skin and speak differently, but our Lord will give me the words to comfort your church, and your town, which I've heard so much about. There seems to be a lot of healing to be done in Solo."

Driving back to Solo, I thought about what JJ had said: "We don't have a clue about the process for obtaining a new rector."

Looking up through my windshield into the clouds, I whispered, "Oh, but JJ, I do. We just ask God to send the right man—married, single, light skin, or dark, it doesn't matter. He'll send us a comforter."

33

His Name Was Satan

CAPP GRATER WAS behind bars in Parchman on Thursday October 20 1960 when Sonny Sartain was taken from his cell and escorted down the long corridor, across the yard, and into the building that housed the gas chamber. (Sartain's execution had been postponed until his shoulder healed.)

I was there, along with Superintendent Harris, the prison doctor, Sheriff Turnbull, and several other official witnesses. One of the men was a Salem district judge, in charge of the proceedings. We sat in wooden chairs and watched through a thick glass window.

One of the state officials asked Harris, "How many prisoners have been in this chamber?"

"This is number twenty-two," Harris said, matter-of-factly. "Most were by electrocution."

Sonny Sartain was brought in and strapped to a chair in the middle of the chamber. One of the guards asked him if he had any last words.

Sartain turned to the window. He couldn't see us, but I felt like he was looking straight at me. Goose bumps sprang from my arms.

"I do have some last words, thank you, guard," he said. "If Martha McRae is behind that window I want her to know she hasn't seen the last of me. I'll be coming back for her. And for Mary and my little boy. Tell her that."

The guard covered Sartain's head with a black hood, then exited the room and secured the door. The judge nodded and gave the command. Nozzles around the chamber's perimeter released a steady cloud of vapor. Sartain arched his back, sucked in the poisonous gas ... and gradually slumped over.

A thought crossed my mind. *You may not have been Satan in the flesh, but you were one of his minions, and I'm sure there'll be others who follow in your evil path.*

On the way out, Superintendent Harris asked me: "Mrs. McRae, do you know what Sartain meant when he made that reference about his 'little boy?'"

"No, I can't say that I do."

I asked him if he might allow me to look down that corridor one last time.

We stopped inside the door to Unit 29. I studied the long row of cells, expecting to conclude my life's chapter with death row. Instead, I heard the inmates passing news from one to the other,

"Father Cain was executed tonight."

"Father Cain got the gas chamber. Pass it on."

"Father Cain was executed."

And on down the line, from one cell to the next, until the news reached a voice I recognized—Capp Grater's.

He screamed, "His name was Satan."

> *Now all has been heard; here is the conclusion of the matter: Fear God and keep his commandments, for this is the whole duty of man. For God will bring every deed into judgment, including every hidden thing, whether it is good or evil.*

Ecclesiastes 12:13, 14

The prosecutor used this map to show the jury Sartain's reign of murders. It was five feet high by three feet.

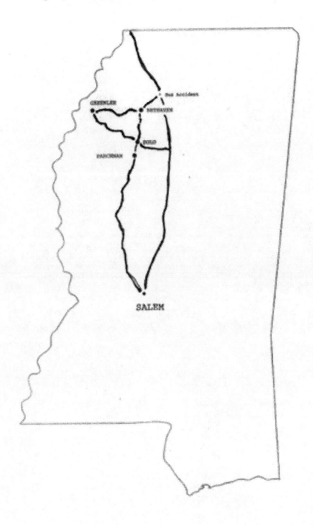

NOTE: In chapter thirty-two, the author used certain concepts and words from *The Mystery of Evil*, an article from Ligonier Ministries and R.C. Sproul. © *Tabletalk* magazine. Also, the phrase and concept "Delivery boy" in chapter twenty comes from a sermon preached by Richie Sessions at Independent Presbyterian Church in February, 2015. "We don't have a soul. We are a soul. We have a body," is a quote from George MacDonald. All phrases known as common were taken from the FreeDictionary domain.

If you enjoyed *The Rector*, please leave a comment on Amazon, next to the book. Here's the tiny URL link:

http://tinyurl.com/govmh7x

Type it into your browser. It should take you directly to *The Rector*.

About the Author

MICHAEL HICKS THOMPSON was born in his mother's own bed. Raised on a small farm in Mississippi, he claims to know a thing or two about strong Christian women, alcoholic men, and Jesus. He graduated from Ole Miss, served in the military, then received a masters degree in mass communication from the University of South Carolina. Married to Tempe Adams for forty-four years, he lives in Memphis, Tennessee. He's the father of three Christian men, and grandfather of four. They call him "Big Mike."

Visit: www.michaelthompsonauthor.com for more information on the author and his works.

He'll be happy to respond to any questions you have, or comments you leave. His blog is titled: *Sweet Tea With Jesus.*

Reader's Guide

IN A BIBLE STUDY OR BOOK CLUB?

Access your free, 6-week guide at

http://www.TheRectorGuide.com.

While inspirational and theology books are more valuable for Bible study groups, *The Rector* is fun to read (and discuss if you're in a group). There are several Biblical doctrines and principles embedded in this entertaining allegory.

Nevertheless, here are the twelve books Michael recommends as infinitely more valuable:

Defending Your Faith, R.C. Sproul
The Reason For God, Timothy Keller
Encounters With Jesus, Timothy Keller
Knowing God, J.I. Packer
Pray With Your Eyes Open, Richard L. Pratt
The Knowledge of The Holy, A.W. Tozer
Evangelism and Sovereignty, J.I. Packer
Know Your Christian Life, Sinclair Ferguson
Facing Your Giants, Max Lucado
Saved From What? R.C. Sproul
The Holy Spirit, Billy Graham
Family Life, Charles Swindoll

Coming next in the *Solo Ladies Bible Study* series:

The Actress

The most famous actress in America, Tullulah Ivey, is in Solo to film a controversial movie. A prominent Solo citizen has been shot and killed outside her bedroom window. A typewritten love note was found clenched in his hand. Martha investigates the who, what, and why of the shooting. It's a twisty, suspenseful murder mystery, embedded with a Paulinian allegory. A new study guide will be available.

Thank you for reading The Rector. Please leave a comment on Amazon next to his novel.
Comments are vitally important to increasing the novel's visibility on Amazon.

CPSIA information can be obtained at www.ICGtesting.com
Printed in the USA
LVOW11s1753200916

505434LV00001B/172/P

9 780984 528271